Two action-packed novels of
the American West!

SIGNET BRAND DOUBLE WESTERNS

LAST TRAIN
FROM GUN HILL

AND

THE
BORDER GUIDON

SIGNET Double Westerns You'll Enjoy

LAST TRAIN FROM GUN HILL

AND

THE BORDER GUIDON

by Gordon D. Shirreffs

A SIGNET BOOK
NEW AMERICAN LIBRARY
TIMES MIRROR

PUBLISHER'S NOTE

These novels are works of fiction. Names, characters, places, and incidents either are the product of the author's imagination or are used fictitiously, and any resemblance to actual persons, living or dead, events, or locales is entirely coincidental.

 SIGNET TRADEMARK REG. U.S. PAT. OFF. AND FOREIGN COUNTRIES
REGISTERED TRADEMARK—MARCA REGISTRADA
HECHO EN CHICAGO, U.S.A.

SIGNET, SIGNET CLASSIC, MENTOR, PLUME, MERIDIAN AND NAL
BOOKS are published by The New American Library, Inc.,
1633 Broadway, New York, New York 10019

First Printing (Double Western Edition), January, 1984

1 2 3 4 5 6 7 8 9

PRINTED IN THE UNITED STATES OF AMERICA

LAST TRAIN FROM GUN HILL

*Based on a screenplay by James Poe
and a story by Les Crutchfield*

Chapter One

IT WAS ONE of those Oklahoma days when the distant hills swim in faint purple haze and the hot, dry wind of late summer sweeps across the prairies, rippling and swaying the endless sea of yellowed grasses. The buckboard seemed to appear out of nowhere, as it rose from a swale and rolled down the near side of a low ridge. Meadow larks fluttered up from the grass before the oncoming horse. The black's neck arched gracefully up and down while his hoofs splashed almost silently into the thick dust of the winding road.

Catherine Morgan drove the swaying buckboard easily, holding the reins in capable gloved hands. Her neatly ironed gingham dress would have stamped her as the wife of a rancher or homesteader except for the fact that she did not wear the trade-mark of those types, the stiffly starched sunbonnet. Instead her thick black hair was bound at the back of her neck with a bright red ribbon. The young boy who sat beside her had his head raised as though he were drinking in the wind like a wild mustang. His eyes were alight with pleasure as he looked first at the smoothly moving horse and then at his lovely mother.

"Touch him up, Petey," she said in mock seriousness. "He's lagging a little."

The boy smiled as he reached for the silver-ferruled whip. There was no need to touch up the lively black, but he snapped the cracker high over the horse's head. He held the whip in his hand and looked far ahead. A hawk hung in the clear sky like a scrap of charred paper, and as the boy watched, it turned gracefully and shot off downwind as though something had disturbed it. Then Petey saw the scarf of dust hanging over the road a quarter of a mile ahead.

Something glinted brightly. "There are two horsemen ahead of us, Mother," said the boy.

She nodded. The sun flashed again from the dust. "Fancy saddle," she said. "Can't be some ordinary saddle tramp."

Petey slitted his eyes as he studied the two men. "Ain't in no hurry either."

"Petey! Your grammar!"

He grinned. "That's the way Pa would say it."

She smiled down at him. "And that makes it right?"

"Well, anyway, he usually does *most* things right."

She did not answer. Her keen eyes had seen something else glint in the dust. One of the men had raised a bottle to his mouth. Her hands tightened on the reins. It was too late to turn back now.

Rick Belden turned in his fancy saddle to look back along the road. A cigarette hung from one corner of his mouth and a tendril of smoke curled up past his half-closed eyes. He stared for a moment and then threw the cigarette away. "Jees, Lee," he said quickly, "look at the filly driving that buckboard!"

Lee Smithers raised a bottle to his loose lips and drank deeply. He wiped his mouth on his shirt sleeve and then turned to peer back through the dust. "Yeh," he said in appreciation. "Here! Catch!" He tossed the bottle to Rick. Rick caught it deftly and pulled out the cork. He drank deeply and then threw the bottle into the grass. His face seemed to tighten under the skin as the rotgut took hold. He fumbled with a saddlebag and drew out another bottle, which he held up to the light to gauge its contents.

The buckboard was within twenty feet of the two men. They both turned in their saddles to eye in bold appreciation the shapely body of Catherine Morgan. There was no indication from her that she resented their searching looks. She nodded shortly as the buckboard passed between them, and did not look back, but the boy could not help turning in his seat to look at the saddle sat in by Rick Belden; it was the most beautiful article of horse furniture he had ever seen.

"Don't stare at them," said his mother.

"It's the saddle, Mother."

"Turn around! They've been drinking."

Rick Belden pulled out the cork of the bottle with his teeth, and his bloodshot eyes stayed staring at the woman's back. He quickly raised the bottle and drained it. He tossed it into the grass. "Another dead soldier gone to hell," he said thickly.

"Jees, Rick!" protested Lee. "That's the third one you finished off today and I swear you drunk most of all three of 'em!"

"Shut up! I always have to pay for them, don't I?" Rick yanked down his hat. "Let's go!"

"It's too damned hot to hurry these horses."

Rick grinned. He looked ahead at the buckboard. "We won't have to hurry them long, *amigo*." He raked the chestnut with his spurs and shot ahead of his companion.

"No, Rick!" Lee yelled hoarsely. "Not that!"

"Come on, you dummy, or I'll have her all to myself!"

Lee hesitated and then he lashed his sorrel to chase after Rick through the shrouding dust.

The hawk hung high overhead, floating almost motionless as it faced into the wind. Catherine Morgan turned to look back down the road as she heard the staccato beating of the hoofs on the sunbaked earth. She snatched the whip from Petey's hand and laid it smartly across the rump of the black. The horse reared a little at the unaccustomed treatment and broke into a smooth, easy run. The buckboard swayed and bounced as it slewed about curves and hit the ruts. The hawk shot off downwind again and vanished toward the distant hills.

"They're gaining, Mother," said Petey quietly. He looked up at her taut face. "What do they want?"

"Be quiet!" she snapped.

The buckboard had reached a wide, flat area of blackened earth where the grass had been burned away. The horsemen were closing the gap. They separated, one on each side of the road, to take advantage of the level ground. Their quirts rose and fell like pistons, and foam flecked back from the mouths of the overheated mounts.

Rick Belden was in his glory. He grinned loosely as he felt the heat of the rye in his guts, and he was excited by the steady driving of the chestnut's powerful muscles. His hat blew from his thick thatch of hair and hung at his back from its *barbiquejo* strap. He glanced at Lee Smithers and yelled in sensuous pleasure. Lee grinned back uncertainly. He wasn't so damned sure he liked this latest escapade of his employer's son, but Rick would ride hell out of him if he failed to play along.

Petey inched closer to his mother. She was driving with all her natural skill, watching each rut and dip in the twisting road, her gloved hands feeling the pull of the game little black. The beating of the hoofs behind them was louder now, and she did not look sideways as Rick Belden closed in on the buckboard and slowed down a little to keep pace with it.

Lee Smithers closed in on the other side and kept on trying to reach the head of the black. He made a wild drunken pass for the bridle and nearly fell from his saddle.

Petey tightened his fists. He had no weapon, not even the clasp knife his father had given him on his last birthday.

Rick leaned over and snatched for the reins. Catherine Morgan stood up, swayed to regain her balance, and then swung the whip with all her strength full across Rick's sweating face. He grunted in excruciating pain and instinctively kneed the chestnut away. He clapped his right hand against the deep slash and shuddered.

The buckboard bounced heavily and Catherine dropped down on the seat. Rick Belden savagely swung the chestnut against the heaving flank of the black and gripped the reins. He turned his head away from the slashing whip and jerked the reins free from her grasp. The black reared as the bit cut his tender mouth. He turned hard to the left. A shaft snapped as the front wheels hit a deep rut in the road and then turned hard. The buckboard tilted, hung for a moment, and then went full over.

Petey leaped and landed on his feet, but his mother was thrown heavily to the ground. She rolled over twice and then lay still in the deep grass, blood trickling from her mouth. Petey jumped into a hollow. He wormed his way into the deep grass and then turned to peer with wide eyes from his hideout.

Catherine Morgan opened her eyes and looked about her with a dazed expression. Her hair ribbon had broken and her thick black hair had cascaded over her shoulders. She felt her bruised face with a trembling hand and then looked up at the two grinning men.

Rick Belden fingered the deep slash in his cheek. "The ornery bitch," he said softly. "Near got my eye, Lee."

Lee nodded in drunken sympathy. He tried to focus his pale eyes on the woman. "She's a looker, Rick. Sure is. Squaw, ain't she?" He hiccuped.

Rick nodded. He swayed a little in his saddle. "Come on," he said.

Catherine tried to get up. She suppressed a groan. Sweat broke out on her forehead. "Petey!" she called.

The boy raised his head. He swallowed as he saw the two horsemen closing in on his mother.

"Petey!" she called again. A spasm of pain contorted her face and she beat a clenched hand against the hard earth. She lapsed into her native Cheyenne as she spoke brokenly to her son.

The boy was badly frightened at the two strange-acting men. His mother spoke to him quickly, telling him to get his father. He stood up and clenched his fists. "No," he said loudly.

Rick swung down from his saddle and stood

spraddle-legged, looking down at the injured woman. He wiped the sweat and blood from his face and grinned.

Petey charged. Rick waited his time, and then swung his left hand, catching Petey alongside the head and knocking him down. "Git, you," he said.

"Go, Petey," said his mother, in Cheyenne. "These men will kill you! There is nothing you can do here! Go and get your father!"

Rick launched a kick at Petey, but the kid rolled away from the boot and wormed his way into the grass. He was gone as swiftly as a frightened cottontail.

Rick hitched up his belt and looked into the steady eyes of the woman. Lee shook his head. "Rick, I ain't so sure . . ." he said uncertainly.

Rick slapped him on the back, driving the dust from his vest and shirt. "Ain't no one to bother us," he said. "Got her all to ourselves."

"What about that kid?"

Rick spat. "Forget him." He leered at the silent woman. He wet his lips. "Now, squaw," he said coaxingly, "ain't no use in fighting. You can't get away. Take it easy and enjoy yourself." He reached toward her. She gripped his right wrist and, dragging it close to her mouth, sank her teeth into his hand. He drove out a boot, catching her on the side of the head, knocking her back into the grass. "Damn you!" he yelped. He licked his wound.

Lee Smithers wiped the sweat from his gaunt face. "She's a wildcat, Rick. Let's turn her loose. There's plenty girls we can get somewheres else. This will only get us into a mess even your pa won't get us out of."

"He can get us out of *any* mess, and don't you forget it."

"Mebbe so, but . . ."

Rick Belden turned angrily toward his companion. "You loco? Look at her! Jesus! Look at them *chichonas!* We won't get many chances like this!"

Neither of them saw the boy crawling swiftly toward Rick's big chestnut as it cropped the grass fifty yards from the overturned buckboard.

Rick hitched up his belt again and bent over the woman. She fought hard and silently, breathing harshly as she held him off. Lee came closer. His excitement got the better of him as he saw clothing ripped from smooth shoulders. He knelt beside Rick. Two pairs of hard, greedy hands were too much for her. Clothing was ripped from her sweating body. The two excited men pinned her down with their knees. She choked in the dust and almost fought free with her last reserves of strength, but Rick Belden smashed her flat with a vicious backhander. She lay still with her breasts rising and falling spasmodically. Rick stood up and looked at Lee with a lopsided grin. "Me first. Keep watch, will ya?"

The wind rippled the long grass. There was no song from a meadow lark. There was no sound but the soft moaning of the wind across the lonely prairie.

Petey Morgan inched toward the chestnut. The sun glinted from facets of the ornate silver-mounted saddle. He looked back toward the buckboard. The black had drifted off downwind and was placidly cropping the grass. One of the two men was standing with his back toward Petey, watching something in the deep grass. The other was not in sight.

Petey spoke softly to the sweat-lathered chestnut in the Cheyenne tongue as his grandfather had taught him to do. The horse whinnied softly. Petey stood up and passed a hand across its nose. The horse sniffed at him. He took the reins and pulled himself up into the saddle. His feet were a long way from the stirrups, but he gripped tightly with his knees and urged the chestnut down into a hollow which shielded his escape from the men. When he rode up the ridge on the other side of the hollow and looked back, he saw the one man still standing there. There was no sign of Petey's mother.

Petey rode hard for Pawley, forcing the big horse to a full-out pace. There was a nameless something within Petey which filled him with terror. He knew a horrible thing was going on back there, but he did not know what it was.

No longer did the prairie seem bright and fresh under the low-riding sun and the hurrying wind, and not one meadow lark was giving voice as he rode on.

Chapter Two

PAWLEY SEEMED TO be dozing under the golden-flecked sunshine of the late afternoon. The metals of the single-track railroad line glistened under the bright light and heat waves shimmered and danced over the rails. Beside the station a blanketed Indian lay asleep on a baggage truck, and his cur dog dozed beneath it. A pig wallowed and grunted in the thick mud beneath the railroad tank.

Three small boys, dressed in their stiff Sunday best, plodded through the dust in their bare feet. Their shoes hung by the laces about their necks. "You think he's in his office, Joey?" anxiously asked the smallest of the trio.

The biggest boy nodded with a superior air. "He's *always* in, Harry. Marshal Matt Morgan don't take no chances on outlaws or anyone else raising a ruckus in Pawley, even on Sundays."

The third boy nodded in agreement. "That's right. I only wish Petey Morgan was with us."

A lone horseman rode slowly up the street. He

stopped in the act of rolling a smoke to watch a derby-hatted cyclist peddle past him. He grinned at the three boys. "Well, I'll be jiggered," he said as he looked again at the cyclist. "A fella is likely to see anything in the big city on a Sunday afternoon."

Joey snorted. "Pawley ain't such a much, mister."

The horseman scratched a match against his belt buckle and looked up and down the almost deserted street. "Used to be back in the late eighties and early nineties." He shook his head and lighted his cigarette. "Why one of these days it might even be plowed under, it's so quiet now." He rode on toward the railroad station.

Joey turned to look down at Harry. "You see? Marshal Morgan tamed Pawley in the old days. You'll learn how it was when he tells you what he had to do to make it like this."

Harry surveyed the street in disgust. "Sure wish it was still like them ol' days. Ain't nothing around here but that dirty old Indian sleeping down there."

Joey gripped Harry by a skinny shoulder. "Another thing, Harry: Mrs. Morgan is an Indian, a sure-enough full-blooded Cheyenne, so don't you say nothing about dirty ol' Indians around him."

Harry's eyes were wide in his freckled face. "Sure enough?"

"Yep."

Harry twisted his face and stared at the Indian

down at the station. "That makes Petey Morgan a half-breed then, don't it?"

Jimmy Tate turned fiercely on the small boy. "Yes, it does! But Petey is our sidekick. Besides, if you ever see his grandfather Keno you won't say anything about Indians or half-breeds."

Joey nodded. "Petey says his grandpa was a Crazy Dog back in the old days, and they were the best fighting men amongst the Fighting Cheyennes."

Harry paled. "I won't say nothing," he breathed.

Joey walked toward the marshal's office. A big poster had been tacked up on the side wall. Harry slowly scratched one bare foot against the other. "That an outlaw on that poster, Joey?" he asked in an awed voice.

Joey shook his head. "Naw! That's Teddy Roosevelt. Him and some jasper by the name of Fairbanks are running for President and Vice-President on the Republican ticket."

"You going to vote for them, Joey? Are you?"

Jimmy spat into the dust. "Him?" he said sarcastically, "He ain't hardly old enough yet, Harry."

Joey frowned. "I *will* vote for him when I'm old enough," he said. "Anyways, right now we came to see the marshal." He stepped up onto the warped porch. "Marshal Morgan?" he called out.

Matt Morgan came to the open door and leaned against the frame, eying the three dusty boys. They looked up at him with wide eyes. There was no low-slung gunbelt about his slim, horseman's waist, but you knew one belonged there.

Matt eyed the boys quizzically. "This a raid, boys?" he asked in a low voice. He tapped his marshal's badge. "I'm still on duty if it is."

"Where's Petey?" asked Jimmy Tate.

"We've been over to your house," said Joey. "He ain't there."

Matt nodded. "He rode out to the reservation with his mother. They had some dances and ceremonies out there and his mother thought he'd like to see them." He studied their disappointed faces. "He'll be back soon. You fellows have a deal with him?"

Harry wet his lips and glanced at the other boys. "Petey was going to show us the six-shooter you used in the olden days when you killed the Bradley Boys."

Matt rubbed his lean jaw. A shadow seemed to cross his gray eyes. "He was, eh?"

"And he was going to show us how you did it," said Jimmy. "Maybe you will, Marshal Morgan."

Matt smiled. "You've heard the story often enough from Petey, I'm sure."

Joey nodded. He placed a hand on Harry's head. "*We* have, but Harry here is new in Pawley. We've been telling him about you, sir. Will you tell us the story again, just for his sake, sir?"

Matt shrugged. He looked up and down the quiet street. Nothing was quieter nor duller than a Sunday afternoon in Pawley. But he himself could take the credit or the blame for that, depending upon which way it was viewed.

"How about it, Marshal?" piped up Harry.

Matt shoved back his hat. "Well, the Bradley Boys were rawhide tough; all horns, hoofs, and rattles they were. Hard case from the word go. They had me covered for sure when I stepped out on this porch."

Harry swallowed. "What happened then?"

Matt walked to a post and thrust two fingers into two holes in the post, about chest height. "You see these two bullet holes, Harry?"

Joey turned. "One was from Jeb Bradley."

"The other one was from Frank, his brother," said Jimmy.

Matt turned and placed his big hands on his hips. "Hey, who's telling the story here?"

Joey looked at Matt. "We're sorry, sir."

"Show us how you did it, Marshal," said Harry.

"We won't interrupt you again," promised Jimmy.

"All right," said Matt sternly. "I'll go on, but I have to have my stage props." He walked into his office and closed the door behind him.

Deputy Andy Bellew looked up at Matt from his game of solitaire. Matt took his gunbelt and holstered Colt from a desk drawer and swung it about his waist with practiced ease. He buckled the belt and then settled it down about his hips. "Target practice, Matt?" asked Andy dryly. "Or maybe the ghosts of the Bradley Boys?"

Matt grinned. "Some of Petey's *amigos* want to hear the story of my fight with the Bradleys." He took out the Colt and unloaded it. He twirled the cylinder. "The old hokey-pokey."

Andy scratched his jaw. "As I remember, that fight wasn't exactly what you could call hokey-pokey."

Matt shrugged. "No, but I don't believe these kids swallow half of it anyhow." He looked toward the dusty front window. It slid up halfway and three noses were pressed against the glass. Matt winked at Andy. He did the road agent's spin with the heavy six-gun, cocking it and then snapping the trigger. He reversed the spin and slid the Colt neatly into its well-worn sheath. He pulled his hat low over his eyes, winked at Andy again, and then swaggered toward the door.

Three pairs of eyes swiveled as one toward Matt. He wet his lips. "Well, here goes," he said under his breath. He raised his voice. "Here I was in my office, boys, when I first heard the ruckus in the street and the shooting." He threw back his shoulders, looked warily toward the door, then opened it cautiously and went into an exaggerated crouch. "I opens the door easy-like." He stepped out onto the porch and pointed down the street. "Down there, where Nick's Ice Cream Parlor is now, there used to be an evil place. Name of the Pink Poodle."

The boys' eyes followed him as he moved behind the bullet-pocked post. Matt pointed upward. "Jeb Bradley was up there, on that balcony

23

across the street with a six-gun and a shotgun. The shotgun was loaded with buck-and-ball . . . nasty stuff. I was out here on the street. Frank Bradley stepped out of that doorway to my right, where the old livery stable was—the one that burned down last year."

Joey shook his head admiringly. "Sure wish I'd been around in them olden times."

Matt straightened up to see Andy leaning casually against the doorframe with a suppressed smile on his face. "Yes, sir," said Matt. "Them sure were the olden times all right."

"Must be all of nine-ten years ago," said Andy dryly.

Jimmy looked at the bullet holes. "Shucks! Don't even get to hear a gunshot around here any more."

"You be glad of that, son," said Matt.

Harry wriggled with excitement. "Go ahead, Marshal. What happened next?"

Matt crouched again. "I was standing like this . . . hands out at my sides . . . so. Well, they had me covered, I tell you. I could hear angel's harps tuning up to welcome me. Like I said: those Bradley Boys were all hoofs, horns, and rattles. Mean as sin and twice as ugly." Matt drew in a deep breath. "Well, there I was all right. I slaps down my right hand." The big brown hand shot down, and the heavy Colt seemed to snap out of the leather. In one fluid motion it was cocked and leveled. Matt slitted his eyes. "I swings from the hips and aims at Jeb Bradley."

24

Hoofs rattled on the hard-baked earth at the end of the street like pebbles in a gourd. Matt turned to look. His mouth opened as he saw Petey riding *á la jinete*, with his knees tight against the sides of the saddle and his feet drawn up close under his buttocks. The big chestnut was at a full pounding gallop, foam flecking back from its mouth. The horse reared and blowed as Petey dragged back on the reins. Petey's eyes were wide with fear. Andy jumped down from the porch and took the bridle. "Easy," he said to the excited horse.

"What is it?" demanded Matt.

The boy opened his mouth and closed it. He swayed a little in the saddle.

"Petey!" snapped Matt. "Where is your mother? *What has happened to her, son?*"

Petey reached for his father with a shaking hand. "Oh, Pa, it was awful."

Matt Morgan paled. He gripped the boy and lifted him from the saddle. *"Where is she, Petey?"*

Petey stared at his father. "Back on the road . . . there was . . . she . . ." The boy broke down into harsh sobbing.

Matt swung into the saddle and reached down for Petey, whom Andy lifted up. Matt placed the boy in front of him. He took the reins and drummed his heels against the sweat-lathered flanks of the chestnut.

"I'll get a horse and follow you!" yelled Andy as Matt rode toward the road which led to the reservation.

"It was just ahead," said the boy over his shoulder.

The wind rippled the yellow grasses. The sun was low over the western hills.

"There's the buckboard," said Petey.

Matt Morgan drew in the blown chestnut and lowered the boy to the ground. He slid down beside the boy and searched the area with slitted eyes. "Stay here," he said quietly.

"There were two men," said Petey.

Matt drew his Colt and loaded it from the belt loops as he walked toward the buckboard. "Catherine!" he called.

There was no sound except the thudding of his boot heels on the hard earth and the moaning of the wind.

"Catherine!"

He looked for her in the deep grass.

"Catherine! Catherine! *Catherine!*"

He stopped short as he saw her, and the color drained from his lean face. She lay with her head on her out-stretched right arm, the long dark hair veiling her face, as though she had gone peacefully to sleep there under the warm sun and wind.

Matt stared unbelievingly at the ripped and bloody clothing and the trampled ground. It told a story of violence and lust. He reached out his left hand toward his wife and then dropped it helplessly. A tremor came over his muscular body.

Petey looked toward his father and then suddenly turned away. There was no need to tell him what had happened to his mother. He rested his head against the ornate fender of the saddle and his body shook as he tried to hold back his sobbing.

Matt slowly knelt by his wife. He carefully pushed the hair back from her face, then covered the bruised body with the ripped and soiled clothing. He picked her up and walked toward the chestnut. There was no way of shielding her ravaged body from the boy.

Then, for the first time, he really saw the elaborately decorated saddle he had ridden out there. He stopped behind the boy and stared at the saddle. "Lift that fender, Petey," he said quietly.

Two letters had been embossed on the skirt leather beneath the fender. "C.B." said Matt. His face tightened. He looked at the boy. "Round up the black, Petey. We're going to take your mother home."

Chapter Three

THE LIGHT FROM the hanging harp lamp shone dully on the silver-studded saddle, which rested on the rail that divided the marshal's office. Matt Morgan's eyes fell on it as he entered. Andy Bellew, Jeb Dobie, and old Keno, Matt's father-in-law, came into the office after him, uncomfortable in their sober suits.

Matt stopped in front of the saddle and eased his collar. Andy and Jeb walked through the gateway and turned to look at Matt. They shifted their feet, looked away, and then turned to look at him again. Only Keno, his dark eyes surprisingly sharp in his aged and weather-beaten face, did not move about.

Matt handed his sack of makings to Keno. The old Cheyenne hefted it. Matt said, "You never could roll a cigarette, could you, Keno?"

The Cheyenne shook his head and watched Matt as he took the makings back and deftly fashioned a cigarette. He placed it in Keno's mouth and then rolled one for himself.

Keno drew the smoke into his lungs and then

expelled it, watching the bluish cloud rise about the lamp. He spoke softly, as though he were addressing the smoke. "I get two friends. Dzi-tsii-tsa, Men of Men. Crazy Dogs. We follow men who did this thing. Maybe many colds we follow them. Many . . . many . . . but we find them. Kill . . . kill . . . *kill* . . ."

Matt shook his head. "There is no need to look for them, my father. I know where to find them."

Jeb Dobie shifted his chew. "You seem to recognize that saddle, Matt."

"I do."

Keno took the cigarette from his lips. His eyes looked like chips of obsidian. "Whose saddle? Where we go? I go and find. Kill."

Matt placed a hand on the old warrior's shoulder. "No," he said gently. "There would only be trouble and you wouldn't stand a chance in a white man's court in that territory."

Keno straightened his shoulders. "My daughter has been sent to the cold Land of Shadows by those men. I go!"

"She was my wife, Keno," said Matt.

Andy walked to the saddle and examined it. "It's a sure enough Pueblo; a real form-fitter."

"Made by Frazier or Gallup," opined Jeb.

Matt dropped his cigarette to the floor and slowly ground a heel on it. "Frazier," he said. "I remember when it was made."

Jeb studied Matt. "Yeh?"

"Whose it is, Matt?" demanded Andy.

Gordon D. Shirreffs

Matt passed a hand over the silver ornamentation. Then he drew back the hand and rubbed it against his coat as though to cleanse it. "This saddle and that chestnut horse are the property of a man I used to work with. A man who was once close to me. We rode the *rio* together. He and I were bunkies about ten years ago."

Jeb quickly raised his head. "Jesus," he said softly. "Not Craig Belden?"

Matt nodded. Andy whistled softly. He shoved back his hat and looked at the saddle. "I'll be damned."

Matt walked to his desk and took a pair of Mattatuck handcuffs from a drawer. He held out a hand to Andy. "I'll need your cuffs too."

The deputy took his handcuffs from where they hung on a rifle rack and gave them to him. "Listen, Matt," he said, "all we have to do is call the sheriff at Gun Hill and he can round up Craig Belden."

Matt shook his head. "I know Craig Belden better than any man. He saved my life in the old days. I know all about what he's *supposed* to be now, but whatever he is now he's still a man. It isn't like him to get mixed up in a thing like this. Another thing: he'd never cover for a man who did."

"I still think—"

"It doesn't matter *what* you think."

"But, Matt—"

"Sit down, Andy," said Jeb quietly.

30

"Jesus, Jeb!"

"You heard me!" Jeb spat. "Listen, Matt, be reasonable. Belden must have twenty or thirty hardcase hombres riding in his *corrida*. It could be any of them."

Matt shook his head. He looked at the expensive saddle. "Andy, you go on down to the station and get me a ticket on tonight's train. I'm going to deliver this saddle personally to Craig Belden."

Jeb shrugged. Keno came close to his son-in-law. "I go too, Matt," he said.

"No!"

"We kill him slow. I know how. Long, long time."

Matt walked away from the old Cheyenne. "He'll be taken care of, Keno. In *my* way."

Jeb Dobie walked to the door, jerking his head at Andy and Keno. Andy shrugged and followed the older man outside. Keno walked to the door and then turned. He eyed his son-in-law with obvious pride. This was the right way after all. The lone warrior on the long, bloody trail of vengeance. It would be as it should be. The way of the Crazy Dogs, the Dog Soldiers, and the Stronghearts, the warrior societies of the Cheyennes. "Maheo ride with you, son," he said, and he was gone.

Matt drew out his Colt and emptied it. He broke open a fresh box of .44/40 cartridges and reloaded the six-gun, never taking his eyes from the saddle. He filled the empty loops of his cartridge belt, buttoned his coat, and then picked up the heavy saddle. He turned down the lamp and stood there in the dimness. "Someone else is going to need the help of Maheo," he said quietly. He walked to the door and closed it behind him.

Chapter Four

GUN HILL was on its nightly prod. Yellow lamplight threw rectangles of light through the dirty windows onto the dusty, littered streets. Somewhere along the main street a piano which had known far better days labored through "When I Was Single," and the uneven notes were curiously intermingled with the mechanical thumping of a coin piano which was beating out "Annie Laurie."

Hip-shot horses dozed at the hitching racks, patiently waiting for their masters. A woman laughed shrilly from an open window on the second floor of Charlie's Place. Three cowpokes raced their ponies along Front Street, and one of them smashed an empty whisky bottle against the stolid face of a cigar-store Indian.

The focal point of the night's celebration was in the Horseshoe Saloon. Smoke hung in rifted layers throughout the big barroom, and the rattling of poker chips came from the curtained gaming rooms. A drunk lay asleep on a bench next to the rear wall and some wag had placed on his chest an empty whisky bottle with a faded paper flower in its mouth.

Rick Belden stood at the bar steadying himself by gripping the neck of a half-full rye bottle. Now and then he straightened up to pour a shot, and then quickly gripped the bottle again before he lost his equilibrium. He eyed himself foggily in the flyspecked mirror. The crusted scar on his right cheek gave him a curious lopsided look. "Baldy," he said loudly to the bartender, "you ought to clean that damned mirror once in a while so's a fella could see himself without looking through a mess of fly crap."

Baldy's fat, soft hands worked at polishing a glass with a dirty rag. "Lots of fellas ain't anxious to see themselves when they're standing on your side of the bar."

Rick raised his shoulders. "Meaning . . . ?" He tried to fix Baldy with a cold, deadly stare.

Baldy spat leisurely. "You heard me."

Rick released his slippery grasp on the bottle and dropped his hand to his Colt. "I oughta put a .44 slug through that mirror," he threatened.

Baldy placed the glass atop a neat pyramid of polished glasses and spoke over his shoulder. "Listen, Belden, I don't give a fiddler's damn who you are. You shoot up that mirror and, by God, your old man will pay for it!" He turned toward the glasses. "As usual," he said in a low voice.

Rick pulled in his gut and jerked down his flopping cowhide vest. "*Mister* Belden," he said.

Baldy turned and eyed Rick in disgust. "*Mister* Belden," he said sarcastically. He looked toward the wide stairway which ascended to the second floor. A lush-bodied redhead was coming down. She stopped at the foot of the stairs and coldly studied the crowd, then she looked at Rick and a change of expression came over her thickly powdered face. Baldy nodded toward Rick and shook his head at her in warning. He made a motion as though downing a drink. She smoothed her gaudy dress over her full hips and walked toward Rick. "Rickie dear!" she said loudly. "I didn't know you came back from Oklahoma! Sure missed you around this dump."

Rick turned and eyed her unsteadily. "Yeh? That so, Minnie? Just *what* did you miss about me?" He grinned loosely.

She placed a hand on his arm. "Do I have to draw you a picture in public, Rickie?" She stared at him. "My God! What lit into you? A wildcat?" She touched the scabbed slash on his face.

He slapped her hand away. "Beat it! Vamoose! I ain't got any time for you tonight, Minnie."

She tilted her head to one side and half closed her eyes. "She must have had nails an inch long. Went right down to red meat, didn't she?"

"Beat it," he said thinly.

Her scarlet mouth drew back over her teeth. "Sure does me good to know someone can hurt *you* for a change."

He bit his lower lip and looked away from her.

She reached out a hand and traced the course of the slash on his cheek. "God, what an incision she made."

Rick whirled, letting his right arm swing up with the momentum, catching her full across the mouth with a backhander. She staggered back, hit a chair, and fell heavily. Her eyes were wide in her white face, and a trickle of blood ran from the corner of her lips. "You dirty sonofabitch," she said thickly.

The batwings had swung open as Rick had struck the woman, and two men had seen the whole thing. The first man was big and solid with pale eyes in striking contrast to his mahogany-hued face. His hat was set square across his low forehead. His companion was smaller, with a muscular and wiry-looking body. His Colt was worn low and tied down. Hired gun was written all over him.

"There he is, Skag," said the big man.

Skag nodded. "On a high lonesome, Beero," he said in a curiously flat voice.

Baldy had not noticed the two newcomers. "Drink up and get out, *Mister* Belden," he said. "Minnie may not be a lady, but she sure as hell is a woman, and even *you* can't get away with hitting a woman in here."

"Go . . ." said Rick. He filled his glass, ignoring the angry looks directed at him from the men in the barroom. Several men stood up and started toward the drunken kid. Then they saw Skag and Beero. Men who had been intently watching the byplay between Rick and Minnie suddenly found an absorbing interest in cards, newspapers, or liquor. Men in Gun Hill walked and talked quietly when Craig Belden's hired guns walked the streets.

Rick looked back at the men in the big room. He laughed loudly. "Yellow bellies," he said. He downed his drink and his body seemed to stiffen a little as the rye took hold. He hadn't yet seen his father's men.

Beero leaned nonchalantly against the mahogany. "Come on, kid," he said cheerfully. "Let's go."

Rick whirled. His face paled a little, but the liquor would talk for him. "Dammit! Who you calling kid?"

Minnie was helped to her feet by Skag. She dusted off her dress and her angry eyes never left Rick Belden.

Beero rubbed his unshaven jaws and grinned. "You sure been on a high lonesome, kid."

Skag leaned against the bar and watched the men in the barroom through the smoke from his dangling cigarette. Men became uncomfortable under his cold eyes.

Beero glanced toward the rye bottle. "Seems as though your old man has been missing something, kid. Something he sets a heap of store by. Something he thinks you pinched from the tack room out at the ranch."

Rick flushed. He glanced at Skag. Skag nodded. "Your old man is on the prod, Rick. Wants you, pronto!"

Rick was scared, and it showed on his scarred face. His gut became queasy. He knew damned well his father would not have sent these two hardcases after him unless he had a good reason, and the reason was clear enough. He reached for the bottle, but Beero moved in surprisingly fast for his bulk, snatched the bottle away, thrust the stopper into it, and then skidded it down to the end of the bar, where it stopped in front of the watching Baldy.

"Damn you, Beero," said Rick. "You take orders from me, you hear? You work for my father."

Beero turned to spit into a garboon. He winked at Skag. "Yeh, Rick, we know who we work for, and he gave us orders to bring you to him, and you'd better come along or—"

"Or what?" challenged Rick.

Beero looked sadly at his big freckled paws and then at Minnie. "Or I'll drag you home by the scruff, kid. You better not start throwing punches neither, because this time you won't be slapping any dame around. Get me?"

Rick pulled down his hat and hoisted up his Levis. He tried to swagger a little as he walked toward the door. Beero looked at Skag and spoke out of the side of his mouth. "The cocky little bastard. I always did like Minnie."

Skag nodded. He flipped his cigarette into the cuspidor and followed Beero toward the door.

"You see what he done to me, Beero?" called out Minnie.

38

Beero turned and waved a big fist. "Sure did, kid. Don't worry, Min. Old Beero won't forget what he done to you." Beero formed a big fist and spat on it.

The batwings swung behind the three men. Saddle leather squeaked in the street and then the uneven pattering of hoofs sounded and died away. Minnie walked to the bar and opened the bottle Beero had slid there. She eyed the bottle. "I'll be damned if I will," she said angrily. "Give me another bottle, Baldy. I won't drink after *him*."

Baldy shrugged. "You'd better look to that mouth, Minnie."

"To hell with it! What do you think he's done this time, Baldy?"

"*Quien sabe?* I know Craig Belden didn't send two gun slicks like Skag and Beero after him just for nothing. That punk! Why, my fifteen-year-old kid could whip Rick Belden with one hand tied behind his back." Baldy idly polished another glass. "Nope, it ain't no little thing he's done this time. He's got something on his conscience."

She laughed. "Him? He ain't got any conscience."

Baldy placed the glass on a pyramid. "Maybe . . . maybe not, but you mark my words, something is going to come of all this . . . *something big*."

The firelight played on the paneled walls of the huge living room, casting alternate patches of light and shadow on the big man who sat facing the fire with his hands gripping the arms of the leather chair. Lee Smithers stood to one side, in the full light of the fire, looking down at Craig Belden. Now and then he swallowed a little.

"All right," said the ranch owner coldly. "Go over the story once more. How did Rick lose my saddle?"

"I already told you, Mr. Belden . . ."

"Goddammit, *I want to hear it again!*"

Lee swallowed hard. "Well, we stopped for a beer or two. You know how it is, Mr. Belden. Well, we come out of the saloon and both horses was gone and so was your saddle."

A log snapped in the fireplace. A waggle-tail clock swung busily to and fro as though in a feverish hurry to get the night's business over with and start a new day.

"That was in Pawley?" asked Belden at last.

"Yes, sir. Pawley. You know how Pawley is."

The dark eyes flicked up to probe into Lee Smithers' eyes. "I know it a damned sight better than you and my son do, Smithers. I know it well enough to know no one is going to steal two horses off the main stem in broad daylight on a Sunday afternoon."

Lee smiled weakly. "Guess someone didn't know the rules, Mr. Belden. I . . ."

"Shut your mouth!" Craig turned his head. "Horses. Must be the boys with Rick."

Lee paled. He looked about the huge room. A

buffalo rug was under Craig Belden's booted feet. Rifles, pistols, and fancy bridles hung on the walls, and every one of them had silver ornamentation or engraving on them. It was one of Craig Belden's fancies, and the missing saddle was his pride and joy next to his son.

Boots struck the outside stairs and thudded on the wide veranda, then knuckles beat a brisk tattoo on the door.

"Dammit!" roared the ranch owner. "You know I'm here!"

The door swung open and Rick Belden walked in, followed by Skag and Beero. Craig studied his son. "Have a nice trip, boy?"

"Yes."

"Came in on the noon train, eh? Took quite a long time to make the few miles home, though."

"Sorry, Pa."

Belden stood up and folded his thick arms. "What happened to the horses you and Lee was riding?"

"Stolen . . . I guess."

"My saddle too, eh?"

Rick wet his lips. "That's about the size of it."

Craig spat into the fireplace. "I don't *like* the size of it, son. *I don't like the size of it at all. Savvy?*"

Rick eyed his father. He nodded shortly.

Beero winked at Skag. Skag felt for the makings, looked at Craig Belden, then changed his mind.

41

Rick felt the white worms moiling in his gut. His head throbbed unmercifully and he was dying for a drink. He'd known all along he'd have to face his father, something he'd never been able to make even a partial success of, and though he had conned Lee into going out to the ranch first to ease the way for him, his old man was more angry than ever.

"Well?" demanded Craig.

Rick shifted his feet. He looked sourly at Lee. "I'll pay for the rig," he said at last.

The older man shook his head slowly and deliberately. "No. The money wouldn't mean a damned thing to me and you know it." His questing eyes seemed to bore into Rick's very soul. "I want that saddle back. Now you'll get it back if you have to ride clear down into Coahuila or wherever in hell it is. Hear?"

Rick nodded. Then he cringed as his father walked toward him. Belden slapped his son heavily on the shoulder, staggering him a little. "Now don't get too worried, son. But if any other man had taken that rig I'd change his face for him." He peered closely at Rick. "Speaking of faces, what the hell happened to you? Cut yourself shaving?"

Rick hurriedly covered his cheek wound with his hand. "Ain't nothing," he said quickly.

Skag tugged at his right ear lobe. "Take a she-bear to cut a furrow like that, eh Beero?"

Beero grunted. "Guess his pappy's saddle didn't

make him the big he-coon he thought he was. Takes more than a man's rump rubbing all that hand-tooled leather and fancy silver to make them Pawley fillies take notice of him."

Rick looked away from his father. Craig looked at the two grinning men and then at his son. "I won't interfere in this, son," he said quietly.

Rick looked down at his fancy boots and then past his father toward the fireplace.

"Did you hear what Beero said, son?" asked Belden, making each word hard and distinct.

"Beero is always joshing."

Craig looked at his two employees. Their grins faded away. But the sting was there, deep and biting, something Craig Belden could not stand; the thought that his only son was not and would never be half the man his father was.

"What's your name?" he suddenly demanded of Rick.

"Belden," said Rick.

Craig shoved the kid toward Beero. "Dammit! Then live up to your name! Go after him, son!"

Rick looked at the broad, impassive face of Beero. He might well be impassive, for he knew what he could do to Rick and two or three others his size and strength in a free-for-all while hardly raising his pulse.

"Go on," said Belden tightly. "Beero, make your play!"

"You joshing, Mr. Belden?"

"You shot off your mouth. Now you back it up. I won't interfere whatever happens."

Beero shrugged. He hitched up his Levis. "Suits me. But I'm plumb scairt to death."

Rick flushed. He ran the back of his right hand across his mouth, then suddenly he rushed the big man, swinging wildly. Beero blocked the blows with his forearms. He looked sideways at Craig.

"Fight back!" snarled the rancher.

Beero shrugged again. He blocked three more blows, straightened Rick with a left, then followed through with a smooth right cross which lifted Rick from his feet and dumped him on a couch. The couch slid against the wall, and a picture fell and bounced off Rick's head.

Skag leaned back and grinned. Beero was neat as sin, could cut a man to pieces or leave him unmarked if he so pleased.

"Get up!" raged Craig Belden at his son. "Go after him!"

Rick shook his head. He got to his feet. Beero eyed him, thick arms hanging by his sides. Skag slowly rolled a quirly and lit up. "Look out, Beero," he said tonelessly.

Rick charged in. Beero again fended off the rain of ineffectual blows, hardly moving his feet and never giving a counterblow until Rick staggered back with sweat streaming from his face and his breath coming in huge gasps.

Skag tapped Beero on the shoulder. "Now," he said.

Beero nodded. "This is for Minnie," he said out of the side of his mouth. He stepped forward, slammed a left into Rick's gut with deep satisfaction, then met the down-coming chin with a perfectly timed uppercut which snapped the head up again. Rick seemed to dance backward on his heels until he hit the wall with a dull thud. He swayed sideways, bumped into Lee Smithers, then fell heavily. Then he retched violently, spewing a sour mess of liquor all over the huge buffalo rug. Tears ran from his reddened eyes and mingled with the blood trickling from his mouth.

Beero looked coolly at Craig. "Enough?" he asked slyly.

Craig nodded.

Beero hitched up his trousers and grinned at Skag. "Know what, *amigo*? I feel like a beero."

Skag opened the door.

Beero looked at Rick again and laughed. "Jesus," he said.

Craig Belden moved swiftly. He gripped Beero by the shoulder and spun him about. He smashed a right to the broad jaw, which drove the big man through the doorway. Beero lost his balance, tripped, and then fell heavily down the veranda stairs. His hat lay on the living-room floor. Belden picked it up and threw it out the door. "My name is Belden too. Remember that, Beero."

Beero felt his jaw. Skag leaned against a post and grinned down at his partner. "Still feel like a beero, Beero?"

45

"Shut up."

Skag grinned again and shook his head.

Craig Belden walked to his son and pulled him to his feet. "Well," he said quietly, "at least you tried. I don't know how you got that slash on your cheek, and I don't give a damn. That's between you and whoever did it. Savvy?"

Rick nodded. He wiped the mess from his face and shirt. His body shook as he walked toward his room. Craig looked at Lee Smithers. "You get your war bag and possibles and go along with my boy. You two get the hell out of here as soon as you can and find that saddle. *Vamonos!*"

Lee left. Craig looked into the fire. His face was hard and there was no light in his dark eyes, but his mouth worked a little before he turned away and walked slowly toward his room.

Chapter Five

THE THREE-CAR TRAIN pounded steadily across the moonlit grasslands, swaying and dipping on the strap iron. The steady throbbing of the exhaust and the clicking of the wheels on the rail joints seemed to have a soporific effect on the male passengers in the baggage coach. Tobacco smoke lifted and wavered and drifted out the open windows.

Craig Belden's saddle lay on the seat across from Matt Morgan. Now and then one of the other passengers, particularly those whose mannerisms and clothing stamped them as Westerners, looked at the ornate saddle and then at the plain-clothed man who sat across from it.

The door at the rear of the coach opened and the conductor ushered in a young woman. One after the other, all of the passengers, with the exception of Matt, turned to eye her in appreciation.

The woman turned to the conductor. "*This* car?"

The conductor shrugged. "We've got only two cars for passengers, ma'am, and you sure can't smoke in the other one. It's against company rules."

"Yeh, you already told me that three times."

The conductor flushed and then hastily shut the door behind him. She stood there, idly twirling a beaded handbag at the end of its long strap. She looked up and down the short aisle. All of the window seats had been taken. A derby-hatted drummer stood up and smiled at her. "Right here, ma'am. Been saving this seat for a lady."

She opened her mouth to speak and then saw the saddle lying across from Matt.

"Sit down, ma'am," said the drummer. He reached for her arm.

She glanced casually at him. "Shut up," she said. "Don't you know a lady when you see one?"

He drew back in mock surprise and yanked off his dusty derby. "Why sure, ma'am. How could I have been mistaken?"

A rancher laughed as she walked past the grinning drummer. She stopped beside Matt's seat. The drummer leaned out into the aisle and eyed her hips. He whistled softly.

She took a cigarette from her bag and tapped it on the back of her left hand. "Pardon me, mister."

Matt did not turn from the window.

"Pardon me, mister," she said in a louder tone.

Matt turned and looked up at her. She was a little startled at the lost look in his gray eyes. She waved her cigarette. He narrowed his eyes. She smiled uncertainly. "All I want is a light, mister."

Suddenly he seemed to come out of the shell he had been in. He stood up, tipped his dusty hat, then took a match from a pocket. He snapped it into light on a thumbnail and held it out to her. She gripped his wrist to steady herself and then drew in deeply on the cigarette. "Can I offer you one?" she asked.

"No thanks. I like handmades."

"Mind if I sit here?"

"Suit yourself," he said tonelessly.

"Yeh," she said dryly. She smoothed her skirt and sat down. Matt dropped down beside her. She winced as the holstered Colt struck her soft thigh. Matt moved away from her. "Sorry, ma'am."

She eyed the saddle. "Forget it. That's a beautiful saddle, mister."

He nodded and looked out of the window at the varying pattern of the lighted windows against the brown and yellow grasses.

"Pueblo, ain't it?" she persisted.

He nodded again.

She turned toward him and drew back her head to study his lean profile. "Talkative, ain't you?"

He looked at her, and once again she felt the impact of his gaze. "I am when I want to be, ma'am," he said mildly.

The train rattled around a sweeping curve and threw her against him. The Colt pressed against her thigh again. "How far are you going?" she asked.

"Gun Hill."

She nodded in satisfaction. "I thought so." She studied him speculatively as though he would be jolted out of his composure at her knowledge of his destination, but his face did not change.

She leaned toward the window to throw out her cigarette, and he gripped her by the wrist, took the butt from her fingers, dropped it on the floor, and ground it out. He released her with the ghost of a smile. "That grass out there is as dry as tinder, ma'am."

She flushed. "I should have known better."

"Forget it."

She leaned back in her seat and studied him. "Cattleman?"

"No."

"Oil man?"

"No."

She smoothed her skirt. "Texas man?"

"Oklahoma."

She laughed gayly.

"What's the joke?"

"At least you answered one question without saying no."

He looked quickly at her and the ghost of a smile seemed to drift across his tanned face.

"I've been riding these rattletraps all the way from Laredo. You ever been there?"

"Years ago."

"I was in the hospital there. I don't like the town, and the hospital stinks."

"So?"

She glanced at the saddle. "I transferred back at the junction and been riding back in that other car, dying for a smoke. Where are you coming from?"

"Pawley."

"You're surely not a businessman, which leaves one job you must have."

He looked at her with amused eyes. "You're determined to find out what I do, aren't you?"

She nodded "You're a lawman."

"Keno." He looked from the window again.

"You don't like ladies much, do you?" His level gaze flustered her again. "Well, dammit, a girl has to make a living somehow. You married?" She tilted her head to one side. "You don't have to answer that. I know."

"You're right."

"Any kids?"

He seemed to soften a little. "One . . . a boy . . . name of Petey."

"I'm glad. This is a good country for men and dogs, but it's hell on horses and women."

"I don't know much about that."

The locomotive whistle sounded. She shivered a little. "Loneliest sound in the world," she said.

"A coyote can sound pretty lonely out on the prairies at night."

"My name is Linda Lewis."

"Pleased. I'm Matt Morgan."

"That's a nice-sounding name."

"It'll do."

51

She looked up and down the aisle. A slightly drunken cowpoke leered at her. She wanted another cigarette, but it was bad enough for a woman to be seen smoking in public, let alone being a chain smoker.

"If you feel like another smoke, go ahead," Matt said. "It doesn't bother me."

"What about the others?"

Matt glanced up and down the car. The drummer met his gaze, tried to grin, then lost all desire to do so as he saw those gray eyes probing into his. Matt took out a match, but she had already lighted up. "I thought you didn't have a light," he said.

She smiled. "I just wanted to sit here."

"Look, Miss Lewis . . ."

"Linda," she said quickly.

"Linda then. I'm not in the mood for conversation tonight."

She flushed, dropped the cigarette to the floor, and stamped on it. She stood up. "Look, Mister Morgan," she said in a low voice, "I don't know what your game is, but if you're a lawman going to Gun Hill with that saddle, and packing a six-shooter under your coat, looking for trouble, you'll sure as hell get all you want. That's one thing I'm certain of."

"So?" he asked coolly.

She leaned toward him. "I happen to know whose saddle that is."

"Why," he said quietly, "so do I."

She stared at him for a moment and then straightened up. "Oh hell," she snapped. She walked toward the rear of the car, ignoring the eyes of the other men.

The drummer swiveled in his seat to stare at her swaying hips. "That guy must be nuts," he said aloud.

Matt turned in his seat to look at the drummer. The man slumped in his seat and pulled his derby low over his eyes.

The locomotive whistle sounded again, echoing and reechoing from the ghostly, moonlit hills.

A scarf of smoke hung low from the stack of the Standard as it rounded a low hill and whistled for the crossing just outside of Gun Hill. Two long and two short, and the echoes had hardly died away when the engineer began braking for the station. The bright morning sunlight shone against the dirty windows of the coaches.

"Gun Hill!" the conductor called out. "The jewel of the prairies! Five-minute stop to wet your whistles, gentlemen! Charlie's Place is a block from the station!"

The train slowed down for the station. The drummer yawned as he looked from the window. "Jesus," he said, "this looks like the end of nowhere." He reached up for his bag and sample cases.

A cowman cut a chew and stowed it in his mouth. "Ain't so bad," he said laconically.

"Gun Hill?" The drummer shook his head. "How'd it get its name?"

"*Quien sabe?*"

"What does that mean?"

"Means 'Who knows?' in Spic." The cowman spat through the open window. "Ain't rightly the name for it anyways."

"So? What *should* it be named?"

The cowman stood up and took his war bag from the rack. "Beldenville!" he said loudly.

Some of the other passengers laughed, and a few of them scowled. There was a reaction from everyone except Matt Morgan. He slapped the dust from his coat, set his hat, rolled a quirly and put it into his mouth as the train halted. He picked up the saddle and walked toward the door.

The girl was standing on the platform of the rear car as Matt left the coach-and-baggage combination. She stepped down onto the platform. The drummer was right behind Matt. He whistled. "Nice ankles."

"Fine-looking filly," said the cowman. "Slender in the pasterns, lithe in the flank, and with a knowing look in the eyes."

"I don't know about that," said the drummer, "but back in Philly we'd call her a nice bit of fluff."

The girl heard him. She looked away.

Matt turned and looked down at the drummer. "You've got a big mouth," he said quietly.

"Say! I don't have to take that, you!"

The cowman gripped the drummer by the arm and shook his head. They watched Matt swing down onto the ballast. He tipped his hat and took Linda's bag from her hand.

"But you have enough to carry already," she protested.

He smiled. "I owe you something for being so rude last night."

She stared at him and then laughed. "You *are* a strange one."

"That's exactly what my father said the first time he laid eyes on me."

They walked toward the street which paralleled the tracks. The drummer followed them with angry eyes. "Who the hell does he think he is?"

The cowman spat. "Forget it. Let that kind of man strictly alone. Strictly alone . . . you understand?"

"Why?"

A cowpuncher limped past them. He nodded. "You listen to what he says, stranger. You'll get to know that type man when you see him out here, providin' you live long enough to get eddicated."

"Come on, I'll buy," said the cowman.

Skag and Beero stood beside a buckboard watching the passengers walking toward town. "There she is," said Skag.

Beero nodded. He threw down his cigar. "Who's the jasper with her?"

"Damned if I know, but I sure as hell know whose saddle that is he's totin'."

"Jesus! It's the old man's!"

"You got perfect eyesight," said Skag dryly. "Not only has he got the old man's saddle but he's got his filly too." He whistled softly. "He sure don't care how long he lives."

Beero hitched up his belt. "I'll handle him. You take Linda out to the ranch."

Skag shrugged. He studied the tall stranger in the dark suit.

"Linda!" called out Beero. "Over here! We been waiting for you."

She stopped and turned to look at the big man. "I'm not going out to the ranch," she said.

Beero's eyes widened. "What do you mean?"

Skag impatiently walked forward. "Come on, kid," he said. "The old man don't like to be kept waiting. Besides, I ain't got all day."

"I'm going to stay at the Harper House," she said.

"Why dammit, Linda," blurted Beero. "The hell you are!"

Matt put down the girl's bag. "You heard the lady," he said.

Beero opened his mouth and then shut it as Skag shot him a hard look. Skag smiled at Matt. He had met his kind before. They didn't scare easy, if at all. "I'll be glad to drive Miss Lewis to the hotel," said Skag.

Skag walked forward and picked up Linda's bag. His flat eyes studied Matt's coat, looking for the gun location: shoulder holster, pocket gun, hip pocket, or standard side holster.

Linda hesitated. She looked at Matt. "Thanks for everything, Mr. Morgan."

"No trouble at all, Miss Lewis."

Skag placed the bag in the buckboard and helped the girl up onto the seat. He swung up beside her, nodded to Matt and drove off. "See you at Charlie's later, Beero!" he called back over his shoulder. He glanced at Linda. "Friend of yours?"

"I met him on the train."

"He's in bad company," he said dryly.

"With Beero? That's a fact."

Skag slapped the reins against the dusty flanks of the horses. "No, I didn't mean Beero; I meant that saddle."

Matt hailed the conductor as he passed by. "What time does the northbound go through here tonight?"

"Nine o'clock. Last train."

"*Gracias.*"

Matt took out his watch and opened the lid. It was exactly nine-thirty.

Beero rubbed his jaw and looked at the saddle. Matt saw that his horse had a *B* brand. "That your cayuse?" he asked.

Beero nodded.

"Craig Belden's spread?"

Beero nodded again.

"Far from here?"

"No. That's a nice rig you're toting there."

"Not my style; too fancy."

"You know who it belongs to?"

"Yep."

Beero's pale eyes narrowed. "Just what is your game, mister?"

Matt placed the saddle on a baggage truck and offered his makings to the big gunhand. Beero rolled a smoke. He returned the sack to Matt, never taking his eyes from him.

"I asked you what was your game."

The hard gray eyes studied Beero through the smoke. "Draw poker most of the time, although I'm also partial to blackjack."

Beero's jaw dropped a little.

Matt flipped away the match. "You go and tell Mr. Belden I'm coming out to see him in a short time."

"You got a handle?"

"He'll know me when he sees me." Matt took the saddle and walked toward the main street. "*Buenos días.*"

Beero stared after him. "Well, I'll be dipped in sheep manure," he said slowly. He walked to his horse and swung up. He touched it with his spurs and rode off, but he kept watching Matt Morgan over his shoulder until Matt was out of sight.

Matt headed for the nearest livery stable. A man stopped forking hay and looked curiously at the saddle. Matt shoved back his hat and wiped the sweat from his face. "I'd like to hire a buckboard," he said.

"You come to the right place, mister. Two- or four-seat; one horse or two?"

"Four-seat and two-horse. I might have to bring some passengers back with me."

"You got a nice load there."

Matt nodded.

"Craig Belden's, ain't it?"

"Yes."

The man leaned his fork against the wall and went to get the rig and team. Matt looked up and down the sunny street. Skag was helping Linda from the buckboard. She was a hurdy-gurdy girl all right, maybe a cut or two above the average of her type, but she seemed to be all right, and a shade brighter than most of her profession.

The liveryman brought the buckboard to the door. Matt tossed the saddle into it. The liveryman whistled sharply. "Holy Jesus! Take it easy on that saddle, mister!"

Matt took the reins. "I don't think I'll need this rig very long."

"Take your time. The longer the better. Business has been slow lately."

Matt rolled out into the street. Here and there along the boardwalk men stopped talking when they saw the saddle. They knew that elaborate Pueblo and the man who owned it. There had been rumors around Gun Hill that it had been stolen.

Signing the register in the hotel, Linda looked through the open doorway and saw Matt pass by.

"There he goes," said Skag.

Linda felt in her purse. "Just what is he up to, Skag?"

Skag shrugged. "*Quien sabe?* All I know is that the old man is sure riled about that saddle being missing. There's something queer about the whole deal, kid."

"Meaning?"

Skag held out his slim hands, palms upward. "Like I said: *Quien sabe?*"

Matt Morgan drove along the winding road to the east. The dry wind rippled the grass and hummed steadily through the telephone wires. Far ahead he could see a fence which seemed to stretch endlessly across the country.

A big sign hung from the sturdy pole gate, and Matt could read the letters easily from quite a distance. "Belden Cattle and Land Company," he said aloud. A pair of immense Texas longhorns had been fastened above the sign.

Matt got down to open the gate and lead the team through. He paused for a moment to look about. In all that immensity of space the only signs of man were the fences and the line of warped telephone poles. Craig Belden had done right well for himself, thought Matt as he drove on, but then he had always known Craig would hew out a niche in the upper brackets. The man coupled an inborn native shrewdness with a driving determination to make a success of whatever he did, and it looked now as though he had reached his pinnacle.

Matt glanced down at the resplendent saddle. Craig Belden had once put every dime he owned into paying for the rig. It had been a sort of a fetish for him, a promise to himself that someday he would rate such expensive finery.

The hill seemed to rise up out of the gathering haze. It was crowned with buildings, and from its summit one could probably see miles and miles of prime grazing land dotted with cattle. Every inch of that land belonged to Craig Belden. Matt whistled softly as he saw the ranch houses. The sun flashed from the revolving blades of a big windmill. Dust was rising from a corral on the southern slope of the hill, and the wind picked up the distant bawling of cattle.

Chapter Six

A STEER BAWLED hoarsely from the corral. Bitter smoke rose to mingle with the choking dust churned up by hoofs and boots. A cowpoke yelled angrily as the steer smashed him back against the fence. The harsh smell of singed hair hung in the air. Craig Belden sat on the top rail with his hat low over his slitted eyes, unmindful of the dust and stink.

Riding toward the corral, Beero stood up in the stirrups to look for his boss. He spotted him, then glanced back toward the road. The stranger was driving fast and would probably reach the house ahead of Mr. Belden.

Beero swung down from his horse and walked toward the corral. He could see Rick Belden out of the corner of his eye. The kid was leaning against a post, and he turned away as he saw Beero. His face was still swollen and discolored. Beero grinned.

"Boss!" yelled Beero above the din.

Craig turned. "Well?"

"He showed up, boss!"

"*Who* showed up?"

"The horse thief."

"You talk like a damned fool."

Beero shoved back his hat. "This hombre comes off the train this morning, carrying your saddle as bold as brass."

"Who is he?"

Beero shrugged. "*Quien sabe?* When I asked his handle he said you'd know him when you saw him."

Craig dropped to the ground. "Rick! Bring my horse."

Rick led his father's fine dun forward. He glanced nervously at Beero and then at his father. He had heard every word that passed between the two men.

"Linda was supposed to be on that train," said Belden.

"She was," said Beero.

"Then where the hell is she? You and Skag was supposed to bring her here."

"She talked Skag into driving her to the Harper House. Said she was going to stay there instead of out here."

The hard eyes held Beero's. "Can't you and Skag do a simple thing like bringing a woman out here?"

Beero hesitated. "Well, she said she wasn't coming, and I wasn't about to drag her, boss."

"Why'd she go to the Harper House?"

There was a faintly malicious grin on the broad face. "I wouldn't know, boss."

Craig Belden flushed a little. He swung up into his saddle. "Who is this jasper with my saddle?"

"Damned if I know. I never seen him before. I do know one thing about him."

"So?"

"He won't crawfish for anyone . . . even you, boss."

"We'll see about that! He better, by God, have a damned good reason for having that saddle."

Beero mounted. He looked casually at Rick. "It wouldn't surprise me none if he did, boss."

The two of them rode up the slope toward the ranch buildings. Rick wet his lips. He touched the crusted scab on his face. There would be hell to pay now, and he wasn't at all sure what his father's reaction would be when he found out what Rick had done. He looked up the slope at the broad back of his old man. He felt an impulse to get a horse and jump up some dust riding out of there.

He had talked his father out of the notion that he and Lee should go off to look for that saddle. That half-breed kid's eyes had been too sharp, and he would be able to give a damned good description of Rick and Lee to the lawmen. Rick had figured he was safe enough in his own territory until the hullabaloo died down.

His throat was dry and his guts churned as he looked up toward the ranch buildings. Who was

64

the man who had brought the saddle back to Gun Hill?

The silver-mounted saddle lay in the dust at the foot of the veranda steps. A buckboard and team stood to one side.

Craig Belden rode toward the house. His face tightened and the blood rushed into it as he saw his treasured rig lying on the ground. He swung down from his horse, with his eyes still on the saddle. Beero slid to the ground. "I'll stick close," he said.

Craig walked toward the veranda, trying to probe the dimness with his eyes. There was someone sitting there, taking his ease in one of the big wicker chairs. An odd feeling came over Craig. He turned to look at Beero. "Take my saddle to the tack room and have one of the boys clean it up."

"But, boss . . ."

"Dammit! Do as you're told!"

Beero shrugged. He stared into the shadows of the porch. It was the stranger from the train all right. He picked up the heavy saddle and carried it away.

Matt stood up as Craig ascended the stairs. Craig stared at him, then shoved back his hat and thrust out a big hand. "Well I'll be damned! Matt! Matt Morgan!"

Matt held out his hand. "How are you, Craig?"

"Fine, just fine. Sassy as a jaybird." Craig Belden threw back his head and laughed. "Matt Morgan!

And I was coming here to hang a hoss thief! This is good . . . really good."

There was no return smile on Matt Morgan's lean face. "It might not be after I tell you why I brought that saddle back."

Craig looked at him quickly. "Sure I want to hear the story of how you got hold of it, but that will keep until we have a drink. Come on into the house." He opened the screen door and looked sideways at Matt. "You find the thief or thieves?"

"No. But I will."

"Sure you will!"

There was deep pride on Belden's face as he looked at Matt for his comments on the big room. Matt saw the massive fireplace, the expensive weapons and other decorations, the fine oil paintings, and the solid furniture. It would have taken him several years to pay for those furnishings out of his marshal's salary.

Craig waved Matt to a chair. "Well, I'll be damned. About ten years, ain't it, Matt?"

Matt nodded. He placed his hat on a side table and wiped the sweat from his forehead.

"You're still the marshal at Pawley, eh?"

"Right."

"I've been meaning to invite you and the wife here for some time. Got plenty of room. We could have a real old-fashioned barbecue and hoedown with all the trimmings. But, well, you know how it is, Matt. Big ranch, other business interests, a little politics."

"Yes," said Matt dryly. "I know how it is."

"Remember the old days along the border? The plans we made sitting around the campfires? Broke as sheepherders, with patches on our Levis and one shirt apiece." Grinning widely, the rancher opened a large mahogany cabinet and looked at the imposing array of bottles of all sizes, shapes, and colors. "Always said you should have stuck with me, Matt," he said over his shoulder. "Hell's fire! Half of all this place would have been yours, but you always took things a little too easy. *Mañana, mañana,* you used to say all the time, when I was itching to get along."

Matt looked about the room. "Well," he said quietly, "you seem to have gotten along, Craig."

Craig took out a cut-glass decanter. "Let's see? Rye is your drink, isn't it?"

"Always was, like yours."

"Yeh, well, I've taken to Scotch the last few years."

Craig filled the glasses and then dropped into a chair, thrusting out his feet, careless of the spurs on the thick rug. "Now don't get the idea it's just money with me, Matt. Land is important to me. Always was. I got me a big *casa* right in the middle of my *estancia,* and my land stretches so far you'd wear out a couple of horses riding around it."

Matt thought back on what he had been thinking as he had approached Craig's spread.

Craig scowled at the rug. "Security, Matt, that's the ticket for a man. Something a man can leave to his son. A boy like mine who won't forget what I done for him."

Matt sipped his rye. It was smooth and mellow, the best that money could buy, and rarely found in local saloons. "You've got a son? I didn't know that, Craig."

"He was only seven when I knew you."

"Where is he now?"

"He's around somewhere. Restless kid. My wife died in childbirth. The boy was raised for a time by her folks while I was seeing the elephant."

"You never mentioned being married in the old days."

Craig looked down at his embossed boots. "No, Matt. It was too painful for me. Died in childbirth like I said, which makes the boy doubly important to me. He's all I got to remember her by, and to keep me from being lonely in my old age. You'll like him, Matt."

"I imagine."

Craig looked curiously at Matt. He raised his glass. "Here's to the old days! *Salud!*"

"*Salud!*"

"Now tell me about my saddle, Matt."

"How did you lose it?"

"Well, my boy Rick borrowed it. He was heading for Dodge or somewhere with an *amigo* of his, Lee Smithers. They stopped in a saloon, and when they came out their horses were gone and so was my saddle." Craig grinned. "I couldn't get over the fact that you had horse thieves still operating around Pawley, Matt."

Matt leaned forward. He ignored the jibe. "What day did they stop in Pawley for those drinks?"

"Let's see? Saturday, was it? No. It was last Sunday, I'm sure."

"The day my wife was raped and murdered."

Craig's eyes widened in horror. "My God, Matt, what are you saying?" He leaned forward. "You've been sitting here all this time listening to me run off at the mouth keeping *that* to yourself?"

Matt looked down at his glass. The pain flooded through him again and there was nothing he could say without betraying how he really felt.

"Is there anything I can do? What can a man say to a friend at a time like this?" Craig raised his glass and then lowered it. He shook his head. "My God," he said softly.

Matt placed his glass on the table. "There were two men involved in the murder of my wife. Possibly the same two men who stole your horses and saddle."

Belden stood up and refilled the glasses. "Go on," he said over his shoulder.

Matt eyed the big rancher. "I brought back your saddle in the hopes that you would help me find those two men."

"Certainly! I'll call a halt on the work here. My whole *corrida* will turn out for the search, and I can get more men from Gun Hill. I'll turn out

69

every able-bodied man in the county to help you. I've got influence here, Matt." Craig filled Matt's glass. "Trouble is those two men could probably walk into this room right now and we wouldn't know them. Gives you an odd feeling, doesn't it?"

"I'll know *one* of them, Craig."

"How so?"

"One of them was marked by my wife's whip. My boy Petey says the lash cut almost to the bone."

Craig's hand tightened about the neck of the rye decanter. "That so?" He picked up the two glasses and turned slowly. He handed a glass to Matt and then sat down. "Just where was this bastard cut?"

Matt drew a line on his right cheek with a finger, from under the eye down to the mouth. "Here."

The Scotch glass suddenly shattered in Craig Belden's powerful left hand. Liquor and blood ran together from the clenched fingers to drip on the rug. Craig seemed heedless of his injury.

"You'd better have that attended to," Matt said. "Cuts leave scars. The wound Catherine gave that killer would mark him for life."

Craig nodded slowly. He opened his fist and let the glass fragments fall to the rug. He took a fine linen handkerchief from his pocket and bound it about his hand.

"Have you seen a man marked that way, Craig?"

Belden turned one end of the handkerchief under the other.

"*Have you?*"

Belden knotted the bandage and pulled it tight with his teeth. His eyes held Matt's as he did so. "No."

"You're sure?"

"My word on it."

Matt nodded. "That's good enough for me. I was in my office the day it happened. There was no report turned in to me or my deputy about any horses being stolen in Pawley."

"The boys were scared, I guess, about me learning about the saddle being taken. I don't give a damn about the horses. I've got hundreds of them in my cavvies. But that saddle is important to me. Rick possibly figured he'd find the saddle himself."

"Maybe. I've got your chestnut, by the way."

"Keep it as a gift from me, Matt."

Matt stood up and put on his hat. He drained his glass. "No, Craig. Thanks just the same. I wouldn't want to have it around. You understand?"

Belden stood up. "I'm going to do everything in my power to help you find those killers."

"*Gracias.*" Matt walked to the door and out onto the veranda. He looked down the long slope across the range land. Craig came out behind him. "I'd

71

like to talk to Rick and his friend," said Matt casually.

"Why? There's nothing they can tell you, Matt. Like I told you, they were in a bar in Pawley. Some jasper stole their horses. That's the whole story they can tell."

"That's all they told you then?"

"Yes."

Matt nodded. He did not look at his old friend. *"Which one of them has a fresh scar across his right cheek, Craig?"*

Belden paled beneath his tan. "What are you driving at, Matt?"

Matt traced an imaginary scar down his right cheek. His eyes were like chips of ice. "One of the two who raped and killed Catherine has the brand of the devil on his face."

Craig tried to return the steady gaze and failed. He looked away.

"Your son is a liar," said Matt slowly. "Those horses were not stolen in Pawley, and those boys never had a drink in Pawley that Sunday."

"So? Maybe you check on every man who does have a drink in Pawley on a Sunday afternoon?"

"No. I don't have to. There are two saloons in Pawley. *They do not open on Sundays.* I closed them myself for Sunday business, and that was months ago."

The wind shifted as they stood there. The big Eclipse windmill turned and began to hum steadily, the huge blades revolving faster and

faster. A mule bawled from a corral and somewhere within the big house a door slammed shut.

"Where is Rick?" asked Matt.

"I don't know."

"I want to talk to him and his partner."

"Now, Matt, don't you go . . ."

"Was it your son, Craig?"

"No! Now you just let me handle this thing,
Matt. I'll see to it. I . . ."

Matt came close to his old partner. "You'll find
those two boys for me."

"Look, Matt, don't you go telling Craig Belden
what to do."

"It's your play, Craig. Either you find those two
boys for me, or I'll find them myself."

Belden looked quickly up and down the veranda. "Look," he said swiftly, "you let Rick alone
and I'll see to it that you get Lee Smithers."

Matt spat. "You haven't changed, Craig. Still
making deals."

"You're not to lay a hand on my son. Understand?"

"I only understand one thing: My wife was
raped and murdered. If those boys did it they'll
get a fair trial. Nothing more; nothing less."

"In Pawley? Don't rib me, Matt. Take Smithers.
Let my boy go. I'm warning you."

Matt looked up at the cloud-dotted sky. "You're
warning me?" he asked softly. "Maybe you should
have seen my wife as I found her, with my boy

standing there hardly understanding that she was gone forever."

Craig's eyes shifted. He glanced down at the bulge under Matt's coat. He looked up again and stepped back.

Matt shook his head. "Don't try, Craig. You never could beat me, and even if you did now it wouldn't save your son. He committed one of the worst of all crimes. Even if you stop me now, there will be other lawmen coming here for him."

Craig looked past his old friend. Beero was leaning against the base of the windmill, slowly rolling a smoke, and his eyes were on Matt. Matt glanced behind him. "You might get me, Craig, one way or another, but you'll never save Rick by killing me."

Craig's jaw thrust out. "You've been doing all the talking. Now you listen to me. I own this country. I own the town. I own the sheriff. Now listen to me good. You take tonight's train out of Gun Hill and don't come back. No one will bother you today if you promise to get on that train."

"I'll get on the train all right, Craig, and I'll have two prisoners with me."

Matt walked down the steps to the buckboard. Beero lighted his cigarette. He looked at Craig. Craig shook his head. Matt got up into the rig. "Nine o'clock tonight, Craig. Either they come to me or I'll come for them. *Adios!*" He slapped the reins against the horses and drove toward the gate.

Belden walked to the edge of the veranda. He watched Matt get down to open the Texas gate, and then drive on. Matt did not look back as he drove down the long slope.

"Beero!" roared Belden.

The big man ran heavily toward the house. "Yes, boss?"

"Get Skag! Move! *Vamonos!*" Craig looked toward the dust rising behind the buckboard. "We've got some fast work to do!"

Chapter Seven

MATT MORGAN DREW the team to a halt across the street from the ugly town hall of Gun Hill. He alighted and slapped the dust from his clothing. He crossed the street and entered the building. A brass plate labeled "Sheriff's Office" hung over a door at the end of the hall. The door was open and a cloud of tobacco smoke drifted out.

A big man with a comfortable-looking paunch beneath his vest sat behind a littered desk. A cigar was clenched in his teeth. He looked up as Matt entered.

"Sheriff in?"

The fat man's little eyes seemed to veil themselves. "Not exactly."

"What does that mean?"

"First you tell me your business."

"I have two John Doe warrants. Rape and murder case. It's customary to let the local sheriff know."

The man rubbed one of his jowls. "Won't be necessary in this particular case, Morgan."

76

"I don't know you. How did you know me?"

"Description of you."

Matt glanced at the phone on the wall. Then he remembered the line of telephone poles along the road to Craig Belden's place.

The fat man inspected his cigar. "I suppose you figure on getting some help from this office?"

"Customary, isn't it?"

"Maybe. Maybe not."

"You mean it's not customary in Gun Hill?"

"Take it any way you want to."

"Who are you?"

"Josh Bartlett."

"Deputy?"

Bartlett shook his head. He turned over the left side of his vest. A star was pinned there. "Sheriff," he said.

"Sheriff Bartlett then?"

Bartlett unpinned the badge and tossed it into a drawer. "Not today, Morgan."

"Just what does that mean?"

Bartlett stood up and brushed the ashes from his vest and trousers. He walked to the window and looked out. "Come here," he said over his shoulder.

Matt walked to the window and looked up the main street. Bartlett placed a fat hand on Matt's shoulder. "You see that big hotel down there? Craig Belden's. That livery stable? Craig Belden's. The general store? Craig Belden's. I can go on for quite a while. Those cattle pens along the spur track. Couple of saloons. So on and so on . . ."

Matt removed the clammy hand from his shoulder. "Including the law hereabouts."

Bartlett flushed. "A man has to take the long view hereabouts."

"Meaning Belden put you into office?"

"That's the size of it."

Matt walked back to the desk, eyeing the immense ash tray full of cigar butts, the ornate and heavy silver fittings of the desk. "I see your hand," he said.

Bartlett sucked noisily at his juicy cigar. He felt in his vest pocket and drew out a match. "I like Gun Hill, Morgan. I like being sheriff." He lighted the cigar and puffed out a blob of smoke. "Maybe someday Belden will relax his grasp on this county. Then maybe things will change. But right now I'm taking the long view, Marshal."

Matt stared at him. "You call yourself a lawman? You damned two-bit politician!"

Bartlett flushed. "Now you listen here! I'm only trying to do things sensibly."

"Bartlett, you stink. What rock did you crawl from under?"

The sheriff walked forward. "Now you listen here! I run this law office. I don't take orders from a half-assed town marshal. Get that straight!" He waved a pudgy fist under Matt's nose.

Matt swung up an open right hand and caught him a hard blow, smashing the juicy cigar all over

Bartlett's chin. Matt wiped his hand on his trousers. "I'm serving these warrants, with or without your help. When I leave Gun Hill tonight those two killers will be with me."

Bartlett wiped his face. His little eyes blazed with frustrated fury. "You'll never get out of here alive."

Matt walked to the door. "Just don't interfere with me, Bartlett."

The sheriff's wet lips drew back. "Me? You make me laugh. I don't have to interfere. You'll learn. I'll spit on your grave, Morgan."

Matt laughed shortly. "That's about the limit of what you can do."

He walked toward the outer door.

Bartlett stuck his head into the hallway. "I'll spit on your grave, you hear?" he yelled.

Matt crossed the street. Bartlett watched him from the window. "Oh, you straight-backed bastard," he said softly. "I'll have a ringside seat when you get your comeuppance." He reached for the phone. "Mr. Belden will want to hear what happened here."

Craig Belden stood at the foot of the steps with his thumbs hooked over his gunbelt. He watched Rick and Lee ride toward him, followed by Beero and Skag. Rick swung down from his horse. Lee hesitated, looked back at the two men behind him, and then slowly dismounted.

"Beero said you wanted to see me, Pa," said Rick.

Craig looked from one to the other of them. "You lied to me about that saddle," he said coldly.

Lee shoved back his hat. "Listen, Mr. Belden."

"Shut up!"

Rick's eyes blinked nervously. "Now, Pa. Wait a minute. That's no way to talk to Lee."

"I'll talk any way I damned please to him and to you too. *I say you both lied to me!*"

The two young men looked at each other. "We was scared, Pa," said Rick in a low voice. "You know I always tell the truth to you."

"You've got a damned good reason to be scared now."

"What do you mean, sir?" asked Lee.

Craig eyed them. "What about that woman at Pawley?"

Rick's face whitened beneath his tan. "We didn't mean her any harm."

"Yeh . . . yeh . . ." said Lee hastily.

Rick raised his head a little defiantly. "You once told me yourself there ain't nothing nicer than a young, good-looking squaw. Why, anyway we didn't really hurt her. She must have fallen or something after we left her."

"*You know who that woman was?*"

Lee waved a hand. "She wasn't nothing but a dirty squaw, Mr. Belden."

"Shut up!"

Lee flushed. "Say," he said angrily.

Craig moved swiftly. He backhanded Lee across the face. The kid staggered back and almost fell. He stared incredulously at the big rancher, and slowly fingered his bleeding mouth. Belden took out his wallet and threw some bills into the dust at Lee's feet. "Get out of here before I kill you," he said in a low voice.

Lee felt for the bills, never taking his scared eyes off Belden. He hastily stuffed the money into a shirt pocket. He mounted his horse and turned it toward the gate. Beero slashed at the horse with his quirt and it buck-jumped, nearly throwing the scared kid. Lee rode fast for the gate.

Belden wiped his hand against his shirt. "Get going, Beero. You too, Skag. I won't need you for a little while. Stay at the bunkhouse until I need you."

The two men led their horses toward the big bunkhouse. Rick Belden shifted his feet in the dust. Craig waited until both men were in the bunkhouse. "I had hoped I'd make a real man out of you," he said at last.

"Jesus, Pa, it wasn't *my* fault!" There was a whining tone in Rick's voice which sickened his father. "I get blamed for everything around here. It wasn't really anybody's fault."

"No? Just keep your mouth shut and listen to me. Listen real close, boy, for your life may depend upon what I say."

"I ain't done anything. I don't like getting accused of things."

81

Belden slapped him hard across the mouth. "I told you to listen." He shoved the kid until Rick was backed up against his horse. "That woman you raped and killed was Matt Morgan's wife. You know who he is? He was my *amigo*. We rode the *rio* together in the old days. You know what that means? No, I guess you wouldn't at that. But maybe you'll understand this: *You killed the wife of the man who was the best friend I ever had!*"

"It was an accident! I swear to that!"

"He's come to Gun Hill to get you and Lee. If he gets you on that train tonight you'll be condemned to hang as sure as you're standing there and there won't be a blessed thing I can do about it. For once you won't have me to hide behind."

Rick drew back his shoulders. "I ain't afraid of him."

"No? Well, by God, a lot of better men than you have been scared by Matt Morgan and with good reason."

"I can handle a six-shooter. You taught me yourself. You said I was good. Remember?"

"Yes," said the rancher slowly. "You're good all right—at hitting tin cans on a fence or blowing the head off a rattler, but you've never faced anything that can shoot back. Worst of all a man like Morgan. He shoots without thinking, as though he had been born to shoot, and he can shoot just as straight while being shot at as you can while shooting at a tin can."

The implication in his father's words struck home to Rick. He wiped his face and looked about a little wildly. "I'll pull out now. I'll hole up in the hills."

Belden shook his head. He looked in the direction of Gun Hill. "No. You don't know his kind . . . the old border breed. He'll track you down if it takes him the rest of his life . . . or *yours*."

"What'll I do then?"

"Dammit! Don't panic! You'll stay where I can protect you. Where I've got something to say about justice."

"What do you want me to do?"

Belden walked toward the house. There seemed to be a weariness in him. "Get Beero and Skag. Circle around the town and sneak into Charlie's Place. Keep those two men with you, and let *them* face Morgan if he tracks you down."

Rick's face was a dirty white. "Yah? And what will you be doing to help me?" He almost screamed out the words.

"I've got to have time to think."

"What about Lee? He was in on it too."

His father turned slowly. "At least you're loyal to a friend."

"What about him?"

Belden shrugged. "Drunk in an hour, dead in two. Maybe that will ease Morgan. It won't ease me." He walked heavily into the house.

Rick looked about as though Matt Morgan

were standing behind him. He wet his lips and gripped his gun butt. Then he mounted his horse and rode toward the bunkhouse. As he rode he jerked out his Colt and leveled it. "Draw, Morgan, you sonofabitch," he said thinly.

Chapter Eight

THREE MEN LEANED against the hitching rack in front of the Horseshoe Saloon, watching the lean, broad-shouldered stranger as he walked toward them from the livery stable. The sun glinted from the badge pinned to his coat. Matt stopped in front of them. "I'm looking for a man," he said. "Name of Rick Belden."

"Never heard of him," said the tallest of the three.

"Stranger to me," said a redheaded man.

The third man eyed the marshal's badge. "How come you want him?" he asked.

"I'd like to have a talk with Rick Belden, or his *amigo*, Lee Smithers."

The tall one shook his head. "Never heard of either of them hombres. You must be in the wrong town, Marshal."

Matt smiled a little. "Right town; wrong people to ask."

The tall man spat leisurely. "That's the only kind we got around here, Marshal."

"So it seems. Maybe this town will be short of

two wrong people about nine o'clock tonight," said Matt quietly.

"Do tell," said the redhead. He yawned. "Well, we did hear an outhouse rumor about some Indian being killed up near Pawley. Right, Jim?"

The tall man nodded wisely. "Didn't pay attention to it though, Red. Hereabouts we don't arrest a man for killing an Indian. We give him a bounty. Hawww!"

Matt stepped in close and swung hard. The tall man sat down hard in the dust and blinked stupidly. Matt stepped back.

"Jesus," said Red. "You had no call to do that."

Matt turned on a heel and walked into the Horseshoe.

Jim got slowly to his feet and felt his jaw. "Got a wallop like a mule," he said ruefully.

"You should have drawed on him, Jim," said Red.

"You loco? You see them eyes of his? Come on. Let's get a drink. I got a feeling we're going to see some fun if he tries to take Old Man Belden's baby boy Rickie on that train tonight."

"Keno," said Red, "but not in the Horseshoe."

Matt stopped at the end of the long bar. The bartender walked toward him. Half a dozen men looked up from where they sat.

"Your pleasure?" asked the bartender.

"Rye."

Baldy placed a bottle and glass in front of Matt.

"Ain't none of my business, Marshal, why you're here in Gun Hill, but I'd like to tip you off to something."

"You're going to advise me to leave town, is that it?"

"You called it."

Matt filled his glass and downed the drink. He felt for his wallet.

"On the house," said Baldy.

"*Gracias.* I don't suppose you know where they are either?"

"Not me! I got a wife and three kids at home."

Matt rubbed his lean jaw. "Isn't there anyone around here who isn't afraid of Craig Belden?"

"Sure," said Baldy loudly. He winked. "Boot Hill is full of them." He laughed and looked at the customers for signs of appreciation, but there were no answering smiles.

Matt turned to look at the customers. Not one man stared back at him. A woman sat in a booth next to the far wall. Matt picked up the bottle and glass and threaded his way between the tables. "Hello, Linda."

"Hello, Marshal. Sit down."

He sat down across from her and filled her empty glass. "What are you doing in a dump like this?"

She smiled ruefully. "Thanks for asking. I've spent a good part of my lousy life in dumps like this."

Matt shrugged. "So have I."

87

"You don't look or act like a damned fool," she said thoughtfully.

"Meaning?"

"Everyone in town knows why you came here. The odds are high against you, Matt."

"Drink up," he said.

"You ought to know better than to play against the house. The deck is stacked."

"I'll take my chances."

"Are you really serious about arresting Rick and taking him away from here?"

"I am."

She raised her head as she heard the distant whistling of a train. "I don't even like to hear them things during the day." She eyed him. "You have just time to make it, Matt."

"It's not going the right way for me, Linda."

She reached across the table and gripped his wrists. "Get out of town, you fool! This isn't the way to take Rick Belden."

"It happens to be my way," he said quietly.

"You'll never leave Gun Hill alive."

He yawned. "People have been telling me that ever since I came here. Tell me, why are you so interested in whether I live or die?"

She released his wrists and sat back. She touched her hair with a deft hand. "I like you. Besides, I have a kind of sympathy for anyone who bucks against Craig Belden."

The train whistled again. He shoved her glass

toward her. "Drink up. Let's talk about something else."

"You know your trouble?"

"Shoot. I'm listening."

She sipped at her rye. "You've got stars in your thick head. I used to know a nice kid, name of Jimmy, who used to say that to me. 'Linda,' he'd say with a grin, 'you're all right but you've got stars in your head.'"

"Is that bad?"

The train was braking into the station. She drained her glass. "That was a long time ago."

"Where can I find Rick Belden?"

Two men were standing at the bar. One of them laughed. The other slapped a hard hand on the bar. "It's the truth, Ben!" he said angrily.

Ben grinned. "You always were a double-barreled liar, Jonce."

"Who you calling a liar?"

"Oh for Christ's sake, Jonce. Calm down. Have a drink."

Linda looked at the two men. "That was how he got it," she said softly.

Matt stared at her. "Who?"

"Jimmy. Just like that. An argument at a bar between him and his best friend. Jimmy died instantly. His friend lived a week."

The whistle blew impatiently.

"You still got time, Matt," said Linda.

Matt shook his head.

The train began to labor out of the station.

Linda eyed Matt. "Stars in the head."

"I asked you where I could find Rick Belden."

"So you did. You really mean to find him, don't you?"

"Yes."

She leaned forward. "I'm not sure where he is but I know where I'd start looking for him," she said in a low voice.

"Fair enough. Where?"

"That hogpen across the street. Charlie's Place. Charlie acts like he owns it, but Craig Belden counts the receipts."

Matt stood up. "Thanks."

"Keep away from the girls over there, Stars in the Head."

"I've got other business."

"Might be better if you did listen to the girls."

Matt shook his head.

"Another thing: don't go walking in through the front door. Someone might make a mistake and start shooting." She filled her glass. "Might not be a mistake at that."

He looked down at her. "Thanks again."

"Forget it. I used to work over there. After Jimmy was gone."

"Keep the bottle. Why don't you get out of town? You're too young and nice-looking to stay here."

She laughed. "First I tell you to get out of town and now you tell me. Thanks anyway, Matt."

Matt walked to the bar and placed a five spot on

it. He jerked his head toward Linda. "Give her what she wants."

Baldy leered. "Man, I'd love to, but my old lady would sure as hell find out." The leer faded from his face as he saw Matt's eyes.

Matt pushed through the batwings and looked across the street toward the saloon. The shades were drawn and the double doors at the front had been closed despite the heat of the day. There was a furtive air about the place. Matt looked up and down the boardwalk. There was no one in sight. He cut across the street at an angle trending away from the front windows of the saloon. He stopped under a wooden awning and rolled a smoke. Then he turned suddenly into the alleyway and walked toward the rear of Charlie's Place.

The yard behind the saloon was littered with refuse. A scavenging dog raised his head to look at Matt and then went on with his business. There were three saddle horses tethered under a sickly tree which rose just behind the big frame building. Each of them bore the *B* brand.

Matt walked to the tree and looked up. It was close to the second-floor porch. He dropped his smoke and stamped on it, then pulled himself up the trunk. One of the horses whinnied softly.

Matt stepped from the tree onto the sagging porch and looked down into the yard. There was no one in sight. He padded softly along the warped porch searching for an open window. He found one at the end of the roof. He tried to peer inside the room, but it was dark.

He eased the window up and stepped cautiously inside. The mingled odors of cheap perfume, sweat, and the unmistakable smell of a woman met him. He blinked his eyes in the dimness.

The room was dominated by a big brass bed. A woman lay asleep on it, her dyed hair tousled about her face. A bottle and glasses were on a marble-topped table beside the bed.

Matt moved toward the door and bumped against a dresser. A large plaster figure of a nude woman fell to the floor and shattered about his feet. The woman in bed rolled over and opened her eyes. "That you, Pinto?" she said.

Matt turned slowly. "Be quiet," he ordered.

She drew a soiled sheet over her full breasts. "Jesus," she said thickly. "Least thing you could do was knock when you come into a lady's bedroom."

Matt wrinkled his nose at the stench in the place. "Sorry," he said hastily. "I'll be back later."

"You just do that, honey. Understand, I ain't feeling too chipper right now but I'll be all right tonight. You just ask for Mae, honey." She dropped her head onto the pillow and was sound asleep in a minute.

Matt eased open the door and looked up and down the dim hallway. There was a stair well at the far end. He padded toward it, then dropped to his knees to peer between the rails. The rattling of poker chips and the clinking of glasses came up to him. Someone coughed. A man leaned against the end of the bar with a glass in his hand. The bartender was cleaning the back bar with a sponge. A swamper was busy with mop and bucket in an alcove just below the stairs.

Five men were seated about a poker table near the foot of the stairway. Two of them were Skag and Beero. A slim man sat with his back toward Matt. He wore a cowhide vest, and his hat hung on the back of his head. As Matt watched, he shoved his cards toward the center of the table. "Deal me out."

Beero looked up. "You ain't going anywhere."

"I heard a noise upstairs, I tell you!"

Skag spat. "Mae's got the shakes again."

"Leave her be," said a bald-headed man.

"Shut up, Charlie," said the slim man. "You act sometimes like you really owned this place." He turned and looked up the stairs. Matt froze. The right cheek was marked by a slash from the corner of the eye down to the sensual mouth.

"You might get your pretty puss scratched again," said Beero.

Rick Belden ignored the big man. He hitched up his belt and started up the stairs. "If I need a drink, Pinto," he called back, "I'll thump a few times on the floor with one of my boots."

Beero laughed. "Be sure it's your boot you thump with," he said. "Hawwww!"

Matt faded back into an alcove. The boots

sounded on the stairs. He flattened himself against the wall and placed his hand on his Colt.

Rick stopped at the top of the stairs and looked down the hallway. A strange feeling came over him. He could hear the swamper working downstairs, the rattling of the chips, the scraping of chairs and heels against the sanded floor. He squinted his eyes in the dimness. There was something alien about the place, although he had walked up and down it many times before.

Rick moved nervously as he heard a sound down the hall. He stepped into an alcove and drew the faded velvet curtain across it. He pressed back against the coats and capes kept there by the girls. He wiped the sweat from his face with shaking hands. He'd best go back downstairs and have a drink, but he didn't want Skag and Beero to see him like this.

Matt had been waiting for the sound of Rick's footsteps. He peered around the corner. The kid had vanished. Then he saw the drapes move and looked down to see Rick's boot toes protruding from beneath the curtains. Matt eased his Colt from its holster and padded down the hall.

"Hey, Rick!" bellowed Beero. "You had plenty of time for a boy like you! Come on down and get back in the game! We need your *dinero!*"

Matt watched the alcove. He saw a rounded shape which must be the kid's head. The Colt rose and fell in a chopping motion. Matt caught him as he fell forward. The drapes pulled down on the wooden bar which supported them, and the bar clattered onto the floor. Matt drew in his breath and looked down the stairs. The game was still in progress.

Matt pulled the drapes from the unconscious kid. He gripped Rick by his thick hair and turned his head sharply to one side. The long scar stood out clearly.

Matt looked at the sensual face and a rage grew in him until he was ready to smash the kid to a bloody pulp or blow out his brains with a soft-nosed .44. He shook a little with tension as he stood up. He got out a pair of handcuffs and knelt to snap them about Rick's wrists. He removed the Colt from Rick's holster and thrust it beneath his own belt.

The game was still going on. A heavy-set man who had been standing at the end of the bar had now moved closer to the table to watch the game. The swamper was walking toward the front of the saloon with his mop and bucket. Pinto, the bartender, was still industriously wiping the back bar.

Matt lifted the kid to his shoulders, settled him, then drew out his own Colt again. He cocked it and walked toward the head of the stairs. He was halfway down when Skag glanced up. The gunhand's jaw dropped. Matt came down a few more steps. "All right down there," he called out. "Up on your feet! Grab your ears! Calf rope!"

The men stood up slowly, watching Matt with wide eyes. The swamper slowly lowered his bucket and leaned the mop against the bar. He wiped his wet hands on his dirty apron and then raised them over his head. Pinto turned slowly. He dropped his cloth and shot his arms up.

The heavy-set man who had been watching the poker game suddenly dropped his arms and made a dash toward a gunrack on the wall. He grabbed a sawed-off, double-barreled shotgun and raised it. Matt fired. The big man jerked as the soft slug tore into him. His finger tightened on the trigger and the gun blasted flame and smoke, the shot tearing out the back of a chair. He fell backward, pawed at the edge of the bar, and then hit the floor. Smoke rifted through the big room and the acrid stench of burned powder made the scared swamper gag and cough.

Matt waved the Colt. "Who else wants to be a hero?"

Nobody moved.

"Lay those guns on the bar. One man at a time," said Matt.

One by one they walked to the bar until the only man still armed was Skag. He wet his thin lips and eyed the man on the stairs.

"Rick Belden committed rape and murder in Pawley," said Matt. "I have a warrant for his arrest. If any of you interfere in what I am doing, you are obstructing the law."

Footsteps sounded in the upper hallway and a woman called out in a frightened voice: "What's going on down there?"

Matt turned his head a little. Skag bent his body, dumped the poker table over in front of himself, then drew and fired over the top of it. The slug rapped into a riser even with Matt's shoulders. Matt fired twice. The bullets slammed through the table, and it rolled sideways on its round top. Skag lay curled up, with his right hand gripping his left shoulder. Blood leaked between his fingers.

Beero swallowed. "You're out of your head, Morgan," he said. "You ain't got a chance. Put down that hogleg and let the kid go."

Mae appeared at the top of the stairs. "That you, Rick?" she called.

"He can't hear you," said Pinto.

"Get back into your room, Mae," said Matt over his shoulder. He eyed the tense men. "Into that back room. All of you. *Vamonos!* I'm getting nervous."

They trooped into the storeroom. Matt walked down to the floor level. He dumped the kid into a chair and looked down at Skag. The gunhand had been sickened by the impact of the heavy slug. Matt picked up Skag's Colt and walked to the room, where the men stood silently watching him. Beero spat. "Hardcase from Pawley," he said.

Matt kicked the door shut in the big man's face and was rewarded with a yell of pain. Matt forced the catch over the hasp and rammed Skag's pistol through the staple. He quickly reloaded his own Colt and then walked to the front of the saloon. A boot crashed against the storeroom door. It wouldn't take long for them to break it down.

The street seemed empty. Matt unlocked the front door and then went back for Rick. The kid was still out cold. Matt hoisted him to his shoulder and walked to the door. He went out onto the boardwalk and looked up and down the street. Sweat broke from his face as he carried the kid toward the city hall.

A familiar fat figure stood on the walk outside the hall. Josh Bartlett's cigar moved from one side of his mouth to the other, and he scratched under his left armpit. "You got farther than I thought you would, Morgan."

"I'll need a cell until train time."

Bartlett shook his head. "Can't give you one."

"I'll lock him up myself. You can make yourself scarce, Bartlett."

Bartlett looked up at the sky. "Locked all the cells and lost the keys."

Matt shifted his burden. Bartlett half closed one eye. "I heard some gunfire down at Charlie's Place. That kid looks banged up. Mr. Belden won't like this, Morgan."

Matt felt the sweat work itchily down his sides. A hopeless feeling began to hover in the back of his mind. Panic was trying hard to force the bit into his mouth and take control of him.

"Nowhere to go," said Bartlett cheerfully. "Train ain't due for six hours."

Matt looked down the street. A faded-gilt sign

hung in front of a rambling two-storied frame building, proclaiming that it was the Harper House. He shifted the kid and started across the dusty street.

Bartlett waddled along behind him. "You've been lucky so far, Morgan, but you should have never touched that boy. You haven't got a chance to hold onto him for six hours. Take my advice. Leave him with me and get out of town. You can hire a horse. I'll take care of the boy. Now leave him be, get a horse, and jump up a lot of dust getting out of Gun Hill."

"Shut up!" snapped Matt. "You run off at the mouth too much, Bartlett."

Bartlett waved a fat hand. "Oh, I was just trying to help out. It's easy to see you'd rather die here in Gun Hill than to get back safe to Pawley."

Matt mounted the steps of the Harper House and pushed open the door. He strode into the lobby, which had a faded and outdated look with its hangings and over-stuffed furniture. He dumped Rick into a big leather chair, and walked to the register counter. The clerk's jaw dropped. His hand still held the key that he had been giving to an elderly man.

Matt turned the register and reached for the pen. "I'll need a room until train time tonight," he said.

The clerk dropped the key. "Wait a minute," he said hastily. "You can't stay here! God's sakes, mister, get out of here and take that kid with you!"

Matt wrote down his name. "What room?"

"My God, mister! They'll turn this place into a turkey shoot trying to get at you. Why . . . you're breaking the law."

Matt stabbed the pen into its holder. "Mister, I *am* the law." He walked to Rick and wearily hoisted him up onto his shoulders. "What room?" he asked again.

"There aren't any rooms for you."

Matt turned. "*What room?*"

The clerk swallowed a little. "Two-oh-one."

Matt took the key from the clerk and started up the stairs. The clerk shook his head. He handed the key he had dropped to the elderly man.

The man's face fell. "Who? Me?" he said. "You loco? I'm dusting out of here."

The stairs creaked under Matt and his heavy burden. The clerk looked up at his back, then toward the outer door, then up at Matt again. He mopped his forehead. "My God," he said softly.

Chapter Nine

THE *B corrida* rode in a compact bunch as they neared Gun Hill. Craig Belden led them, with his hat pulled low over his burning eyes. They thundered over the plank bridge, and the rumbling of the hoofs was like the rolling of thunder on hot summer nights.

Belden drew rein when he reached the main stem of Gun Hill. Dust floated ahead of the riders as they halted their horses and waited for the boss's next command.

Beero left the shade under the porch roof of Charlie's Place and walked toward Craig Belden, wetting his lips.

"How did he get him?" asked Belden.

Beero waved a thick arm. "We was holed up in Charlie's Place. Somehow Morgan Indianed in the back way. Rick goes upstairs to see Mae. Morgan buffaloes him up there. Morgan gets the drop on us as he comes downstairs."

Craig Belden sat stiffly in his elaborate saddle. There was no sound other than the occasional stamping of a horse, the grinding noise of a bit, and the squeaking of saddle leather. One of the *vaqueros* spit hard into the dust. "Jesus," he said. "*One* man."

Beero's pale eyes narrowed. "Maybe you'd have done better if you was there, Luke?"

"Maybe."

"Shut up," said Belden. "Go on, Beero."

"Dewey, the bouncer, tries to get his hands on the scater-gun behind the bar. Never had a chance. Morgan's bullet catches him in the guts. Skag tries next. Morgan creases Skag's shoulder."

"Skag?"

Beero nodded. "Sure, Skag is fast. Fast as chain lightning and eleven claps of thunder, but Morgan is faster."

"I could have told you that," said Belden dryly.

"Well, anyways, Morgan won't get anywhere."

"Meaning?"

Beero grinned. "He's treed."

"Where?"

"The hotel clerk told me. Morgan has Rick in room two-oh-one. Second floor front."

The dark eyes turned toward the Harper House. A front window was open and a dingy curtain flapped in the hot breeze. Belden moved his horse closer to the hotel and reined him to a halt in the middle of the street. He looked up at the open window and yelled, "Morgan!"

Matt Morgan pulled the curtain back.

"Where's my son?"

Matt turned. He shoved Rick toward the window. The kid was still dazed. He blinked stupidly as he looked down at his father.

"Rick!" yelled Belden.

"Yeh, Pa!"

"You all right?"

Rick fingered the lump on his head. "Yeh," he said sourly.

Belden nodded in satisfaction. Kneeing his horse back toward his waiting men, he beckoned Beero to him. "I want four or five of the boys, the best rifle shots, to get up on the roofs of the buildings where they can cover that hotel. No shooting unless I say so. Savvy?"

Beero nodded.

Belden dismounted and handed the reins to Luke. He walked toward the Harper House.

"You going up there alone, boss?" called Beero.

Belden spoke over his shoulder. "He's only one man," said he contemptuously.

He stopped just below the open window. "Morgan! I'm coming up for a palaver."

Matt looked down at his old friend. "Leave your six-shooter."

Belden unbuckled his gunbelt and hung it over a hitching rack. He walked into the hotel and slowly climbed the stairs. The door of room 201 was open. Matt sat on the edge of a dresser out of the line of fire from the window. Rick lay on the bed, his right wrist and right ankle handcuffed to the bedposts.

Craig stopped in the doorway and looked at

Matt. "I told you to get out of town, Matt. You won't get anywhere doing this."

"I've done all right so far. No one thought I'd even find him, and they figured if I *did* find him I'd never capture him. There he is, Craig, all trussed up for market day."

"*What* market?"

"The court in Pawley."

The dark eyes studied Matt. "I always gave you credit for having more than average sense, Matt. You know you'll never get away with this."

Matt shrugged. "I've done all right so far."

"Fool's luck!"

"Maybe. Is that all you've come up here to talk about?"

"Isn't there any way we can settle this before the shooting starts?"

"Sure. Just let me do my duty."

Belden looked at his pale-faced and battered son. "You're forcing my hand, Matt. Let's be reasonable about this. After all, old friends should understand each other."

"I understand only one thing right now, Craig. That punk there raped and killed my wife. He'll go to trial if this is the last thing I'll do on earth."

"It probably will be."

Matt glanced toward the window. "Another thing: you can hole me up here, and shoot all you want to, and the last thing I'll do when the chips are down will be put a slug through his head."

Belden wet his lips. He felt inside his coat. "I've

got money, Matt. More money than I'll ever need. I'll make you a wealthy man, Matt, in exchange for that boy's life."

"No dice."

Belden held out his big hands pleadingly. "I'll do anything you ask me to, and I'll see that the boy repays you somehow, if it takes him the rest of his life."

"He can't bring *her* back, Craig."

Rick raised his head. "He never gave me a fighting chance, Pa," he whined. "Why, I could have . . ."

"Shut up," said his father coldly. "You're damned lucky he wants to take you for trial. If it had been *my* choice . . . well . . . it doesn't matter."

Matt leaned back. "You through now, Craig?"

"No. There's something I want to get across to you. He's not much to be proud of, God knows, but he's all I've got, Matt. *You're not going to take him away from me.*" He waved a hand toward the window. "There are twenty men of mine out there. Men who'd charge hell with a bucket of water if I told them to."

"Nice odds," said Matt dryly.

"So help me, Matt! I'll kill you myself!"

Matt looked at Belden's waist. "With what?"

The blood rushed into the rancher's face. He moved a little, to where he could see one of his men on the roof of the building across the street. The man raised his rifle and looked inquiringly at his boss. Belden nodded quickly and stepped to one side.

Matt jumped from the dresser. There was the sound of a breaking stick from across the street and a slug smashed into the mirror right where he had been sitting. Glass sprayed across the room. Matt drew his Colt and leveled it. "I ought to kill you, Belden."

Craig smiled thinly. "You see how it is?"

Matt nodded. "It took guts to signal that rifleman while you were standing here, but then you always did have guts aplenty."

Belden looked down at the gun muzzle. "You won't shoot," he said, "which is more than I could say for myself."

"Get out of here!"

Belden shrugged. "Take it easy, Rick. It won't be long. Keep your mouth shut. Don't rile *Mister* Morgan."

He left the room and walked down the hall. They heard his boots on the thinly carpeted stairs, silence as he crossed the lobby, and then the slamming of the front door.

Rick yawned. "Do me a favor, lawman," he said. "Step in front of that window. The sun hurts my eyes."

Matt holstered his Colt. He glanced at the deadly window and then at the big bed. He raised a foot and shoved it against a wardrobe. It teetered, and a second boot toppled it over. It crashed on the glass-littered floor. He gripped the brass bed and skidded it toward the window.

"What the hell!" yelled Rick.

A rifle cracked flatly. The slug smashed into the wall, showering the cringing kid with plaster. Matt ducked to one side as another slug whined through the window and ricocheted from the brass head-rail and thudded into the ceiling.

"Pa!" roared Rick. "Make them stop! It's me under the window, Pa!"

Matt grinned. "Cry, baby, cry," he said in a singsong voice. "Daddy's gone a-huntin' to save little Rickie's skin."

A sudden quiet fell over the street. Matt took a chair and tilted it back against the wall so that he could see part way down the hall. "That's better," he said. "I never did like unnecessary noise."

Craig Belden paced back and forth on the boardwalk in front of Charlie's Place, slapping his quirt against his thigh. Now and then he looked up at the hotel. Some of his men lounged in the hot shade watching him.

Beero rolled a smoke. "What now, boss?"

"Shut up! I'm thinking."

Skag came out of the saloon, his left shoulder bandaged. His eyes were cold as he looked at the open window in the Harper House. "Let me go up after him," he said.

"You've had enough of him, Skag."

107

Skag spat. "It'll take more than that tinhorn marshal to send *me* to Boot Hill."

"He damned near did," said Luke dryly. "Couple of inches lower, Skag . . . rest in peace."

"Maybe you think you can buck him?"

"Maybe I can."

"Ain't no one stopping you from walking across the street, hombre."

Belden whirled. "Dammit! Shut up! If some of you men are game you can try him."

Beero hitched up his belt and threw away his cigarette. Skag rubbed his hand on his gun butt. Luke grinned. He stroked his heavy mustache both ways.

"You might get him," said Belden thoughtfully.

"*Might?*" said Luke. "Cinch."

The hotel clerk came through the crowd. "He's rough as a cob," he said.

The three men removed their spurs. "Ready?" said Beero.

"Keno," said Luke.

Skag nodded. He started across the street, angling away from the line of sight of Morgan's window. They reached the far side and padded down the wooden sidewalk. Luke eased open the front door of the hotel and the three of them walked into the deserted lobby.

Skag stopped at the bottom of the stairs.

"You're already plugged, Skag," said Luke. "I'll go first."

Skag slowly shook his head. "He's all mine. A

bullet in the belly for him." He led the way up the stairs.

Matt Morgan let his feet drop to the floor. He eyed the hallway. There was no one in sight, but he had felt, rather than heard, something on the stairs. His years along the border had honed and whetted his instincts. They hadn't failed him yet; pray God they wouldn't now.

Rick Belden raised his head a little, eyed Matt, then he dropped his head and turned away. The curtains fluttered in the window. It was quiet; it was too damned quiet.

Matt moved closer to the doorway. There was a blind spot to his left, but he'd have to step out into the hallway to see if anyone was standing there. He cocked his Colt. Rick was breathing steadily, but Matt knew the kid wasn't asleep.

Minutes ticked past. Something moved down the hall. Matt stepped outside of the room, whirling and crouching to thrust his Colt forward at waist level, elbow close to his side.

Skag stood at the top of the stairs, Colt in hand. His jaw dropped as he saw Matt.

Beero and Luke stood on the stairs with only their heads visible.

Matt fired three times. The roaring of the shots slammed back and forth in the confined hallway. Leaping tongues of flame and smoke shot toward Skag. His lean body jerked as three slugs rapped into his chest an area which could be covered by the space of one hand.

Beero and Luke plunged down the stairs.

Skag dropped his gun hand, and the Colt fell from nerveless fingers. He stared incredulously through the rifted smoke, then swayed backward, grabbed for the newel post, opened his mouth, and sank. Blood gushed from his gaping mouth. A wide stain spread across the front of his shirt. He coughed thickly and rolled backward. His body thudded on the stairs, and he crashed against the bottom post and lay still.

The smoke wavered and flowed toward the stair well. Blood was soaking into the faded carpet. Having reloaded, Matt went into the room and cautiously peered down at the street. There was nothing in sight but a wandering yellow cur dog. The wind raised a dust devil which meandered down toward the corner and vanished as swiftly as it had appeared. A tattered newspaper floated high in the air.

Matt went back to his chair. He rolled a smoke and lighted it. Then he opened his watch and placed it on a small table next to him.

"Think you're pretty good with a cutter?" asked Rick.

Matt waved a hand. "Passable."

"You're a goner, Morgan. I know my old man. The only way you'll leave Gun Hill is in one of Sam Houghton's pine boxes."

Matt yawned. He drew on his cigarette. He

tilted his head to look at Rick. "What makes you so sure you won't be fitted into one of those pine boxes, here or in Pawley?"

Rick paled. "Damn you!" He rolled over to stare unseeingly at the faded wallpaper.

Matt rested his head against the wall. So far he had managed to counter all of Craig Belden's maneuvers. Luck had been with him. Maybe fool's luck, as Belden had said. It would be a long wait until train time.

Craig Belden stood at the front window of Charlie's Place, moodily watching the hotel. He had heard the sharp rattle of gunfire.

The back door opened and Beero walked in, wiping his face.

Craig turned. "Well?"

Beero reached for a bottle sitting on the bar. "We made it to the top of the stairs all right. Skag insisted on leading. He got to the top first." Beero drank from the bottle and then wiped his mouth. "Morgan came out into the hall like a jack-in-the-box. He fired so damned fast it almost sounded like one shot. Skag takes all three slugs in the chest. Never got a shot off. I never seen anything like it. Me and Luke dusted that place fast."

"What about Skag?"

"With three slugs in his chest he ain't going nowheres."

Belden slapped a hand on the bar. He stared

through the flyspecked window. "Damn him! Why don't he give up?"

Beero took another drink. "Rushing him won't do no good. We might get him but he'll take plenty of good men along for pallbearers in hell."

Craig glanced up at the bar clock. "Time is running out. He can't stay treed forever. Where are the extra men I wanted?"

"Over at the Horseshoe."

Craig nodded. He pulled down his hat and walked toward the back entrance. Beero watched him and then took the bottle to the window. He looked up at the hotel.

Pinto mopped the bar. "What do you think now, Beero?" he asked.

"*Quien sabe?* I think that ornery polecat is sitting up there laughing at us."

"Yeh."

Beero turned. "He'll be laughing on the other side of his face before long," he said. "I never seen the old man so damned determined."

The clock pendulum swung steadily back and forth.

Chapter Ten

LINDA SAT AT the end of the bar watching Baldy taking bottles from a case. Humming softly, he wiped each one of them with a cloth and then placed it on the back bar.

"You never miss a thing, do you?" she asked.

Baldy shrugged. "Never can tell when you need extra stock, Linda."

She looked toward the door. "Doesn't seem to be much drinking going on."

"Not now, but wait until all the killing is over. You'll see. They'll cinch up their nerves and ease their consciences with liquor. It's always been that way."

She toyed with her glass. "There's one man dead already. How many more do you think will die today?"

"*Two* dead," said Baldy. "You forgot Skag."

"*Him?* He wasn't a man."

Baldy eyed her. "Matter of opinion. Reason there ain't no buying right now is because the man who killed both those jaspers is penned up in a hotel room waiting to get killed too."

"There's a real man . . . Matt Morgan."

"Ain't many like him."

The batwings swung open and a man came in. He tipped his hat to Linda and she looked away. It was the loose-mouthed drummer from the train.

Baldy leaned against the back bar. "Morgan has the real killing instinct."

"Don't kid yourself, Baldy."

"Two dead men in less than an hour and a half? Seems to me you're kidding yourself."

"They went after him, didn't they? They were the real killers."

Baldy spat. "Women!"

The drummer nodded. He eyed Linda appreciatively. "You lonesome, kid."

"I haven't been lonesome since I was twelve years old."

"How about a sociable little drink with me?"

"Later, honey."

The drummer winked at Baldy. "Double bourbon."

Baldy poured the drink and the salesman took it to the front of the saloon. "Don't want to miss anything," he said.

"And you won't, you—" said Linda in a low voice.

"Now, Linda," chided Baldy. He leaned close to her. "You don't believe Morgan will actually get away with it, do you?"

She shook her head. "But I'd sure like to see him do it. Just to see the look on Craig Belden's face."

"Yeh, I get the point, kid."

She emptied her glass and picked up her handbag. "I know one thing: if Matt Morgan can get Rick out of Gun Hill to stand trial in Pawley, it will really hurt Craig. It might be the only thing in the world which could hurt him."

"Where you going, kid?"

"To my room."

Baldy stared. "In the Harper House? You loco?"

The drummer turned slowly. "You mean you're going into that hotel where Morgan is holed up?"

"You get the idea, honey."

"But why?"

"I live there. It's as simple as that."

Baldy winked at the salesman. "She's joshing. Linda is a great one for the joshing. She might go into the lobby, but she sure won't go up them stairs."

"Yep," said the salesman. "Forget it, Linda. I'll buy you that drink."

Craig Belden opened the rear door of the saloon and stood there watching them. Several men seated at tables looked expectantly at him. Craig Belden paid good wages to those who did his dirty work.

Linda opened her handbag and took out a roll of bills. "Here's a hundred bucks says I'll not only walk into that hotel but also upstairs and talk to Matt Morgan in his room."

The drummer grinned. He placed his glass on the bar and drew out his wallet. "You got yourself a bet, sister." He counted out his money. "All I can chance is fifty bucks."

Linda looked at Baldy. "You want a piece of this?"

"Hell, I don't like to take your money."

"You won't."

Baldy shrugged. He hoisted his apron and counted out fifty dollars. "I hate to do this to you, kid. But fifty bucks is fifty bucks. Who holds the money?"

"Put it into the cash register."

Baldy looked at the salesman. "Fair enough?"

"O.K. with me."

Baldy whistled softly as he turned toward the cash register. He saw Craig Belden and the tune died away on his lips. Linda and the salesman turned to look at Craig.

Craig walked toward the bar. "Before you try to win that bet, Linda," he said quietly, "there are a few things I'd like to know."

The salesman gulped his drink. "I'm in no rush," he said hastily.

"Me neither," said Baldy. "Drink, Mr. Belden?"

Belden shook his head. He took Linda by the arm and walked her to one of the gambling rooms. He drew the curtain behind them. She turned to face him. "Well?"

"Why didn't you come out to the ranch?"

"One beating from you is plenty for me."

"I was drinking. I lost my temper."

"So? Because that punk kid of yours tells filthy lies about me you have to take *his* word for it? I tried to reason with you, but you believe anything he says."

Craig waved a hand. "He's my son."

"That covers everything he does, doesn't it? No matter how low or how rotten he is, the fact that he's Craig Belden's son makes up for everything," she said bitterly.

"He's my son, I tell you!"

"What was I to you? Nothing? Another possession you could smash and throw away if the mood struck you?"

"You know better than that."

She faced him defiantly. He raised his big hands and then lowered them helplessly. This was something new to Craig Belden, just as Matt Morgan's stubborn opposition was new, and it had shaken his confidence in his power.

He gripped her by the arms and drew her close. He wanted to tell her how much he had missed her, but it was an impossibility for a man like him. Instead he crushed her to him. She made no response. Her eyes looked steadily into his and he could see something there he had never seen before. "It's all over, Craig," she said quietly.

"What do you mean?"

She turned away from him and rearranged her

dress. "You're always so sure of yourself, aren't you? In the past all you had to do was whistle and I'd come running like a fool. Hit me and then pat my head to let me know *I* was forgiven."

He slowly shook his head.

"I lay in that stinking hospital for ten long days. I went a long way from here so people in Gun Hill wouldn't know what kind of a man you really were. Well . . . it worked, not for you but for me, because if no one else around here really knows you, *I* do. I've had enough of you, Craig. God knows I stuck it out long enough."

"But you came back," he said quietly.

She studied him. "Yes, because of something you once told me I came back to find out if you really mean it."

"What was it, Linda?"

"You said you would marry me."

He shook his head. "I can't do that."

"Then it's all settled. Somehow I knew you'd never keep your word."

He leaned back against a gaming table and studied her. "Just why are you going into that hotel?"

"I'm staying there."

"The bet you made was that you'd talk to Morgan. Why?"

"I met him on the train. He isn't an ordinary man, Craig. I knew he was coming here to face you and I knew you couldn't trample him underfoot as you have so many others."

118

LAST TRAIN FROM GUN HILL

He absent-mindedly rubbed his holster. "Now you listen to me, Linda. I know Matt Morgan better than you ever could. He rode with me years ago. I once considered him my best friend. I don't want to see him die. But Rick is up there with him and no man on earth is going to take my son away from me no matter what he did. The only way Matt Morgan will get out of being killed is by me getting Rick back safe and sound."

"So?"

"You want to save Morgan's life, don't you?"

"I don't want to see anyone get killed."

Craig nodded. "Which is your room?"

"Number two-oh-four, across the hall from his."

He took her by the hands. "Go up there. Talk him into leaving Rick and coming to your room. Make some kind of a signal to my men so that they can get to Rick. I'll give you my word that Morgan will leave town tonight on that train, safe and sound."

"*Your* word?" She laughed.

His face grew hard. "Don't rile me, Linda."

"You *are* in a tight spot, aren't you? But you don't really want to kill him."

He released her and looked away. "It's up to him, or to you, Linda."

"You really love that rotten kid of yours. I didn't think you had it in you to love anyone but yourself."

"Cut it!" he snapped. "Just make up your mind

119

right now as to whether you want to save Morgan's life or not!"

"Supposing he doesn't fall for this strategy of yours . . . or ambush . . . whichever it is."

"You let him make up his own mind."

She walked to the door and looked back. "Well, I've got to change into my working clothes. I need a job and I have to look my best."

He drew her back fiercely. "You're not going back to work in one of these dumps. Don't over-play your hand, Linda. I'm not a patient man. You'll only leave me when I tell you to leave me. Now get going."

"I never thought I'd ever feel sorry for you, Craig, but somehow I do. I can't explain why."

He turned away from her and felt for his cigar case. She looked at his broad back for a moment and then let the drapes fall across the doorway. The drummer and the bartender watched her walk to the rear entrance and leave the saloon.

"There she goes," said Baldy.

"You think she'll really go up there?"

Baldy shrugged. "She's got more guts than most men I know."

They walked to the front door and looked along the shaded sidewalk. Linda appeared from the alleyway farther down the street. She paused to adjust her hat, lifted her skirt to clear the deep dust, and walked toward the Harper House.

Men watched her from rooftops and doorways

as she walked steadily toward the hotel. She looked as though she had been out for an afternoon stroll and was returning to freshen herself up for the night's activities.

Chapter Eleven

THE PALE-FACED HOTEL clerk looked up as Linda entered the lobby. Two of Belden's men lounged in chairs with rifles across their thighs.

"My key please," she said.

The clerk stared at her. "Now?"

"I have a room, two-oh-four, remember? I also paid in advance."

He glanced toward the stairs. "Sure, miss. Sure. But you can't go up there now."

"Do you know who I am?"

"Certainly."

"Then give me my key or Mr. Belden will hear about it."

The clerk looked at Luke. Luke shrugged. "Let her go," he said. "Maybe Morgan needs company." He grinned.

Linda took her key. "Matt Morgan won't bother a woman," she said. "He isn't a Belden, you know."

The clerk looked quickly at the two men. "Take it easy, ma'am!"

She walked to the foot of the stairs and saw the

stains on the stair carpeting. She bit her lower lip as she started up.

The clerk looked at Luke. "Maybe I'd better get out of here."

Luke yawned. "Stay right where you are."

"Why?"

"Might be more guests, eh, Joey?"

Joe laughed. "Yeh—pallbearers."

Craig Belden left the Horseshoe with the extra men he had hired. They walked across the street and into Charlie's Place. Belden ordered drinks for them and had Beero pass the word along to the men watching the hotel that they must be alert for a possible signal from Linda. Then he took up his post at the front window of the saloon with a cigar clenched between his teeth.

Matt hit the floor with his heels. The kid stirred. Matt drew and cocked his revolver. He peered warily into the hallway. Linda stopped at the head of the stairs and raised her arms. "Don't shoot, Marshal. It's only your late traveling companion."

He let down the hammer of his Colt and holstered the weapon as she came toward him. "Well?" he said.

"We're neighbors, Matt." She looked past him into the room.

Rick rolled over and grinned at her. "Linda, honey!" He winked. "You got a smoke?"

She opened her handbag and took out a pack

of tailor-mades. She thrust one into his mouth and lit it. She saw the livid scar on his face, the bruise marks left there by Beero's beating, and the lump where Matt Morgan had buffaloed him.

Matt leaned against the side of the door. "You'd better leave," he said.

Linda surveyed the messy room. "Some party." She started toward the window, but Matt gripped an arm and whirled her around. "You want a slug in your pretty head?"

"I think they'd know the difference between us."

"Get out of here."

Rick drew in on his cigarette. "Linda, doll," he said cockily, "you see my old man, you tell him I'm tired of waiting for him to spring me out of here."

"Mr. Morgan is tired too," she said.

"Him?" Rick laughed. "He's tired of life, period."

Linda walked into the hall. She glanced over her shoulder as she stopped in front of her door and unlocked it. "Matt!"

"Yes?"

"Come here."

Rick said, "You made a hit with her. Better go."

Matt crossed the hallway and looked into her room. Linda was behind a screen stripping off her dress. He saw her smooth, bare shoulders. "Hand me that red dress from the wardrobe, Matt. Can he hear us?" she asked in a low voice.

"I doubt it."

She pulled the dress over her head. The odor of lilac overhung the mustiness of the room. The wardrobe was hung with her few dresses. Lingerie lay carelessly on a chair.

"Come closer," she said.

Matt walked to the screen.

"You can get out of this mess if you'll listen to me."

"Shoot."

"Turn him loose."

"No."

"Play it smart, Matt!"

"I said no."

"There's a rainpipe down the back of the building. It's strong enough to hold a man."

He shook his head. "It's not my way."

She bit her lip. "I didn't really have to change," she said. "I made a bet, a rather silly one now that I think back on it."

"Keep talking."

She fiddled with her hair. "I said I would come up here and talk with you."

"You've won the bet then."

"Won't you listen to me? Get out of here before they come in after you."

"You're wasting your breath."

She looked toward the open window. "There isn't much time left."

"How do you stand in this thing?"

"What do you mean?"

"I need your help."

125

She came from behind the screen and turned her shapely back toward him. "Button me, honey."

He buttoned the dress and smoothed it down.

She turned and smiled. "You've done that before for a woman," She saw the look in his eyes and she flushed. "What do you want me to do?"

"Don't listen to that tinhorn, Linda!" yelled Rick.

"I need a shotgun," said Matt tensely. "A six-gun won't get me out of here."

She shook her head. "You'll need a troop of cavalry and a Gatling gun to get past those cold-gutted sharks down there."

"Just get me a shotgun."

"I can't do it, Matt. I'm not like you. I don't want to die."

He walked to the door. Then he turned and eyed her coldly. "Get out of here and stay away until it's all over."

Her eyes filled with tears. "I'm sorry, Matt."

"Forget it. Maybe I'm asking for too much."

"Anything else but that, honey."

Matt stood in the hallway. She came out behind him and locked the door. As she passed room 201, Rick rolled over. "Don't get mixed up in this thing, Linda!" he yelled.

She looked away from him.

"You hear me, Linda?"

She walked toward the stairway.

"Linda!" yelled Rick. "You hear me?"

"Shut up!" she yelled back. She hurried down the stairs.

Rick took the cigarette from his lips and flipped it out of the window. He turned to look at Matt. "She's loco about my old man, Morgan. She won't do anything for you. She knows which side her bread is buttered on."

Matt sat down in his chair and rolled another cigarette.

Rick lay back on the bed. "Won't be long until they come after you, Morgan. I'm going to enjoy hearing you beg for mercy. Man, I hope I can get some licks in on you."

Matt lit his cigarette and blew out a cloud of smoke. "That'll be the day," he said quietly.

"I'll give you a personal going over," Rick boasted.

Matt spat. "You talk too much for a fighting man, sonny."

Linda paused at the bottom of the stairs. Luke whistled softly as he eyed her. "My, my, our Linda has some fine feathers," he said.

Joe stood up. "Morgan say anything?"

She shook her head. "Rick wanted a cigarette. I gave him one." She closed the door behind her.

"Well, I'll be damned," said Joe.

Craig watched Linda as she came from the Harper House. He looked at Beero. "Stay here and if Linda goes back to the hotel again you let me know pronto."

Beero nodded.

Belden walked to the bar and poured a drink.

"She's heading for the Horseshoe," said Beero.

Craig looked up at the clock. He emptied his glass and then refilled it. Pinto opened his mouth to speak and then saw the look in Belden's eyes. He industriously mopped the back bar.

Linda walked casually into the Horseshoe twirling her handbag at the end of its strap. The drummer looked up from a game of solitaire. "O.K. O.K. So you changed your dress. Not bad either, but we don't know if you talked with Morgan."

She leaned against the bar, hardly listening to him. "Have it your own way. I did talk with him though. It wasn't a decent bet anyway."

"Who cares about that?"

She turned. "I do!"

Baldy placed a bottle in front of her. "He's right, Linda. How do we know you talked with him?"

"Isn't my word good enough?"

"Not for a hundred bucks it ain't."

"Forget it then."

He studied her. "What's up, kid? I've never seen you like this before."

"I'll tell you! That poor fool sitting up there in that room without a chance of getting away with what he plans to do. That's what's bothering me."

"Like I said before: The man is a born killer. He

likes this sort of thing. Wearing that tin badge makes him think he's God Almighty."

"No. He's right in what he wants to do. It's the people of Gun Hill who are wrong. Not one person in this Godforsaken town will lift so much as a little finger to help him, all because they're scared to death of Craig Belden. *Mister* Belden! It makes me sick and ashamed of myself for being like all the others."

"He won't be here long, one way or another, and Craig Belden will be the king bee in Gun Hill for a long time yet."

"Get out the spondulicks," said the salesman eagerly. "She lost, didn't she?"

Linda took out her cigarettes. "You're like all the rest, Baldy. You talk as though Craig Belden was God. He's only a man. I ought to know if anyone does, and he's no different from Matt Morgan up there in that hotel room, a man standing up to his ideals. They're just men after all."

"Very touching," said the salesman. "Where's the mazuma, Baldy?"

Baldy turned to the cash register. A man sitting at the rear table got up quickly and walked into a back room. He reappeared with Lee Smithers. Lee blinked as he looked about the saloon. He swayed a little as he wiped his mouth with a dirty sleeve. "This hombre can prove whether or not she was in Morgan's room," said the man with Lee.

"Yeh?" asked the salesman. He grinned as he

looked at Lee. "He doesn't look as though he could prove his own name right now."

"Shut up, you," said Lee. He looked at Linda. "You say you saw Rick up there?"

She nodded.

"Notice anything different about him?"

She laid a slim finger against her right cheek. "He's got a nasty slash here."

Lee nodded. "She was up there all right. Who's buying?"

"What does that prove?" demanded the salesman.

Lee swayed a little. He glared at the salesman. "I'm Rick's *amigo*. You seen Rick since he come back to Gun Hill from Oklahoma, Linda?"

"No."

Lee waved a hand. "Then she was up there all right."

"That's good enough for me," said Baldy.

"But not for me," said the salesman. "I think you're playing me for a patsy."

Lee hitched up his belt. "She says she been up there, she's been up there. You want to make something out of it?"

"Take it easy! I was only joshing."

"You bet you were, tenderfoot!"

Lee shoved back his hat and staggered a little as he headed for the bar. "Another thing: he say he was going to try and take me too, Linda?"

"He didn't say. Why would he want you?"

Lee grinned. "'Cause I was with Rick in Oklahoma and I was in on the whole deal."

Linda looked quickly at him. "Just why does Morgan want you and Rick?"

"You don't know?"

"All I've heard was that Rick killed someone in Oklahoma."

Lee braced himself against the bar and felt for his sack of makings. "You ought to hear the whole story."

The man with Lee nodded. "Lee already told me. He was with Rick Belden all right. Jesus, you ought to hear Lee tell about it."

Baldy placed the betting money in front of Linda. She picked it up. "Give me a bottle of rye, Baldy." She took the bottle and beckoned to Lee. "Come on, Lee. I want to hear the whole story . . . in private."

Lee grinned loosely. He followed her into one of the gaming rooms.

"What's she after?" asked the salesman.

"*Quien sabe?*" said Baldy. "It's her business. She seems awfully interested in Morgan. Don't ask me why. I mind my own business. Let's buy, gentlemen. I ain't here just to be sociable."

131

Chapter Twelve

THE SUN WAS dying over the western hills in an agony of rose and gold. The wind was shifting steadily. It blew down the main street of Gun Hill scattering papers and dry leaves. The halyards hanging loosely from the warped flag pole in front of the town hall slapped steadily. Wind-caught doors slammed here and there. The heat of the long day began to dissipate slowly.

A rifleman moved about restlessly on top of Charlie's Place. He looked at the western sky. "Won't be too long now, Chuck," he said.

His companion spat toward the street below. "Won't be hot up here now. You think he'll ever make that break?"

"It's quite a while until train time."

They looked at the dark window of Matt Morgan's room. There was no sign of life there. The curtains flapped in the rising wind.

Men shifted about at their posts in doorways and rooftops. Here and there a lamp was lit along the quiet street, throwing yellow rectangles of light onto the yellow dust. Someone had begun preparations for the night's meal in a restaurant near the railroad station, and the odor of beef stew was mingled with that of wood smoke. A buckboard rattled across the plank bridge and the thudding of the hoofs died slowly away.

The stores were empty of customers and the storekeepers stood on the wooden sidewalks in front of their establishments and looked toward the Harper House. Only the saloons seemed to be busy, but there was no tin-pan music coming from them. Probably for the first time in the history of Gun Hill there were no horses hitched to the many racks along the street. A lone buckboard stood near one of the livery stables with the horse still in harness, forgotten by the liveryman, who was standing in a bar forgetful of his duties.

Craig Belden raised his head and looked at the wall clock in Charlie's Place. The pendulum swung steadily to and fro, marking off the time. Craig took a cigar from a silver case and placed it in his mouth. He scratched a match on his belt buckle and lit the cigar. He looked up at the clock again and then walked to the front window to watch the second floor of the Harper House.

The clerk in the lobby of the hotel closed his ledger and placed the pen in its holder. He looked up the dark stair well and he seemed to feel as though the shadows were moving ominously closer to him. He raised the wick in the Argand

133

lamp which stood on the counter behind him. Luke and Joe still sat, holding Winchesters, in a dark part of the lobby. Now and then they drew in on their cigarettes, lighting up their lean faces.

The dark splotches on the stair runner were almost invisible now, but the big stain at the bottom of the stairs where Skag had ended his death fall seemed black as ebony.

Matt Morgan shifted in his chair. The hotel seemed deserted except for him and his prisoner, but he knew better. He moved quickly as light came in from outside. Then he realized someone had hung a lamp where it would throw rays against the open window. They weren't missing a trick.

Rick moved. "Hey, Morgan?"

"Yes?"

"There any way I can make things up to you?"

Matt did not answer. The kid's voice had a quality which irritated him.

Rick shifted on the bed. "Maybe we can make a deal?" he asked hopefully.

"No deals."

"It was an accident. We had too much to drink. You know how it is. We didn't know what we were doing."

"No . . . *I don't know how it is.*"

"Be reasonable."

Matt's feet struck the floor. "Reasonable? After

134

what you did? You won't worm out of this one, Belden."

He walked to the window and looked down, careful not to silhouette himself against the light. Lamplight dotted the street, but there was no sign of life. There was a lone buckboard in front of the livery stable. Charlie's Place was dimly lit. It seemed as though his besiegers had vanished, but he knew better.

"You still figuring on making that nine o'clock train?" asked Rick.

"Why not?"

"You don't have much time. You'll have to make your move before too long."

"There's plenty of time left."

"Yeh?"

"It's my worry, Belden."

"Sure is. What time is it?"

Matt walked to the table and picked up his watch. He opened the lid. "Eight o'clock," he said.

Rick made his move. He kicked out with his unfettered leg, striking Matt just above the groin. Matt gasped and doubled over in time to meet a smashing blow to the jaw. He half fell over Rick. Rick snatched at the holstered Colt. Matt slashed his left hand across the kid's eyes and dropped his right hand to grip Rick's wrist. They tensed with the strain. The kid had strength and he was desperate. Matt was weary from his long train trip and the tension he had been under since the death of his wife.

Matt felt for Rick's throat with his left hand, but Rick forced down his chin. His teeth sank into Matt's hand. Matt jerked it back and Rick drove his head up against Matt's face. The blow was stunning. Tears flowed from Matt's eyes and he felt a trickle of blood from his nose.

Matt straightened up and dumped the kid over the side of the bed so that he sprawled half on the floor. Matt ripped out his Colt and cracked the kid sharply over the head with it. Rick yelled in pain. Matt stood up and placed the Colt on the table. He pulled the kid up on the bed and gripped him by the throat. He thrust his bloody face close to Rick's and tightened his grip. He relaxed it for a moment.

"For God's sake, don't kill me!" gasped Rick.

Matt tightened his grip again deliberately, feeling the kid's body tense beneath him. "What did *you* say when my wife pleaded for her life, or didn't you give her a chance, you bastard?"

Rick's hand tore at the wiry fingers. Matt held on, knowing how easy it would be to finish the killer off there, and then make his break for freedom alone. The kid went limp and Matt let go his hold.

Matt wiped the blood from his face and felt a rush of sweat break out on his body. He shivered a little.

If Rick Belden was dead, the best thing for Matt to do was make his break when he heard the train and keep the last cartridge for himself, for he knew that Craig Belden's vengeance would be a terrible thing.

Matt sat down weakly and felt his nose. It wasn't broken but it had been a close thing. He sat there looking at Rick. Then the kid moved and groaned a little.

Rick felt his bruised throat. He could not understand why the implacable man who sat there had not killed him.

"No," said Matt quietly. "That would have been *too* easy. I know an old Cheyenne who wanted to come looking for you, and if he had found you, you would have died *his* way. Maybe the little torture fires. He can keep a man alive a long, long time, in agony."

The wind whispered through the window and fluttered the faded curtains. The bedsprings creaked as Rick tried to move away.

"No," said Matt. "It won't be the quick way out, nor the Cheyenne way of dealing with a woman-killer. It will be the way of justice, which in a way, is the cruelest of them all.

"First comes the long waiting in the stinking jail. Then a long-drawn-out trial to make sure you are guilty. Every man in that courtroom will know you are guilty, but it has to be done legally.

"Then comes the sentencing. That will sicken you, Belden, because you haven't got the guts to be a real man.

"Then you'll be taken back to your cell for another long stretch. Meanwhile they'll be busy

137

erecting the gallows outside. Hammering and sawing to make it just right, according to the specifications. The hangman will be called in with his basket of ropes. Special ropes, made of Kentucky hemp, beautifully and smoothly woven. Inch-and-one-eighth rope. He stretches it with weights until it's just exactly an inch in circumference. He oils them like he would a fine gun."

Rick turned his head away.

"He gets about a hundred dollars for the job, and is underpaid at that, because he's a specialist. At least *most* of them are. Some of them are bunglers."

Rick jerked. "What do you mean?"

Matt leaned back in his chair. "Three or four years ago they hung Blackjack Ketchum at Clayton, New Mexico. Blackjack was quite an hombre. *Muy hombre*, as the Mexes say. They made a mistake on the drop through the trap door."

"What happened?"

Matt rubbed his battered nose. "Tore his head off."

Rick gasped. He trembled violently. "I don't want to hear any more."

Matt leaned forward. "They test the ropes with two-hundred-pound sandbags. Then comes the cold dark morning when they call for you. Your hands will be lashed behind you and they'll walk you to the gibbet, if you *can* walk, but they'll get you there all right, one way or another. It won't make any difference what you say or try to do. You'll get there on time.

"You'll go up the stairs with the witnesses watching you. The black cap goes over your head."

"Damn you! Shut up!" screamed Rick.

"The noose goes around your neck. Fourteen turns, all legal-like. Then comes the last few seconds of waiting. An eternity, it is said, although how any living person knows about that is beyond me. Your whole life is supposed to flash in front of your eyes, and there must be some nasty scenes you'll see, Rick."

"Jesus . . . oh Jesus!" screamed the kid. He pulled the pillow over his head.

Matt could not stop. "Then there will be a thump as the trap doors open. You'll hit the end of that rope like a sack of potatoes. You alone will know what happens then. I'd say the rope would cut into your Adam's apple like a white-hot knife. Your eyes will pop and your tongue will shoot out."

Rick moaned softly.

Matt stood up. "Maybe a prayer will shoot through your mind that last second. No one will hear it, maybe not even God, for he's turned his face away from you, Belden."

Rick began to sob, but there was no pity in Matt Morgan, nothing but the desire to hurt him without laying a hand on him. "Then they'll cut you down and the coroner will certify that you are dead and that justice has been carried out. Into the pine box next. They'll haul you to Boot Hill, and maybe say a few words over you. Into the grave. Clods rattle on the box lid, but *you* won't hear them. Then they'll finish off the fill in a nice smooth mound."

Rick shook as he tried to drown out the cruel words.

"Rest in peace," said Matt. "Gone from this earth to his reward in heaven . . . or hell."

Matt turned away and leaned against the wall, trying to control himself. Minutes ticked past. Matt walked into the dark hallway and crept to the head of the stairs. A lamp was lit on the clerk's desk, but there was no sign of anyone down there. The faint odor of tobacco smoke drifted up.

Lee Smithers wiped his mouth with a shaky hand. He filled his glass and looked across the table at Linda. "So far as we knew she was just a dirty squaw." He hiccupped. "Of course the whole thing was Rick's idea."

"Naturally."

"But he's my *amigo*."

"Sure . . . sure . . ."

Lee downed his drink. "Morgan ain't going to get my old *amigo* out of Gun Hill."

Her upper lip curled a little. "So? You're going to save Rick?"

He blinked his eyes and tried to focus them. He wanted to be *muy hombre* in front of her. "Yeh," he said.

"How?"

He squinted, trying to look shrewd and dangerous. "Oh, it can be done all right. I ain't telling anyone, but old Lee knows how to do the job. I *can* do it too, Linda. You bet your sweet little life on that!"

She stood up and looked down at the drunk.

"How about another bottle?" he asked. "After all, you didn't know what Rick and me really done until I told you."

She picked up her full whisky glass. "Sure," she said. "Have this one on me, you filthy scum!" She threw the whisky full into his bloated face.

He got slowly to his feet as she left the room. He wiped his cheeks and looked about the room. He walked to the drapes and pulled them aside. "I'll show her, the bitch," he said to himself. "I'll show up Morgan and that bastard Craig Belden. They'll know who *I* am and what *I* can do tonight."

He walked to the rear of the saloon and opened the rear door. He glanced once more at Linda and then walked down the dark alleyway toward the rear of the Harper House.

Linda stood at the end of the bar and her hands trembled so much she gripped the edge of the mahogany.

"Drink?" asked Baldy.

"No."

"On me. You look peaked, Linda."

"I am."

"Got some special stuff. Too good for these

bums." He bent under the bar and took a sawed-off double-barreled Greener from the shelf. He placed it on the bar right in front of her. "Blasted thing is always in the way."

She looked at the deadly weapon. "Why do you have it at all, Baldy?"

He took out a sealed bottle and placed it on the bar. "That there gun is short on looks but long on results. Looks ugly and it is. Twelve-gauge Greener loaded with Blue Whistlers with split wads. Can cut a man nigh in half at ten or fifteen feet. You can have your six-guns for close range. Me, I'll take my old Greener. Ain't no man in his right mind will stand up to one of them. Regular cannon, that is."

He uncorked the bottle and poured her a drink. He sniffed the mouth of the bottle. "Have one yourself, Baldy." He grinned. "Don't mind if I do." He filled a glass for himself. "Drink up, it will do you good."

"Thanks." She pressed a hand against her brow. "I've got a lousy headache. You have any of those powders here?"

"Sure, kid. Hold on a minute." He bustled to the end of the bar and opened the gate. He ducked into a rear room.

Linda downed the shot, looked at the few men in the bar, then snatched up the shotgun. She held it close to her side and pulled her gaudy shawl about it to conceal it. She walked quickly to the door and stepped outside. She hurried to the alley-way and stepped around the corner.

Baldy came out of the back room and looked for her. "Where'd she go?"

A customer grinned. "I never ask a lady where she's going when she's in a hurry."

Blady scratched his bare pate. "Where the hell is my Greener?"

"Damned if I know."

Baldy picked up Linda's empty glass. "You don't suppose?" he said.

"What?"

"She took it."

"I didn't see her."

Baldy wiped the cold sweat from his face. "Queer," he said. He climbed over the bar and walked to the door. He looked up and down the street, shrugged, and went back inside. Baldy was a man who took things as they came and kept his mouth shut, which was probably why he was the best-liked bar critter in Gun Hill.

The brass pendulum of the big wall clock swung steadily to and fro, with the lamplight glinting on it. Craig Belden sat at a table near the front of Charlie's Place where he could see the Harper House. In the past hour men had come into the saloon, had reported, then had a drink and left to return to their posts.

Belden toyed with an empty glass. An unlit cigar was clenched in his strong teeth. Beero sat at another table, idly shuffling and reshuffling a deck of cards. Now and then he looked at his boss. He looked up at the clock and then at Pinto. Pinto held out his hands, palms upward, and shrugged.

Belden shoved the glass back and stood up, throwing the cigar into a garboon. The clock showed half past eight o'clock. "Wait here," he said curtly to Beero. He went outside.

Beero walked to the window."

"Where's he going now?" asked Pinto.

"Toward the hotel."

"You're loco!"

"Dammit! Then come see for yourself!"

Every man in the dim saloon walked to the front window to watch Belden as he crossed the street and paused on the sidewalk. Then he entered the lobby.

Matt Morgan stood up as he heard the heavy tread on the stairs. He stepped into the hallway. This was no stealthy approach. Light wavered in the stair well, casting strange shadows on the faded wallpaper.

"About time someone came for me," said Rick.

Craig Belden appeared at the top of the steps. He placed the Argand lamp on a hall table and slowly unbuckled his gunbelt. He draped it over the newel post and looked toward Matt.

"What is it now?" asked Matt.

"Palaver." Craig held out his empty hands. "No dirty work."

"Come on then."

Matt stepped aside to let the rancher enter the room. "No lights," said Matt.

"I'm not anxious to get a bullet in my head."

"Well?"

Craig turned slowly. "Matt, you owe me a life. Have you forgotten that?"

"I haven't forgotten La Honda, if that's what you mean."

"I do. At that time you said you'd never forget what I did for you."

"I haven't. I know what you're driving at. You want a life for a life."

"Exactly."

"It can't be done."

"Listen, Matt! Figure it this way: it will pay off the score you owe me. I don't know whether my boy killed your wife or not. I've never begged for anything in my life before and you know it. I'm humbling myself before you. Let me have my boy and I'll call your debt even."

"You didn't lose anything by saving my life. But look at what I have lost because of this animal you raised instead of a man."

"Don't you understand?" pleaded Belden. "He's all I have left from her, Matt. Surely that means something to you? Maybe I've failed as a father, but the boy had no mother to raise him."

"Has mine now?" asked Matt softly.

Craig smashed a fist into his other palm. "I understand how you feel, Matt, but taking this boy

away from me won't bring your wife back to you.
There's not a chance for you to get out of Gun Hill
tonight. It will cost you your life."

"I've talked enough."

"Listen, Matt! You've got a son of your own.
What about *him* if anything happens to you?"

"What about *him?*"

Belden came closer to Matt. "He'll be on his
own. No mother and father. Have you considered
that?"

"Yes," said Matt quietly. "I've done a lot of
thinking about that."

"Well?"

"I'm still going through with what I started to
do. It's my belief, my way of life, and I hope to
God I'm right in it."

"Revenge isn't that important, Matt."

Matt stared through the dimness at his old
friend. "It all depends on who gets the revenge,
doesn't it? Well, I'm taking revenge, as you call it,
and no matter what happens to Petey he'll know
what kind of a man his father was. He'll know I
tried to make your son pay for what he did. He'll
know too that I didn't run out on my duty."

"You're loco!"

Matt shrugged. "Maybe . . . maybe not. I do
know this: Every time my boy would look at me in
the years to come he'd remember that I had my
hands on one of the scum who raped and killed his
mother and that I didn't have the guts to bring
him in. You think I want that boy to grow up hat-

ing me? Look at the son you've bred. He doesn't give a damn for his father or he would have tried to make you proud of him instead of becoming a stink in the nostrils of decent men."

Craig Belden raised his hands and then dropped them. He turned silently away from Matt, looked at his son, then walked out into the hall. He paused at the head of the stairs to get his gunbelt, picked up the lamp, and walked heavily down the stairs.

Matt went to the window. He heard the hotel door slam and watched Belden walking purposefully across the street. "Beero!" roared Belden as he neared the saloon.

The big gunhand opened the door of the saloon. He looked up toward Matt, then stepped aside as Belden stamped in.

Lee Smithers looked up and down the dark alleyway. The moon was due to rise soon, but there was enough time for him to get his job done before he would be seen. He tried the lock on the door of the storage shed behind a general store. He picked up a piece of iron rod and forced it down behind the hasp. It broke free with a grating noise as the rusted nails and screws gave way. He paused for a moment to see if the noise had been heard.

He walked inside and knocked over a box, skinning his shin. He cursed. He lit a match and looked about until he found a big can of kerosene.

He shook it and nodded as he felt the weight. It was at least three-quarters full.

Lee staggered a little as he walked toward the rear of the Harper House. He scouted up a cross alley and looked up and down the main street. There was no one in sight but a shawled woman walking slowly toward the door of the hotel. He tried to focus his eyes on her, gave up the attempt, and sat down for a moment as the alcohol he had drunk threatened to take control of him.

He felt in his pocket for a box of matches, grinned inanely to himself, and then made his way back to the can of kerosene. He hummed a little as he carried it to the rear of the hotel.

Lee looked up at the second floor. Not a room was lighted. He found a newspaper and formed two long spills from it. There was a partly open window at one end of the ground floor. He took the cap from the can and poured about half of the kerosene across the sill. Then he walked down to the other end of the hotel and pried up a window with a stick. The rest of the kerosene was dumped in there.

Lee wiped his sweating hands on his dirty shirt and lighted one of the spills. He shielded the little flame with a hand until it caught hold, then waved the paper about until it flared up. He threw it into the room.

Lee grinned as he ran toward the first window. He lit the second spill, waved it about, then heaved it in. The wave of flame roared back at him, and he staggered and fell down. "God," he said, "this ought'a be a real barbecue for sure. Good old Rick. He'll sure thank me for this."

He set off at a staggering run, looking over his shoulder now and then at his handiwork.

Chapter Thirteen

LINDA PAUSED FOR a moment at the door of the hotel. She drew her shawl tightly about her, snuggled the Greener closer to her side, took a deep breath, and walked into the lobby.

Luke looked up at her. "Not again," he said.

Joe eyed her appreciatively. "Ain't no one up there worth while, kid. Stay down here with a couple of real men."

She kept sideways to them, hoping to God they couldn't see the shape of the shotgun against her body. "You fellows like a drink?" she asked.

"Hell yes," said Luke.

"It's upstairs."

"You go get it then, honey. I sure ain't going up there."

She walked to the foot of the stairs.

"Nice ankles," said Joe.

"Always got your mind on the fillies," said Luke.

"What else is there besides liquor?"

"You got me there, sonny. Hurry up and get that whisky, Linda."

She started up the stairs. Joe winked at Luke,

then he ran over to the foot of the stairs and peered up at her. "Man," he said softly. "No wonder old man Belden likes her."

There was a draft in the stair well. It caught her shawl and whipped it back. Joe saw the butt of the shotgun. "Hey!" he yelled. He started up the stairs, then thought better of it. He turned to Luke. "She had a scatter-gun under that shawl."

Luke laughed. "What she got under that shawl ain't no shotgun."

Joe shook his head. "I saw it, *amigo*."

Luke stood up and glanced through the front window toward the saloon. "Man, oh man," he said thoughtfully. "Wait till old man Belden gets his hands on that conniving bitch."

Matt Morgan raised his head. There was someone on the stairs. He peered into the hall and then breathed easier as he saw Linda. She hurried toward him. "Come out here," she said softly. She took the Greener from under her shawl and placed it in his hands. "God forgive me," she said.

"Thanks, Linda, but why ask God to forgive you?"

She looked at him in the darkness. "Because of what will soon happen," she said simply.

"This may cause you plenty of trouble, Linda."

"Trouble? I've lived with it most of my life, and I'm so used to it that I wouldn't know how to act if I wasn't in it from day to day."

"I'm sorry to hear that."

"Why? You had nothing to do with it."

Matt pushed over the top snap to open the breech of the Greener. He could see the dull brass bases of the two cartridges in the dim light from the stair well. He drew one out. "Split wads," he said quietly.

Linda pulled the shawl up about her shoulders as though she had felt a chill.

Matt replaced the shells in the chambers and snapped the breech shut. He put the safety catch on. "Thanks again," he said. "What made you change your mind about helping me?"

"I heard the whole story," she said. She looked away. "About your wife, I mean."

"So?"

"Lee Smithers told me."

"*Where is he?*"

"You can't get him too, Matt!"

He gripped the shotgun. "I'll be back for him."

"Matt, why don't you get out of here while you have time? You can't beat Craig Belden."

"Let me alone," he said tensely.

"You're sure to get killed. Everyone in Gun Hill knows that except you. You should see them out there. They're waiting in the saloons and along the side streets for the main event to start. It's to be a big night in Gun Hill. The vultures are gathering. The human race stinks!"

"It's not as bad as all that. You can't judge everybody in this country by the people here."

"You forget I'm practically an authority on the subject."

Matt leaned the shotgun against the wall. "Maybe you haven't met the right kind of people."

"Like who?"

"My wife," he said quietly. "I have never met anyone who didn't like her."

She stared up at his face in the dimness. "Matt, was she very beautiful?"

"To *me* she was. That was all that mattered."

"Yes."

Matt suddenly raised his head. "Smoke," he said.

She turned quickly. "In the hotel?"

"Yes, I'm sure of it."

She gasped. "What happens now?"

"They're trying to force my hand. By God, I didn't believe Belden would go this far."

"He'll do anything to win," she said bitterly.

He looked down at her. "You'd better get out of here."

"What about you?"

He smiled. "*Quien sabe?* They haven't licked me yet."

He took her by the arm and hustled her toward the stairs. She looked up at him. "Good luck, Matt." He bent and kissed her. For a moment she wanted to cling to him, but she turned quickly and hurried down the stairs. The smell of smoke was stronger on the first floor. She walked right into the arms of Luke. He gripped her hard by the shoulders. "Come on, honey," he said grimly. "Craig Belden will want to have a few words with you for what you just done." He hustled her toward the door.

Craig Belden looked up and down the street and nodded in satisfaction. "Everything set, Beero?"

"Sure thing, boss. Not even a gnat could get past the boys."

"Keno."

A woman yelled from across the street. Craig whirled. He saw Linda being dragged toward him by Luke and Joe. "Damn you!" she shouted. "Let go of me!"

Luke waved a hand at Craig. "Mr. Belden!"

Craig walked toward them. "Yes?"

"She smuggled a shotgun upstairs to Morgan."

"*What was that?*"

Joe pulled his head back from her raking nails. "She gave Morgan a scatter-gun, boss."

Luke twisted Linda's wrist, forcing her down on one knee. Craig pushed his hired hand aside and pulled her up on her feet close to him. "Did you?" he demanded hoarsely.

She laughed in his face. "Yes, damn you! And I hope Matt Morgan empties both barrels into you!"

His hand cracked across her face. She fell back against Luke.

"Go ahead," she said defiantly. "It's the only way you and that rotten son of yours know how to handle a woman. With the back of the hand or the heel of the boot. I'm praying that Matt Morgan makes it, Craig."

He raised his hand and then lowered it. "A dozen shotguns won't help him now," he said harshly.

A man yelled from behind them. "Look! The hotel is afire!"

Beero ran toward them. "Jesus," he said. "The whole damned back of the lower floor is in flames. You can smell kerosene all over the place."

Craig lifted his clenched fists. "How the hell did this happen?"

A cloud of smoke drifted toward them and they heard the subdued crackling of the flames as they ate into the sun-dried wood.

"Get the fire pumper!" someone yelled.

"No use," said an older man. "Won't do a bit of good. The hoses are rotted clear through and the new ones is still on the way from the East."

Belden looked up and down the street. "You men take cover! Those flames will expose you to his fire! Get back and watch for his break! Pronto!"

He walked toward the hotel. "Morgan! Matt Morgan! Come out of there! The place is ablaze! You won't have a chance if you wait much longer!"

Firelight showed through the lower windows of the building. The upper floor was still dark. Smoke hung in the lobby. A steady roaring of flames began to be heard above the crackling of the wood. Glass shattered as accumulated gas blew out a window.

"Matt!" roared Belden. "Come out with your hands up! You can't live in there!"

There was no answer from Matt Morgan, and only the flames seemed to answer Craig Belden as they chewed into the wood and furnishings of the hotel. The firelight reflected from the eyes of the horse hitched to the buckboard, making them moist jewels. Up and down the street the people looked in fascination at the devouring flames. Men with Winchesters in their hands and Colts hanging by their sides were waiting for the silhouette of Matt Morgan to appear in the doorway of the hotel. Each one of them was sure he'd drill the marshal before he reached the middle of the street. Craig Belden paid well when a job was done to his satisfaction.

Linda Lewis stood across from the burning building with her shawl hanging loosely about her white shoulders. There was a red mark on her face where Craig Belden had struck her. Her lips were parted, breathing a silent prayer as she waited for the next move in this game of death.

The people of Gun Hill stood well back from any possible line of fire but close enough to see as much of the forthcoming drama as they could. Some of them admired Craig Belden; some of them put up with him as a necessary evil; some of them feared him as they would the devil. One thing they all had in common; none of them liked him. A good many of them hoped the gutty marshal would make it to the station with his prisoner, but none of them would have been foolish enough to have taken a bet on it, even with the best of odds.

There was one man who was enjoying the holocaust more than anyone else. Lee Smithers stood at the corner next to Charlie's Place, his tongue making a continual circuit of his wet mouth. The firelight reflected in his eyes, giving him a half-mad, half-shrewd expression. Now and then his right hand would hover over his pistol butt.

Chapter Fourteen

THE SMOKE WAS drifting through the upper hallway of the Harper House. The odors of burning wood and cloth, mingled with the stench of kerosene, hung thickly throughout the building.

Matt Morgan stifled a cough. The time had come to make his move and there would be no going back. He unlocked the handcuffs which held Rick's ankle to the bed. Rick drew up his leg and rubbed it. "Looks like you're all washed up, Marshal. Burned up, I mean. Get it?"

"Shut up."

Matt unlocked Rick's wrist from the bedpost and snapped the open cuff about his own left forearm. He mercilessly dragged the kid to his feet. He gripped him by the front of his shirt and drew him closer. "Now you listen to me, sonny. You're going to walk nice and peaceable-like close to my side. You make a break—" Matt gasped in pain as Rick brought a knee up into his groin. Rick swung with his left, catching Matt alongside the head.

Matt was staggered. He pulled the kid toward

him. Rick was laughing like a madman. He kicked savagely at Matt, then cut at his face with the edge of a hand, trying for the eyes. He butted with his head and Matt felt a tooth break. His mouth tasted of blood.

They swayed back and forth, Rick having the edge. He kneed and kicked, gouged and bit. They went battling back to the wall and Matt's right hand struck the barrels of the shotgun. They grappled chest to chest in the swirling smoke, savagely gasping and grunting.

Matt gripped the Greener and raised it. Rick closed his left hand about the barrels. He slowly forced them up and across Matt's throat, driving him back. Matt's head struck the wall and he felt the barrels crushing against his larynx. Spots seemed to dance before his eyes. In a last wild effort he kneed the kid and felt the pressure slacken.

Matt jerked the shotgun from Rick's hand and kneed him again. He smashed the gun against Rick's head. The kid went down on his knees and nearly dragged Matt down on top of him.

Matt pulled him to his feet. He rammed the twin muzzles up under Rick's chin. He thrust his face close, and blood and saliva flew from his mouth and flecked the kid's cheeks. "You make another move and I'll touch off both barrels!"

Rick's eyes were filled with fear. He tried to talk, but the relentless pressure under his chin made it impossible. A faint sound came from his

mouth. His eyes widened with horror and Matt
suddenly realized the room was alight. He turned
his head to see a runnel of flame licking along the
hall carpet. Already the wallpaper was smoking,
and even as he watched it broke into flame.

Rick found his voice. "We'll never make it
now!"

Matt dragged the kid after him into the hallway.
He stopped as he saw the stair well. The wall beyond it was a mass of flames roaring up toward the
skylight.

Rick pulled back. "No!"

Matt grinned but there was no humor in his
eyes. "You either walk, sonny, or I'll drag you
down. Take your choice." He yanked viciously at
the handcuffs.

They staggered toward the stairs, but even Matt
felt a qualm of fear as he looked down. Flames had
almost consumed the wall hangings near the
clerk's desk. The right-hand stair rail was ablaze
from top to bottom and patches of fire were hun-
grily consuming the runner. It was a tunnel of
flame to safety.

The big front window of the hotel crashed to
the ground outside. A cloud of smoke poured up
the stair well.

"Matt! Matt Morgan!" The voice seemed to
emanate from the roaring flames as though someone was calling from the gaping doorway of hell
itself.

There was a crashing noise from below and

flames billowed high, licking at the left-hand rail. A whirling volcano of fat sparks and burning fragments soared up the stairway.

"Matt! Matt Morgan!" The voice seemed louder now. "You can't let that boy burn to death! I'm coming in!"

"It's Pa!" yelled Rick. "He'll save me!" He tried to shield himself behind Matt.

The heat scorched Matt's battered face. He started down, dragging the scared kid behind him. Flames licked about his boots. The stains left by Skag's blood seemed to be liquid in the light.

Matt plunged down the stairs. Rick grabbed for the rail and screamed in pain as the melting varnish came off on his palm.

Matt plodded across the lobby with his head bent and his right arm across his eyes as though he were walking into a norther. The big front door was outlined in flames. There was a crash behind them and a blast of heat as the roof fell in on the staircase and blocked it with a mass of embers and burning beams.

Another blast of heat seemed to propel the two of them through the doorway and out onto the boardwalk. Here and there small fires had started on the walk.

A roar went up from the watching people as they saw the two men come out of the flames.

Craig Belden started forward, but Beero gripped him by the arm. "Jesus, boss!" yelled Beero. "The

Gordon D. Shirreffs

place is ready to collapse! He's smoked out now!
We got him, by sin!"

Matt instantly thrust the muzzles of the shotgun
up under Rick's chin. He looked at Craig Belden
and tightened his grasp about the small of the
stock. Their eyes clashed through the drifting
smoke.

"Don't make me do it, Craig."

Rick screamed, "No, Pa! No! He means it!"

Belden raised his big hands as though to reach
out for Matt, and then dropped them. "Don't play
the fool, Matt. You can't make it."

Matt looked toward the station and saw the silent men of the *B corrida* standing in his way with
ready rifles and pistols. "One move by any of your
men, Craig, and I'll touch off one of these loads.
Tell them to move back out of the street."

Craig tried to outstare him but it was no use. He
knew Matt Morgan and what he was capable of,
and so far in this game Matt had held all the aces.
But his luck would run out; it had to between
there and the station.

Their eyes seemed to be fencing as they stood
there, thrust and riposte, and it was Craig Belden
who at last turned away and looked at his hardcase *vaqueros*. The firelight glittered on their eyes
and on the barrels of their rifles. Craig shook his
head and motioned them back. Hammers were let
down to half-cock on Colts and Winchesters as the
men drifted slowly back toward the sides of the
street.

162

Matt jerked his left hand. "Come on, Rick. We're on the way."

Sparks darted through the thickening smoke like fireflies. The wind shifted a little and drove the smoke back toward the hotel as though it were opening a pathway for Matt and his prisoner.

There was no movement among those watching as Matt forced Rick down the center of the street.

Craig Belden stood there with his hands resting on his hips, leaning slightly forward as though waiting for a leash to be slipped, but he knew better than to make a sudden move. Matt Morgan would act not only as the captor of Rick Belden but also as jury, judge, and executioner in a matter of split seconds. It wouldn't take much pressure from Matt's trigger finger to blow Rick to hell.

Josh Bartlett stood behind a post, watching the slow movement of Matt and Rick toward him. Now and then his little eyes swiveled toward Craig Belden. An unlit cigar was in Bartlett's wet mouth and he moved it slowly back and forth.

The sidewalk in front of the Horseshoe was lined with people, and Baldy had deserted his post to see the final phase of the drama. His eyes widened a little as he saw his Greener in Matt's hands. He looked across the street toward Linda, and nodded to himself as though he had forgiven her for what she had done.

Minnie looked down from her second-story window in the Horseshoe. Her hand touched the bruise on her cheek as she saw Rick Belden. Sud-

denly she turned away and threw herself on the
bed, clasping her hands over her ears to drown out
the expected gunfire.

Matt kept his eyes on the closest of Belden's
men. Belden himself, the man most to be feared,
was somewhere behind them, but Matt did not
dare turn to look for him.

The buckboard was still standing in front of the
livery stable. Matt forced Rick toward it. Rick
walked in stilted fashion as though trying to raise
himself up and away from those deadly muzzles.

Matt stopped beside the buckboard. "Get up
into the left seat," he said quietly.

The kid moved slowly. The shotgun now was
pointed at the base of his skull. He sat down on the
seat with his hands flat on his thighs. A trickle of
sweat cut pale rivulets through the grime on his
battered face.

Matt walked around the back of the buckboard
and the shotgun never wavered away from Rick.
Matt stepped up into the right-hand seat and
looked at Sheriff Josh Bartlett, who stood just beyond the horse's head. "Unhitch him," said Matt.

Bartlett slowly took the cigar from his mouth.
His eyes swiveled from Matt to the slowly approaching Craig Belden.

"Pronto!" barked Matt.

Bartlett raised a fat hand and dabbed weakly
at his plump jowls.

"Do as he says, Josh!" called Belden.

Bartlett clumsily untethered the horse. His face glistened wetly in the light from the burning hotel.

"Stand up nice and tall, sonny," said Matt out of the side of his mouth. He took the reins in his right hand and held the shotgun in his left, forcing the cold muzzles up firmly into the soft hollow under Rick's chin.

"For God's sake!" husked Rick.

"Shut up!"

Lee Smithers peered quickly around the corner. He nodded as he stepped back drawing his Colt to check it. Then he hurried toward the alley which led to the railroad tracks.

Matt slapped the reins on the rump of the horse. It moved slowly forward. Men crowded back against store windows and into doorways as the buckboard rolled past, swaying a little now and then as it hit the ruts.

Rick rolled his eyes. "For God's sake, Morgan," he gasped, "take that thing away from my throat!"

"Stand still and you'll be all right."

Craig Belden walked down the center of the street with his hard eyes fixed on his son and Matt Morgan.

They reached an intersection. A swaying figure stood part way down the block, looking at them. "Hey, Rick! Hey, *amigo!*" he yelled. "Don't you worry none, boy! Old Lee will get you out of this! Don't you worry! Hear?"

"That Smithers?" asked Matt quietly.

"Yes."

Lee whirled and darted back toward the closest alleyway.

"He ought to be riding with us," said Matt.

Rick blinked his eyes as the wheels hit a deep rut, forcing the shotgun hard against his throat. "You got enough on your hands now, Morgan. You ain't going make it with me. You'll see. Pa ain't licked yet."

Matt spat. "You sure got a big mouth," he said. "Your pappy never teach you any manners? He never ran off at the mouth like you do."

Craig Belden increased his pace behind the buckboard.

"You aimin' to rush him, boss?" asked Beero as he hurried to keep up with Craig.

"Not now, you damned fool! Our time is coming. He can't fox us much longer."

"It's only two blocks to the station, boss."

"Dammit!" growled Belden. "I've got eyes!"

There was a sudden roaring noise and then the crackling collapse of timbers as the front wall of the Harper House tilted forward and then crashed into the street behind the crowd which was slowly following behind Craig Belden and his hired gunhands.

The horse shied and blowed as he heard the crash of falling timbers. A blast of gas carried sparks high over the street and one of them landed on the horse's withers. Matt drew in on the reins as the horse thrashed his head back and forth. The shotgun muzzles never moved from Rick's throat.

A fresh outbreak of sweat greased the kid's scarred face.

"He's ready to bolt," husked Rick.

"Shut up!"

All eyes were on the panicky horse. It seemed as though the calmest person in Gun Hill was Matt Morgan.

"Damn you!" said Rick.

"Damn you too," said Matt calmly.

The horse moved on. They had crossed the intersection of the first street and were approaching the street which paralleled the railroad tracks. A familiar figure stood at the mouth of the last alleyway before the end of the block. It was Lee Smithers, swaying a little as he tried to clear his senses and focus his bloodshot eyes on the two men in the buckboard.

"I hope for your sake, sonny, that your drunken *amigo* doesn't try anything," said Matt softly.

The horse had stopped again. It tossed its head as it fought the bit.

Matt looked back. The onlookers had stopped following the buckboard, leaving Craig Belden and Beero standing in the middle of the intersection. The rest of Belden's men moved back at an imperative wave of his hand.

Lee Smithers squared his shoulders and walked out into the street. He reached the center, directly in the pathway of the horse and buckboard, then turned slowly and deliberately to face toward the vehicle. His right hand hovered over the butt of his six-gun.

"That's Smithers for sure?" asked Matt.

"Yes."

Matt slapped the reins on the rump of the horse and it moved toward the silent figure in the street.

"All right, Morgan," said Lee. "You can stop right there."

"Get out of the way, Smithers."

"You heard me, Morgan."

Rick swallowed. "For God's sake, Lee," he called shakily, "don't start anything! You can't help me now! *Get out of the way!*"

The blazing hotel cast a weird light over the scene.

"Come on, Morgan," challenged Lee. "Let's see just *how* good you are."

"Damned fool," groaned Rick.

Lee hitched up his belt and swaggered forward. "Don't you worry none about me, Rick boy. How about it, Morgan? I was in on that deal with Rick. You want to draw on me?"

Matt halted the horse.

"Stay out of this, Smithers!" yelled Craig Belden. "Get out of the way!"

"You had your chance, Belden," said Lee. "Now it's up to me."

Craig Belden spoke over his shoulder to his men. "Keep back, all of you."

Matt handed the reins to Rick. "Drive," he said. "He's right in the way."

"Drive, damn you!"

"Lee," pleaded Rick, "get out of the way."

"Drive over him if you have to," said Matt coldly, "but keep this rig moving."

Rick slapped the reins hard on the horse. It moved on.

Lee spat to one side. "Come on, Morgan. You yellow? You going to draw or not? I'm asking you for a fight, law man."

Craig Belden moved quickly forward. "Get out of the way, Smithers, or I'll kill you."

Lee grinned. He wet his loose lips. His eyes seemed to roll in their sockets. "All right!" he screamed. He whipped out his Colt and threw himself forward on his belly.

Matt dropped his right hand and drew his Colt. Even as Lee's Colt exploded twice it was matched by the triple roaring of Matt's six-shooter. Rick threw up his left hand to shield his face from the flashes of Matt's gun. Craig Belden ran forward, clawing down a hand to grip his Colt, drawing it and cocking it in one easy motion as he thrust it forward to fire at Lee.

Rick swayed against Matt as Matt's body jerked with the impact of one of Lee's slugs. Smoke swirled about the buckboard. Lee Smithers looked up and grinned. "You got Rick easy enough, law man," he said. He coughed and when he spoke again his voice seemed thicker. "Wasn't so easy with me." He got slowly to his feet and peered through the wreathing gun smoke as though trying

169

to see through a thickening veil, then he pitched forward to fall heavily on his face in the dust.

Matt looked down at his left shoulder. There was a widening dark stain on the coat. Rick turned toward Matt, shoved the shotgun aside and looked full into Matt's face with unseeing eyes. There was a bluish hole under the kid's left eye. Rick swayed backward and fell from the buckboard, dragging Matt with him by his handcuffed wrist. Matt knelt beside the dead young man. The horse shied and then reared, and ran swiftly down the alleyway dragging the bouncing buckboard behind him.

Matt holstered his Colt and drew out the handcuff key. He unlocked the cuffs, freeing himself forever from Rick Belden. He stood up and swayed a little, then started walking toward the station. A far off sound came to him; the faint whistling of a locomotive in the dark hills.

Matt drew out his handkerchief and wadded it, forcing it under his blood-soaked shirt. He winced at the pain of the wound.

"Jesus!" said a bearded man. "Did you see that? Lee shot his pal Rick."

"The hell he did!" said a storekeeper. " 'Twas Morgan killed Rick Belden with the shotgun!"

"Yore loco!" said another man. "That double-gun never went off!"

A young cowpoke spat. "It was that drunken louse Lee what done it," he said. "Killed Rick and wounded Morgan. How the hell Smithers ever got up off the ground with that load of lead in him from both Belden and Morgan is beyond me."

Craig Belden looked at Matt's slowly moving figure, and then he looked down at Rick. He knelt beside the boy. He took off his coat and placed it over Rick's face. There was a brightness in Craig Belden's dark eyes. Linda watched him and then looked away.

Matt pressed his hand against the wound. There was an intolerable dryness in his throat.

The train whistle sounded again, low, long-drawn and melancholy sounding, awakening the echoes in the dark hills. There was a far off flash of yellow light as the headlight showed itself. The locomotive was laboring up the grade now, with an increased throbbing of its exhaust.

"He went right on to the station, Mister Belden," said Josh Bartlett, "just like nothing had happened."

Craig Belden nodded. He started down the street walking with long swinging strides, and there was cold hatred on his dark face.

The train whistled for a crossing; two long and two short.

Matt Morgan crossed the tracks, faintly, visible in the headlight of the approaching train.

The locomotive pounded across a switch and blew for the station. Then it passed the end of the street and shut off the view of the station. A scarf of thick cinder-laden smoke settled down about the cars.

Gordon D. Shirreffs

Matt Morgan walked along the platform as the engine braked to a halt. A station attendant opened his mouth to speak to Matt and then closed it as he saw the taut white face of the law man.

The cars banged together and the noise of escaping steam and rattling couplings drowned out everything else.

The locomotive headlight picked out the tall form of Craig Belden as he passed in front of it. He turned toward the platform with his boots crunching on the ballast. "Matt Morgan!" he called out.

Matt turned slowly. The conductor was stepping from one of the cars. He saw the two grim-faced men standing there, stared for a moment, and then got back on the car platform.

Craig Belden came up the ramp, walking slowly now, with his arms swinging easily at his sides. His eyes never left those of Matt Morgan.

"It's all over, Craig," said Matt steadily.

"No, it isn't, Matt. *I told you* . . ."

"It *is* over, Craig. I'm sorry that it didn't work out my way."

"Your way? I told you I'd kill you if anything happened to that boy."

Passengers peered from the car windows at the two big men. They saw the two set, hard-lined faces. Smoke and steam drifted between and about the two men giving them an unreal quality, but there was nothing unreal about their voices and the holstered six-guns by their sides. The conduc-

172

tor opened his mouth and shut it at a gesture from the station attendant.

"Stay where you are, Belden," warned Matt. "Don't force my hand. Your son is dead."

Craig Belden stopped and studied the wounded man who faced him. There was no pity on his face.

Beero rounded the front of the locomotive followed by Luke. Luke worked the lever of his Winchester to load it but Beero thrust up the barrel of the saddle-gun. "No," he said quietly. "It's between the two of them now. *Showdown*."

Josh Bartlett stood behind the two of them. "Beero is right, Luke. This is the way it should be."

Linda Lewis came around the rear of the last car and stopped to watch Craig and Matt. Her right hand rose to rest against her white throat.

Craig walked forward again, his boot heels ringing hollowly on the planks of the platform.

Matt raised his left hand. "All right, Belden, if this is the way you really want it, you draw."

Craig stopped. He nodded. *"This is the way I want it."* His right hand swept down, gripped the big six-gun and whipped it out, thumbing back the hammer. He fired. Matt bent into a crouch and his Colt came out in a fluid motion to rap twice. Craig Belden squeezed the trigger of his gun. The slug sang thinly past Matt's head but he did not move away. He fired once more and raised his head to look at Belden.

Belden took one step forward. "I wish . . ." he

said thickly, and then he pitched forward. His Colt flew from his open hand.

Matt walked toward his old friend. He knelt beside Craig and rolled him over. He opened Craig's collar. "Craig?" he asked softly.

Craig Belden opened his eyes. "What's the name of that boy of yours, Matt?"

"Petey, Craig."

"Matt . . . you raise him right. You . . . understand?"

"Yes."

"But you would anyway. It . . . would be . . . your way." Craig Belden closed his eyes. He stiffened a little, then opened his eyes to smile at Matt. Then he was gone. Matt stood up and looked down at Craig Belden. He turned to look at Linda Lewis who stood behind him.

"Board!" called out the white-faced conductor. The engineer hastily pulled the whistle cord.

Matt walked to the car and swung himself aboard. The train pulled out slowly, wreathing itself in steam and smoke. Beero and Luke looked up at Matt as he passed by them but there was no emotion in their eyes.

Linda had knelt beside Craig. She raised his head and cradled it in her arms. She moved slowly back and forth as though holding a baby.

The lights of the cars made flickering patterns on the back of the girl in the red dress and shone on the calm, dead face of Craig Belden.

The locomotive headlight picked out the shiny

ribbons of rail and the yellowed grasses on each side of the right of way.

The whistle shrieked for a crossing. Two long and two short, echoing back from the hills, which were just being faintly silvered by the rising moon. The train drove on with increasing speed through the night with the harsh puffing of the Standard's exhaust, trailing a scarf of smoke and sparks clear to Gun Hill.

THE
BORDER GUIDON

Chapter 1

THE BITTER January wind swept across the parade ground of Fort McComber, slashing tiny pebbles and grit against the drab post buildings and rattling the flagpole halyards in mad frenzy against the tall warped pole. The flag streamed tautly in the wind, as hard as a sheet of metal, while the outer third of it was whipping itself into bright rags.

First Sergeant Daniel Timothy Gallagher, Provisional Company A, First United States Dragoons, left his quarters and braced himself against the battering of the wind as he fought his way across the *caliche* of the parade ground, wincing as pebbles stung his mahogany-hued face. The wind was howling in its insane triumph, and the sound of it was enough to make an Irishman think uncomfortably of banshees.

He struggled under the sagging ramada that shaded the officers' quarters when the molten Arizona sun beat down upon the isolated fort. Maybe the banshee *would* howl that very night, he thought, for death itself hovered in the officers' quarters of Fort McComber.

He fumbled for the handle, opened the door, and was propelled into the hallway by a wild gust of wind. He closed the door and placed his broad back against it. His eyes and nose were full of grit—even his thick reddish dragoon mustache was caked with it. Above the dry astringent odor of the desert wind he could smell the mingled odors of carbolic and sweat, sour vomit, and the sickly odor of approaching death.

Gallagher slowly passed his hands down his shell jacket and trousers to free them of dust. The orange dragoon stripes on his trousers were faded and threadbare—there had been no issue of new clothing since the war had begun

5

somewhere in South Carolina, at a city named Charleston, at a fort named Sumter. That had been ten months ago, and it seemed as though the United States had quite forgotten isolated Fort McComber in Arizona and the handful of men who formed Provisional Company A.

A door opened slowly, emitting a flickering glow of yellow light, and the miasma in the hallway seemed to become thicker. The thin yellowish face of Medical Orderly Olney Little stared at Gallagher.

"Well," said Gallagher.

"It's worse than I thought, Sergeant."

"Get on with it, man!"

Little passed a hand across his sweating face. "It's typhoid, Sergeant."

A cold hand seemed to pass down Gallagher's spine. "Ye're sure?"

The orderly nodded. "The captain has all the symptoms: rising temperature, nausea, loss of appetite, headache, and nosebleed. Pains in the back and limbs. Pink spots on the abdomen."

"Could it be something else?"

Little's washed-out grey eyes blinked. "No."

"Ye are not a doctor, Little."

The man seemed to grow in stature. "I was . . . once," he said quietly.

"Ah!"

The orderly nodded. "You'd never have medical orderlies or company clerks in the Army if doctors and educated men didn't drink, Sergeant."

Gallagher nodded. "What happens now?" he asked with a new respect for the failure who stood before him.

Little passed a hand across his forehead again. Bright beads of sweat stood out on his sallow skin. "The symptoms usually appear from eight days to two weeks after infection. During the third week the fever begins to drop and the patient suffers from weakness, tremors of the muscles, delirium, and weak heart. This is the dangerous stage, Sergeant."

Gallagher added rapidly in his head. The commanding officer had come down with the sickness the second week in January, and now the month was drawing to a close. "Now," he said quietly.

"Yes."

"Is there any chance?"

"He is not a young man, Sergeant."

Gallagher nodded. He ground a big freckled fist into the palm of his other hand and listened to the wild wind scrabbling at the walls and roof of the quarters. Suddenly his hair seemed to rise at the nape of his neck as he heard an eerie moaning sound in a minor key below the roaring threnody of the wind.

Little smiled whimsically. "It is not the banshee, Sergeant Gallagher. It is the captain."

"Can I go in?"

The orderly passed a hand across his forehead again. "It is highly infectious."

"The breath? I will stay far back."

"Not the breath. The body discharges are said to carry the disease."

"Ye do not look well, Little," said Gallagher, eying the orderly closely.

"I have been on duty for twenty-four hours."

"They did not think enough of us at headquarters to allow us a surgeon," said Gallagher bitterly. He walked into the sick room, and the aura in it was enough to make his strong stomach moil within him.

Captain, Brevet Colonel, D'Arcy Hastings Eustis, lay flat on his back, looking up at the fly-specked ceiling with wide eyes that did not seem to see. His thin hands plucked steadily at the sweat-damp sheet—the skin on them seemed like that of a freshly plucked chicken. They were hands that once could swing a heavy issue Chicopee saber easily in left and right moulinets, thrusts, and slashes. Now they could not snap a match. The officer's classic face seemed etched in marble, and the fine thin nose stood out from the sunken face like that of a Roman bas-relief.

How old was he? thought Gallagher. He looked over sixty. Gallagher had ridden with him for almost ten years, from private up through the grades to first soldier, from Texas to New Mexico, from New Mexico to Utah, from Utah to California, and back again to New Mexico. There was no better Indian-fighter on the wide frontier where a handful of men in blue held off thousands of hostiles and taught them respect for cavalry, mounted rifles, and dragoons, with the emphasis on the last.

The room reflected the personality and character of D'Arcy Hastings Eustis. His fine Castellani saber hung over the beehive fireplace. A cased pair of dueling pistols lay on the chipped marble-topped table beside the bed, and ranks of medicine bottles, glasses, and spoons surrounded the morocco leather case. There were a number of fine pencil drawings hanging on the walls. Gallagher knew every one of them for he had often seen the captain sketching on his pad, even as he rode through the Big Country. The drawings on the walls were almost a history of the captain and his company of dragoons. His violin was in its case and on its shelf; many a night the officer had played for his men about the campfires in mountains or desert, with the soft music vying with that of the whispering wind and the muted howling of the coyotes.

The officer moved a little and looked at Gallagher, but the big noncom had the impression that Captain Eustis was looking right through him to something that could be seen only by a man who was waiting for the Angel of Death. Then Captain Eustis sang softly in his fine voice:

> "Oh, the dragoon bold! He scorns all care,
> As he goes the rounds with uncropped hair;
> He spends no thought on the evil star
> That sent him away to the border war."

Many a time had Gallagher heard the officer sing that song. Every time the going got rough and the chips were down he would sing that old ballad in defiance of fate.

Gallagher wiped the sweat from his face. It was stifling hot in the little room.

"I won't keep you long, Gallagher," said the officer quietly.

"There is no hurry, sir."

The officer shook his head. "But there *is*." His voice trailed off. He turned his head a little and then placed a thin hand on his forehead.

"The dispatches have not come in yet this week, sir," said Gallagher. He hated to tell the old man that, for the captain had been waiting months for orders to leave Fort McComber and join the rest of the Army, wherever the fighting was thickest against the rebels. Gallagher had it in his mind that D'Arcy Eustis would be up and about if those orders had come. Had they forgotten the old man after all these years of service to his country?

Eustis nodded. "Where is Mister Artenis?"

"In his quarters, sir. He is not feeling well." Why tell the old man his second-in-command was filthy drunk and had been so for days?

"And young Mister Tyrel?"

"He has gone out with a detachment to look for the courier from New Mexico, sir."

Eustis nodded. "A good soldier, that boy. Not a dragoon as yet, but a good soldier. He will do well." The gray eyes twinkled. "When I am gone it will be Sergeant Dan Gallagher who will forge him into the fine Damascus steel of a real dragoon."

Gallagher reddened. "Ah, sir!"

The eyes closed. "Let me see the dispatches when they arrive. I want to sleep now."

Gallagher saluted and spun about. He walked into the dim hallway. The orderly lay flat on his face near the outer door. Gallagher knelt beside him and rolled him over. He placed a big rough hand on the yellowish forehead and swore softly. The little man was burning up with fever. There was a trickle of blood coming from his nostrils. Gallagher unbuttoned the man's shell jacket, pulled up his thick woolen undershirt. The thin belly was stippled with faint pinkish spots. "For the love av Heaven," breathed Gallagher.

He carried the little man into an empty room and covered him with several blankets. Gallagher shoved back his forage cap and eyed Little. It was typhoid, sure enough. It was what had frightened Mister Artenis into a three-day drunk and what had caused a shadow of fear and panic to hover over the isolated outpost. They all knew that something more than just a fever had attacked Captain Eustis.

As Gallagher walked outside the wind battered at him. It was a hell of a place, this Fort McComber, a fort in name only in southern Arizona, surrounded by great hairless mountains, dull leaden in color, that seemed to brood over the vast desolation below them. The place was out on the Devil's hind limb and had only one reason for its existence—it kept the Tonto and Chiricahua Apaches from sweeping the hated white-eyes from that country. McComber did not protect the mines or the small towns that had been slowly springing up throughout the territory since the Mexican War. McComber was there to keep the travel routes open by the use of its long arm of forty hard-pratted dragoons. The duty had developed into an almost personal feud between Klij-Litzogue—Yellow Snake, predatory war leader of the Tontos—and First Sergeant Dan Gallagher. The odds were about even on them.

But now that the war was on there seemed little reason for McComber's occupation. In the past six months frontier post after frontier post had been abandoned, stripped of their garrisons of regulars who were needed in Virginia, Tennessee, and New Mexico. Indeed, most of the First Dragoons were in another theater of war, and Company A was with the regiment. It had been a belly blow to the old man who had commanded Company A for so many years when he found out that the company designation had been given to a newly formed unit, to keep the regiment up to full fighting strength, while his company, *the* Company A, had been redesignated as a "provisional" company. But they still had their old guidon despite the fact that some company calling itself A was riding with the regiment. As far as Captain Eustis and First Sergeant Gallagher were concerned the dragoons garrisoning forgotten Fort McComber were Company A, First Dragoons.

"They've forgotten we exist," said Gallagher bitterly.

He walked toward the guardhouse and kicked open the warped door in his cold anger.

"Jesus!" said Corporal Hallahan, "do ye have to kick down yon door, Dan?"

"Shut yer gob! Have ye seen any sight of Mister Tyrel?"

"Divil a one, Dan."

Gallagher shook his head. Tyrel had the makings of a good dragoon, but he was young, impetuous and hungry for glory, and such men were fair game for Yellow Snake. He played a waiting game. He had the time and the patience, and the country fought for him better than it did for the white soldiers.

"He has been gone a long time," said Private Henry.

"Aye," said Hallahan.

Gallagher nodded. The young shavetail had but ten men with him, and one skilled noncom, Corporal Heinrich —hardly enough for a fight with the Tontos. They had become increasingly bold of late. *They knew.* They had seen post after post abandoned. They had seen the funeral pyres of stores, blankets, medicines, saddles, tents, spare uniforms and all the other impedimenta of an established garrison rising above the empty barracks and buildings. Post after post, like beads widely spaced on a thin string, had been abandoned, and the Apaches had swept in again to the country where they had fought with, and been defeated by, the men in blue. Chiricahuas, Warm Springs, White Mountain, Mohave Apaches, Jicarillas, and the ultrapredatory Tontos had come into their own again. Gallagher had it in his mind that they were laughing silently at Fort McComber and its pitiful garrison of a handful of slowly demoralizing dragoons.

"Why are we left here in this outpost of hell?" growled Private Kitridge. "The rest of the regiment is gone. The whole damned territory, from the Colorado right clear to the Rio Grande, hasn't a garrisoned post in it except for Fort McComber."

"True," said Hallahan sourly.

There was no use in telling them to shut up. They were right. Forts Buchanan, Breckenridge, McLane, and Mohave had been abandoned. Arizona was now the bloody playground of Apache, Paiute, Mohave and Navajo. Between Fort Yuma, on the California side of the Colorado River, and possibly Fort Craig, on the northern Rio Grande in New Mexico Territory—somewhere between four hundred and four hundred and fifty miles—there were no United States troops to hold the hostiles in check or to prevent the Confederates taking over the whole kit and caboodle. Latrine rumors had it that the rebels already were invading New Mexico, and if they invaded New Mexico, Arizona would be next.

"Maybe they forgot we're here," said Private Henry.

"Yellow Snake hasn't," said Kitridge.

They all looked at each other.

"Go get my horse and saddle him," said Gallagher to Henry.

"You don't mean to tell me you're riding out there, Sergeant?"

"Don't ask questions! Get the bloody horse!"

"And ye go out and patrol the rounds," said Hallahan to Kitridge.

"In this wind? You're loco!"

One of Hallahan's big hands gripped the front of Kitridge's shell jacket and twisted it, pulling the big dragoon to his feet, and Hallahan's right fist smacked neatly against his jaw. "Git!" roared Hallahan.

The dragoon scuttled from the room. Gallagher impatiently walked outside to wait for Henry to bring him a horse. When the big bay came it seemed listless. Gallagher swung up into the McClellan and checked his Enfield musketoon. His Navy Colt was holstered at his side.

The wind lashed across the mesa top, sweeping tumbleweeds ahead of it. Some of them were banked high against the corrals, stables, and barracks. Vast whorls of yellowish dust hung against the dull sky. The rutted road to the east was hard to distinguish. Gallagher tied his orange scarf about his nose and mouth and hunched in his saddle. The wind muttered obscenely in his ears, and the foul thoughts it placed in his mind sickened him. He drove off the feeling of impending doom and disaster and rode on into the sweeping dust clouds, a big man, as hard as lignum vitae and spring steel.

red blossoms, and half of the escort went down on the dusty road. A horse reared and threw its rider. Another took the bit in its mouth and raced back the way the party had come. Troopers milled around. Mister Tyrel shook his...

◆◆ *Chapter* 2

THE WIND died away as he descended the side of the mesa toward the dry watercourse that snaked along the foot of the elevation. He peered through irritated eyes toward the flatlands east of the watercourse. There was a movement out there, but it was hard to distinguish. In a little while he made out the dusty blue of uniforms. He grinned. Mister Tyrel had found the dispatch rider. Gallagher's fears had been for nothing.

He urged the bay on, but the big mount was strangely listless. Gallagher wiped the dust from his face and mustache. It was then that he saw the quick, almost indistinguishable movement on top of the low mounds that paralleled the road on each side. Coyotes perhaps? But they were rarely seen in the daytime and never that close to humans.

Gallagher stood up in his stirrups, wishing to God he had the captain's fine Vollmer field glasses.

Mister Tyrel was riding easily, with reins in his left hand and his right hand resting gracefully on his hip. Behind him clattered the escort. About half of them were greenies, fish, new rookies from the East, while the remainder, with the exception of hard-bitten Corporal Heinrich, had little experience in Indian-fighting other than scattered skirmishing.

Gallagher stared at those mounds and suddenly knew what was moving on them. Apaches! He stabbed the bay with his spurs and swung his clumsy Enfield musketoon forward and capped the nipple.

Mister Tyrel saw Gallagher and waved at him.

Gallagher thrust his Enfield toward the mounds and yelled at the top of his voice. It was too late. The dull-colored heaps of earth and ragged brush sprouted orange-

14

red blossoms, and half of the escort went down on the dusty road. A horse reared and threw its rider. Another took the bit in its mouth and raced back the way the party had come, but a lead slug was faster than the horse, and its rider died with a bullet in his back.

Tyrel freed his saber and Colt and tried to rally his men, but it was no use. They broke for the open road. Instantly half-naked figures, crouched low on ponies, lanced out of the thick brush and cut in from both sides, like the horns of a crescent.

"Don't run, for God's sake!" bellowed Gallagher. "Stand! Stand and fight man to man! They cannot stand that!"

But it was no use. Panic had saddled up and now rode stirrup to stirrup with the routed dragoons. Apaches closed in and rifles and pistols cracked at short range, like shooting fish in a barrel. Corporal Heinrich reared up in his saddle as a pipe-axe struck home through his forage cap fair into the top of his skull and blood and brains spurted against the fresh, sunburned face of Mister Tyrel.

"Stand and fight!" screamed Gallagher. Then he was into the melee like a madman. His Enfield cracked, and the slug drove into the chest of a screaming brave. He reversed the weapon, stood up in his stirrups, and brought the butt down hard on the skull of another buck, driving him to the ground. The stock shattered, but the barrel was still there, and it did yeoman work while the bay drove hard against the lighter Apache ponies, guided by Gallagher's strong thigh pressures.

The musketoon barrel slipped from his sweating grasp. He hurled it full into the face of a buck whose nose was smashed beneath the impact. The buck's eyes stared into Gallagher's like those of a demon peering from a smoky window of hell itself. There was no mistaking those eyes. It was Klij-Litzogue!

The fight broke like a bloody fistula on the flats. The bucks screamed in sheer ecstasy for the success of their ambush, but they were paying for their minor victory now—paying it out in cold hard cash to the screaming, battling Irishman who yelled insanely as he whipped out saber and Colt and went to his work like a butcher cutting meat. *"I've come to stay!"* he roared as he stood up in the stirrups and laid about himself with his bloody Chicopee saber.

The one man drove them back; the big man with the three orange stripes and diamond of a first soldier on the faded sleeves of his jacket. Finally, he sat his weary horse alone in the blood-spattered road. But Yellow Snake urged his warriors on. Mister Tyrel had been unhorsed, but he swung up on the back of another bay and spurred it toward Gallagher, through the milling warriors and past his dead and wounded escort, for none of them were on foot or horse by now.

They let him pass part of the way through, and then Yellow Snake, with blood masking his face, stood up in his leathern stirrups, drew a short mulberry wood bow back to his ear, and released the thick cane shaft. It struck Arnold Tyrel full in the breastbone and stayed there quivering as he rode toward Gallagher with nerveless hands still tangled in the reins.

As the officer passed him Gallagher prepared for an Apache charge, but nothing Yellow Snake could do would make those sullen bucks charge the redheaded madman sitting the big bay in the center of the road. Slowly they drew back. There was other, more enjoyable work to be done now. The mutilating of the dead after they had been stripped; the skull crushing of the dead and severely wounded; the binding of the lesser wounded for transport to Yellow Snake's hidden rancheria in the Diablos, where they would be delivered into the greasy hands of the squaws for their final work with knife and fire.

Gallagher turned the bay and rode slowly toward the distant figure of Mister Tyrel. The officer still sat his horse, and as Gallagher drew near he turned, smiled a little, then fell heavily from the saddle.

The yellow lamplight flickered steadily in the draft, casting shadows on the whitewashed walls of the little dispensary. Gallagher wiped the sweat from his face, gripped the scalpel and began to cut.

"Not too deep, Gallagher, for the love av God!" husked Hallahan in Gallagher's ear.

"Ye've been in the medical alcohol, ye scut," growled Gallagher.

"A man needs a drink, Dan!"

The blood ran down Gallagher's hands as he gripped the cane shaft and began to work it free from bone and flesh.

"Agghhhh!" screamed the officer.

Hallahan and Private Devito's hands held him down as he writhed in excruciating agony.

"Agghhhh!"

"For the love av God, Gallagher, hurry!" cried Hallahan.

" 'Tis out!"

He held the bloody flint arrowhead in his big reddened hands. "Close," he murmured. Then he stared closely at the arrow point. He turned, and dipped it into the pinkish water of the basin, and then rinsed it. He held the point close to the lamp, and his stomach turned over within him.

"What is it, Dan?" asked Hallahan in a low voice.

Gallagher looked at the officer. He was unconscious. "Poisoned arrow," said Gallagher quietly.

"Ye mean that?"

"Aye!" Gallagher held it close to Hallahan. "See the brown gummy stuff on the point?"

Hallahan nodded.

"They take the fresh liver av a deer and cast it upon a hill of great red Sonoran ants, and the ants fill it with their poison as they bite into it. Then the liver is dried and mixed with grease, and other foul substances for aught I know. They carry it in wee bags and daub it onto their arrow points. They can kill game with these points, and eating av the meat does not affect them."

"And a man's meat, Dan?"

"Gangrene, Mike."

"There is no hope?"

Gallagher looked at the white naked chest of the young officer, laced with coagulating streaks of blood. "In a limb we could halt it by amputation. What can we do with that wound?"

Devito finished bathing the deep wound with a strong carbolic solution and then placed a pad upon the wound. He bound it about the officer's body. He looked up at Gallagher. "Will you tell him, *Sargento?*"

Gallagher wiped his face. "I do not know."

"If it is gangrene he will know soon enough," said Hallahan. "The poor lad!"

Gallagher walked outside carrying the dispatch case he had found attached to Tyrel's saber belt. It was dark, and the wind was still moaning as it swept across the naked mesa and battered insensately at the fort as though to drive it from the mesa as it drove tumbleweeds helter-skelter miles and miles across the lonely country.

He looked to the east. None of Tyrel's men had come in. It was now hours after the fight, and Gallagher did not expect any of them. He strode over to the quarters that Lieutenant Millard Artenis shared with Mister Tyrel. He opened the outer door and stepped into the hallway that divided the two rooms of the building. The left-hand doorway showed a thin line of yellow light beneath it. Gallagher tapped on the door with a big hand. There was no answer. He tapped harder. Still no answer. "Mister Artenis!" he called out.

It was quiet in the room; it was *too* quiet.

"Mister Artenis!"

There was a faint rustling noise within.

"Mister Artenis!" Gallagher almost added, *"Dammit, sir!"*

He waited a few minutes and then opened the door. The stench that flowed out was enough to sicken a man who had come from the wind-swept atmosphere outside. Sour liquor slops and sweat intermingled with other odors.

A candle guttered in the neck of a bottle and the light glistened on a set of Spanish half-armor and a morion helmet that hung on one wall. Mister Artenis had found it deep in a canyon of the Daiblos while on patrol and had removed the dried bones from within and given them Christian burial in the post cemetery. Gallagher had wondered at the time how long that spider-infested armor had been lying there in the loneliness, saved from rusting destruction by the dry air.

The officer sat on his rumpled bed with his back straight against the wall and his hands flat on the coverlet at each side of his hips. His brown eyes stared straight ahead of him fixedly. His thin hair hung over his sweating forehead, and was pasted to it in a tangled pattern. He had on his long dragoon trousers and high shoes but was naked from the waist up; beads of pearly sweat worked down through the sparse black hair on his chest.

"Mister Artenis, sir!"

The brown eyes looked at Gallagher but they did not see him.

Gallagher looked about the room. The man had not been out of the quarters for several days, except perhaps to go to the sanitary sinks behind the quarters, but even so the room stank of urine and sweat. Several empty bottles lay on the floor. Another, half full, was on the table. Gallagher walked over to the table and looked down at the officer. "Mister Artenis?" he said.

"What do you want, Gallagher?"

"The captain is taken bad, sir. Mister Tyrel was wounded by Apaches while escorting the dispatch rider. We lost twelve men counting the dispatch rider. I have the dispatches here, sir."

Artenis wiped the sweat from his face. "Hand me the bottle," he said.

Gallagher resisted an impulse to pull the man to his feet and smash in his drunken face.

"You Irish sonofabitch, hand me the bottle," said Mister Artenis in a flat clear voice.

"Mister Artenis, the lieutenant is in command now and is the only officer left able to command." Gallagher glanced at the bottle. Typhoid had laid Eustis low, and an arrow had dropped Mister Tyrel, but that had been no fault of theirs, while this drunken scut lay in his quarters.

Artenis moved quickly. His left hand came up with a

cocked double-barreled derringer; the twin muzzles looked almighty big to Gallagher. "Hand me the bottle, Gallagher."

"Ye have to take command, sir!"

The brown eyes looked as hard and as unreasoning as the twin muzzles of the little gun with the big bite. *"The bottle."*

Gallagher shrugged. He picked up the bottle with his right hand and walked toward the bed.

The gun came up and centered on Gallagher's flat belly. "I ought to kill you, you Irish sonofabitch! You goddam loyal patriotic bastard!"

Gallagher stared at the man.

"Wear the blue, Irishman! Salute the Stars and Stripes! Do your duty to your adopted country!"

"I will that, sir," said Gallagher quietly.

"Do you know something? People like you are riffraff. The gutter sweepings of Europe."

"Aye," said Gallagher slowly, "call me names, sir. And ye lie here in a drunken wallow whilst the captain is dying and Mister Tyrel has nothing but long agony before he too dies as sure as fate."

"It's useless to talk to you."

Gallagher stepped back and placed the bottle on the table. "I feel the same way about ye, sir, beggin' yer pardon. But there is work to be done. This foreign filth, as ye call me, has his duty to do. The dispatches have come in. The captain is hardly capable av holding his command. Will ye take the dispatches, sir? For the last time, I'm asking ye?"

"And if I tell you to go to hell?"

The big Irishman turned ever so slowly. "I will take command here, sir."

Gallagher opened the door and stepped into the hallway. For a long moment ice-locked blue eyes clashed like tempered steel with the amber-hard eyes of the officer. Artenis at last turned away. "Get out of here," he said thinly.

Gallagher closed the door behind him. His great hands opened and closed, then he left the quarters and walked toward Captain Eustis' quarters. The wind raged across the lonely fort. There were long and deadly miles between it and any other fort still flying the flag of the United States. A cold, unholy feeling came over Gallagher, and there was a fleeting impulse within him to get his horse, some rations, and his weapons and grease out of there for Mexico or perhaps California, and to hell with his duty.

▶▶ *Chapter* 3

OLNEY LITTLE was dead. His thin birdlike hands clutched the rough edges of the gray issue blankets, and his wide-open eyes stared up at the ceiling of the dark cold room. Although his face was drawn and sunken there was a look upon it almost of relief, for Olney Little, once a doctor of medicine, was through with the bottle and the world forever.

Gallagher drew the blankets up over the set face of the little man. He had never paid much attention to the medical orderly. The Regular Army had a good leavening of his type. Educated men who had jousted with the bottle and had been unhorsed time and time again until home, wives, children, friends and respect all vanished in an alcoholic haze.

Gallagher closed the door and walked across to the captain's room. Captain Eustis was awake. The candle-light postured and danced on the whitewashed walls. The case of fine dueling pistols had been opened, and the light glinted from the exquisite silver chased barrels and the ivory and ebony inlays of the graceful and slender butts. They were the officer's most prized possession next in importance to his violin. Gallagher had never known the old man to use them except for shooting at marks, and their accuracy matched their appearance.

Captain Eustis eyed Gallagher. "You seem to get bigger every year, Gallagher."

" 'Tis the fine Army food, sir."

Eustis smiled wanly. Then a slight spasm seized him. He fought for control. "You have the dispatches?"

"Aye, sir."

"Read the important ones to me. You can take care of the routine matters." Eustis indicated a chair. "Sit

22

down. We have been comrades too long to stand on formality."

Gallagher sat down at the table. Officer and non-com, gentleman and tough Irishman, they had been friends for ten years. Gallagher opened the case. There was a dark patch of blood on the cover. He turned the case so that the stain could not be seen by the officer. He riffled through the contents. Routine matters, most of them, pertaining to allotments, requisitions and other matters now of little importance. Gallagher mentioned each of them in turn and placed to one side at a wave of Eustis' thin hand.

There were two items left in the case: a sealed official letter and another smaller envelope. He opened the sealed letter first and looked up at the officer. Captain Eustis had dropped off into one of his comalike dozes. Gallagher eyed the address on the official envelope: Captain D'Arcy H. Eustis, Provisional Company A, First United States Cavalry, Fort McComber, Territory of New Mexico.

"Cavalry is it?" he said harshly. "Some stupid ass av a clerk at Fort Marcy does not know we are dragoons!"

He scanned through the dispatch and his face paled beneath the reddish tan of it. He looked up at the captain and then down at the dispatch once more. It was long-winded but the gist of it was that Fort McComber was the last occupied U. S. military post in Arizona, and Company A. was the last unit of the United States Regular Army still on duty there. Federal forces in New Mexico proper were expecting an attack by a column of Texas mounted rifles whose obvious objective was to advance north up the valley of the Rio Grande, defeat the Federal forces, occupy Albuquerque and Santa Fe, capture Fort Union with its vast supply of military stores and rally Southern sympathizers to the Confederate flag. Definite information from secret agents in Southern New Mexico indicated that a unit of Texas mounted rifles was already advancing west into Arizona, with the objective of capturing Tucson and, later, Fort Yuma, California, on the Colorado River. This was all part of a plan to conquer the West Coast for the Confederacy.

Information received by Federal officers in New Mexico had indicated that the column advancing into Arizona was not well equipped, but that they expected to find better arms and equipment *in* Arizona. A large store of military equipment—Sharps, breech-loading, carbines, Springfield muzzle-loading rifles, Colt revolving pistols, all with ammunition, as well as six brass mountain howitzers, with charges, projectiles, friction primers and all necessary accessories, had supposedly been shipped in November, 1861, from Fort Coulter to Fort Breckenridge, for transshipment to Fort Craig in New Mexico. The smaller supplies were immediately shipped to Fort Craig where they were stored until January, 1862, when they were opened and it was discovered that the cases contained only rocks and sand. There was no record of the brass howitzers ever having been received at Fort Breckenridge, nor had they ever arrived at Fort Craig.

This indicated either that the equipment and guns had been lost or destroyed by enemy agents or sympathizers or, what was infinitely worse, that they were hidden somewhere in the vicinity of Fort Coulter ready to be picked up by the rebel troops now thought to be advancing into Arizona. The possession and use of the guns and equipment by the enemy might very well tilt the scales in their favor in their intended invasion of California.

Gallagher read the last paragraph aloud in the quiet room.

"You will therefore immediately upon receipt of these orders destroy all untransportable government property at Fort McComber, render all facilities useless, blow up all post buildings, and abandon the area. You will then take your command, in its entirety, and institute an immediate and intensive search for the missing equipment in the vicinity of Fort Coulter, and either satisfy yourself *conclusively* that the cache has been destroyed, or destroy it yourself, if it is impossible to withdraw it from the area, to prevent capture by the enemy.

"Upon completion of this mission, you will take your command either to Fort Yuma, California, on the Colorado River, or to Fort Craig, New Mexico Territory, on

the Northern Rio Grande, to report for further duty . . ."
Gallagher's voice trailed off. The impact of the dispatch
had struck him like a dose of grape at point-blank range.
He knew Fort Coulter well enough. It was to the west,
across malpais country and through rough hills. A hard
journey on man and beast. There was something else, too.
Fort Coulter had been built in the Diablos for one reason,
and only one reason. It was in the very heart of the
country once fully dominated by Klij-Litzogue and his
predatory Tontos. Since the post had been abandoned in
the fall of 1861 Klij-Litzogue had again ruled that country
with bloody hands. *If he got his hands on those weapons
and munitions. . .*

But if the rebels got the weapons it would be far
worse. Then nothing could stop them in their sweep to
the Pacific Coast. It was likely they would advance west
via the Great Southern Overland Route, through La Mesilla, Apache Pass, Dragoon Springs and Tucson. That
gave the dragoons one advantage; they were closer to Fort
Coulter than the rebels were.

"Aye," said Gallagher bitterly. "Some advantage!
With a sick commanding officer, a drunken second-in-
command, and a dying shavetail for officers while we
have nought but thirty-odd dragoons left on the post."
Not enough to hold the post; not, by a damn sight,
enough to force a march to Fort Coulter on an important
mission which might, in the long run, by a twist of
malicious fate have a definite effect on the final result of
the war itself.

Gallagher tugged at his thick mustache. Christ, but he
wanted to get back to the regiment, whether it was called
cavalry or dragoons or anything else, for that matter.
"First Cavalry," he said sourly. It would not rest well
with the old man, either.

Captain Eustis opened his eyes. "Well, Gallagher," he
said quietly.

Gallagher read the dispatch. The officer lay there for a
long time looking fixedly at the ceiling. "First Cavalry,"
he said in a remote voice. "For eighteen years we have
been the First Dragoons. It will be hard to remember

that we are now cavalry. At least we are the *First* Cavalry
—that is as it should be."

"Your orders, sir?" asked Gallagher.

Another long pause. "They will be obeyed to the letter. We will take no wagons to Fort Coulter. Each man
will carry forty rounds for the musketoon and twenty
for the Colt revolving pistol. Issue any extra revolving
pistols so that each man will have two, as far as the
supply lasts. Extra ammunition will be carried by mules.
Two hundred rounds reserve supply for musketoons. Fifty
for the Colts."

Gallagher eyed the officer. His face was sheet white and
drawn. It was hard to recognize him except for the great
eyes.

"Mister Tyrel will be in charge of the destruction of
government property and of the blowing up of the buildings. Mister Artenis will be in charge of the post until I
am on my feet."

Gallagher stood up. It wasn't likely Captain Eustis
would be out of his bed for many a day. Meanwhile those
stores at Fort Coulter would perhaps be lost to the
United States, either to Klij-Litzogue or to the rebels.
There was little time to waste. Yet they could not leave
the old man. And it was certain he could not travel, even
in an ambulance, across that country.

Eustis looked at Gallagher. "I rely greatly upon you,
Gallagher. Mister Artenis is a good officer, but he has
his weaknesses."

Yes, sir," said Gallagher. *God yes!*

The wind moaned piteously about the quarters, and
the candles guttered crazily in the searching draft.

Captain Eustis slowly sat up and looked directly at
Gallagher. The big Irishman's skin crawled at the look on
the officer's face. It was almost as though a man cold in
death had suddenly sat up in his casket at a wake. "It
may not be that I will lead the company to Fort Yuma or
to Fort Craig, Sergeant. But I *will* lead them until I am no
longer able to."

How long, oh God?

"This company is Company A of the First Dragoons,

no matter what Washington has decided to redesignate us. The company has been assigned a dangerous mission. Most likely a hopeless one, but we will obey those orders to the letter!"

To the last man, and there were hardly enough of them left to go around if Klij-Litzogue caught them on the march.

"The company, when it reports for duty, at whichever camp, post or station it reaches after the completion of its mission, will ride in *under the company guidon.* If there is *one* man left, and *one* only, *that man will return the guidon to the regiment,* Sergeant Gallagher!"

"Aye, sir!"

For a moment it almost seemed as though D'Arcy Hastings Eustis would get up from that sweat-soaked bed and stand ramrod erect as he always did when taking over the company from First Sergeant Daniel Gallagher after morning roll call.

" 'Tis impossible," breathed Gallagher.

"If there is *one* man left, and *one* only, *that man will return the guidon to the regiment,* Sergeant Gallagher!"

"Aye, sir."

The wide eyes held Gallagher's attention as though hypnotizing him. *"But only when the mission has been completed successfully,* Sergeant Gallagher!"

"Aye, sir."

Then the officer fell back. Gallagher waited. A chill seemed to creep into the room. The candle flames bowed and postured in some meaningless ritual of their own.

The man was very still, though his eyes were still open.

The wind brushed against the walls.

Gallagher stepped close to the bed. The officer did not move. Gallagher bent close to the dry lips. He placed a hand on the captain's forehead, then took up his left wrist and held it with a big finger on the pulse. He placed the hand gently beside the still body and then slowly drew the damp sheet up over the face.

Gallagher turned and snuffed out all but one candle. He closed the lid of the dueling-pistol case and picked up the dispatches to put them in the case. It was then that he remembered the smaller envelope in the case. He held it up to the candle and saw that it had been addressed to the captain in a fine handwriting, no doubt that of a woman. Penciled at the bottom of the envelope, in strong masculine handwriting, was the forwarding note. The letter had originally been addressed to Captain Eustis in care of Fort Marcy, Santa Fe. Gallagher replaced it in the case. It would have to be returned with the captain's effects to his next of kin. Odd that Gallagher had never heard the captain mention any "next of kin" in all the years they had known each other.

He walked to the door and opened it. He glanced back at the bed, then closed the door behind him. As he stepped out under the ramada he heard a mournful howling out on the mesa. A coyote. He walked toward headquarters. The howling came again, faintly and dismally, almost lost in the whining of the night wind. Gallagher stopped and listened, with the wind drying the sweat on his face. He had never heard a coyote that close to Fort McComber, but then it didn't sound quite like a coyote either. The pitch of the howl was different. He had heard a sound like that before somewhere.

It wasn't until he was in the dark headquarters, feeling for a candle lantern, that he remembered where he had heard that sound before. It had been in Ireland when his father had died during a cold winter night. His big hands fumbled as he lighted the candle. "Ah, Gallagher," he said thickly, forcing back the strange thoughts in his Irish mind, "there are no banshees. At least none in America."

The howling came softly once more, and then it was gone.

▶▶ *Chapter* 4

THE WIND had died away by the time of the false dawn and the softly graying light flowed over the desert country and across the naked mesa to Fort McComber, last garrisoned outpost of the United States in the vast part of New Mexico Territory known as Arizona. There was a loneliness about the drab little collection of buildings, set in their straight rows and alignments, as though a meticulous child had been playing in that Godforsaken spot and then had been driven away by the brooding melancholy of the atmosphere.

Lonely and forbidding, there was nothing else to call it, thought Dan Gallagher as he walked toward the first of the two barracks buildings. He had been up all night going through the files, destroying material that could not be taken along; placing important papers—and there were few enough of those—in a dispatch box. He had written out a plan of destruction, and now it was time to get the garrison ready for their mission.

Mike Hallahan met him at the door of the barracks. " 'Tis fine news I have for ye, Dan," he said quietly.

"So? I could use a bit of fine news." Dan shoved back his forage cap. "The old man is dead, Mike."

Hallahan nodded. "I knew it. The banshee was about last night."

"Bull crap!"

The corporal eyed Gallagher. "Ye know it was, Danny," he said wisely.

"Get on with yer news!"

Hallahan waved a hopeless hand. " 'Tis me platoon, Dan. Nine av them pulled out last night sometime betwixt tattoo and the first light av dawn. Kitridge was behint it. I know."

Gallagher stared at him as though stunned. "Ye mean it?"

"Aye! I was tired. I've been on a lot of fatigues, Dan, as ye well know, what with the shortage of trained non-coms. I slept like a baby. A few minutes ago I got up and saw that they had taken their musketoons and gear. I went to the stables and twelve horses are gone. They tuk enough for mounts and three besides for carrying water and food."

"Do ye think we can run them down?"

Hallahan's face tightened. "Out there, Dan? Klij-Litzogue owns that country, and well ye know it. Besides, there is something else ye should know."

"Go on."

"Ye'd best come to the stables."

Hallahan lighted a lantern he took from a hook near the door and led the way along the low-roofed stables. He stopped at a stall. "Take a look at Big Pat," he said quietly.

Gallagher walked into the stall, spoke softly to the big bay, and then took the lantern from Hallahan. He held it up to study the horse. There was a pussy discharge from the nose and eyes, and the eyes were inflamed. "Jesus God," said Gallagher. He looked at Hallahan. "Is it mayhap farcy, do ye think?"

Hallahan slowly shook his head. " 'Tis glanders, Dan."

"And the rest of the mounts?"

"*All* of them, Dan. They have fever and swollen lymph glands, and they all have lost weight. There is only one exception. The captain's bay, Shannon. Ye know we keep him in a special stall in the old storehouse beside the corral because he fights with the other stallions."

Gallagher walked out of the stall and to the outer door without looking back at the dying animals. They would *all* die. If it had been farcy, a milder form of glanders, they would live, although still infected, but this was not so, according to Mike Hallahan, and no man knew horses better then he did.

Gallagher placed the lantern on the ground.

Hallahan. "We'll have to burn the stables, Dan."

Gallagher did not answer. Hallahan did not know of the dispatch that would send all of them to their deaths in the distant Diablos, on *foot* now.

Hallahan looked to the east where the growing light of day was etching the wolf-fanged mountains darkly against the coming of the sun. "What do we do now, Dan?"

Gallagher quietly told him of the orders.

Hallahan wiped the sweat from his face. "To go there is to die, Dan."

"Aye."

"But there is nothing else we can do."

"No."

"It has been a long trail together, Dan."

Gallagher nodded. "Where is Sergeant Caris?"

"In the hospital, Dan. Taken hard with fever he was."

Gallagher looked quickly at Hallahan. "When was this?"

"Yesterday. He is not the only one."

"How many others?"

Hallahan hesitated. "Corporal Nellis is down too, and Privates Carmody, Dudzik, Jonas, Barents and Schiel."

"Typhoid?"

"I think so."

Gallagher felt the invisible belly blows of fate. He wiped his face with his bandana. "And Mister Tyrel?"

"Bad, Dan, very bad."

"Is there nothing good?"

"Only a man's duty, Dan."

There were no officers left, fit to do their duty. There were no horses to carry the company on its mission. There was hardly anything left of the company.

"What are your orders, Sergeant?" asked Hallahan.

Gallagher straightened up. He was the first soldier. The man with the three stripes and the diamond. The ramrod placed against the spine of the company. Gallagher was not afflicted with typhoid, gangrene, or alcoholism. He wasn't licked yet. He grinned wryly. Poor consolation that was.

"Sergeant?"

Gallagher turned. "Have the trumpeter blow first call."

"There is hardly a squad left to answer it, Sergeant."

"Blow it!"

Gallagher strode toward headquarters, and as he entered he heard Hallahan's voice blasting Trumpeter Farrington out of his bunk.

The sun was well up. The shooting was over. The corpses of the diseased horses lay at the bottom of the deep cleft just south of the post boundaries. It had been more merciful to kill them while they were still on their legs. But nothing is more painful to a horse soldier than to have to kill his mount.

The typhoid had almost full control now. The rations had been poor for some time, with very little variety. The men had been weakened by their substandard diet, and the disease had caught hold. None of the sick could be moved. There were no horses to move them. There were not enough men left on their feet to guard them if they *were* on the move. If they stayed at the fort, and there was nothing else they could do, the few men able to fight would hardly be enough to hold off an Apache attack.

Gallagher had had charges placed in the various buildings—enough to destroy them and not harm the hospital. A detail had been piling extra equipment together in the big corral down the slope from the stables. It was equipment that could not be moved. Yet all of Gallagher's preparations seemed useless to him. The whole bloody business seemed useless. What more could be expected of him?

He walked to the edge of the post and looked to the west, toward the invisible Diablos. Heat waves shimmered and danced across the flats. After the cold night it had suddenly become unseasonably warm, almost like summer, but that would not last. He walked the boundaries of the post buildings, slowly, lost in thought, trying to find some way of obeying his commander's last orders, but he could not.

He stopped on the low rise to the east of the post and looked across the low country below the mesa. There was a faint suggestion of dust far out there. Perhaps a wind devil. It would not be Apaches. They would not herald their approach with banners of yellow dust.

He walked back in headquarters. It was quiet in there. The company guidon rested in its stand against the wall behind the company commander's desk. Gallagher studied it. He had ridden behind it for ten years and had heard it snap in the dry winds of summer and the icy blasts of winter. He had seen its bright colors against the dun of the sterile desert and against the lush green of the mountains.

The guidon was swallow-tailed, colored half red and half white, and attached to a nine-foot lance. The white letters "U. S." were emblazoned on the red upper half, and the red letter "A" was on the white lower half. The captain's last order had been that the guidon should be returned to the regiment where it belonged, *after* the mission had been accomplished.

"How?" asked Gallagher quietly. He threw up his hands in a gesture of despair.

Mister Tyrel shot himself at sundown—twenty-two years old, with but six months service on the frontier. He was a soldier, but not yet a true dragoon. He would be buried next to Captain D'Arcy Eustis who had served his country well for over thirty years and had died forgotten, still wearing the blue. The long trail from the United States Military Academy, the Seminole War, the Mexican War, as well as years of duty in Indian-fighting country had ended for him at forgotten Fort McComber.

The darkness that night was complete. Beyond the faint yellow lights in the hospital and guardhouse there was nothing but blackness . . . and the howling of the wind. Three men died of typhoid in the hours before dawn.

Gallagher awoke to see gray light creeping in through the windows of the headquarters office. He got up from his cot and pulled on his shell jacket and shoes. Another day of indecision. What was the use of trying to keep this parody of a military post going?

It was much lighter when boots thudded against the wooden porch in front of the headquarters and the door swung open. Gallagher turned from the window where he had been looking to the east, to where he had seen that threadlike and persistent line of yellow dust the day before until dusk had hidden it.

Lieutenant Artenis stood there. His face was pale beneath the tan, but the man was sober.

"Good morning, sir," said Gallagher.

Artenis nodded. "The dispatches?"

"On the captain's desk, sir."

"How is he, Sergeant?"

Gallagher stared at the officer for a moment. "He is dead, sir."

The brown eyes flicked up. "Is Mister Tyrel any better?"

"Mister Tyrel is dead, too, sir. Gangrene." There was no sense in saying "suicide", and clouding the memory of a dead man. Gallagher had entered it on the books as death by gangrene, brought on by the poisoned arrow of an Apache. Maybe it really didn't make any difference. Maybe no one would ever know either way, for it seemed as though every man and everything at Fort McComber would be lost with no record.

Artenis sat down and looked through the dispatches. He spent a long time reading the vital one, then walked to the map on the wall and studied it. Gallagher watched him. There was something odd about the man. At last Artenis turned. "There is no question of this dispatch being obeyed of course, Sergeant."

"The lieutenant is now in command. Captain Eustis' last command was that the order was to be carried out."

"Corporal Hallahan told me about the horses."

Gallagher nodded.

"Then you agree that it is hopeless to carry out this order?"

"It is the *lieutenant's* decision, sir."

"Then it will *not* be carried out."

"Yes, sir."

"What's wrong with you, Gallagher?"

"Nothing . . . , sir."

Artenis looked through the window. "There is no hope

for any Union troops in Arizona now that the Confederates have invaded New Mexico and Arizona. It is my intention to surrender this post to them."

Gallagher glanced at the guidon.

Artenis did not turn. "We are not far from the route the Confederates will take to the west. There is no hope for us at this time with typhoid raging here, no horses, and not enough men to defend the post."

Gallagher wet his lips and waited.

"I want you to bear witness that the situation here was impossible, in case there is a military court, Sergeant."

Gallagher eyed the straight back of the officer. There was something else coming. Gallagher could feel it.

Artenis turned slowly. "I intend to surrender the fort. At that time I will resign my commission in the United States Army and take service under the Confederate States of America."

That was it! That was what had been bothering the man all this time. It had not been the typhoid at all.

"Well, Sergeant?"

Gallagher eyed the man. "Why do ye wait until then to resign?"

The brown eyes half closed. "What difference does it make?"

"If ye turn over this post as an officer of the United States Army, then resign and take service with the Confederacy, ye will stand trial for treason if ye are captured by the United States forces."

"*If*," said Artenis quietly.

"Suit yerself, lieutenant."

Artenis rubbed his freshly shaven cheeks. He eyed Gallagher. There was a glint of fear in his eyes. There was a sneaky streak in the man. Suddenly he sat down and began to write. He signed the sheet with a flourish and sanded it. He looked up at Gallagher. "This is my resignation."

"Ye want me to witness it?"

"Not yet."

"Why, sir?"

Artenis smiled. "Look out of that window."

It was light enough for Gallagher to see that mysterious wraith of dust once more.

"Those are Texas mounted rifles, Gallagher. On their way here to occupy this post."

"So?"

"I have known for some time they were coming here."

"So."

Artenis leaned back in his chair. "I have already been offered a commission in that command."

"The lieutenant was pretty quiet about that fact when the captain was still alive."

"There was a reason."

"I can imagine." Gallagher closed his hands into great hard fists. "We have been at war with the Confederacy for ten months. Why did ye not resign at the beginning av the war?"

Artenis toyed with the letter opener on the desk. "Did you know what duty I was assigned to just before I joined this company?"

"No, sir."

The brown eyes had a glint in them. "Until I came here to Fort McComber, I was quartermaster officer at Fort Coulter."

The impact of Artenis' statement hit Gallagher like an Apache lance—the transshipment of arms and munitions from Fort Coulter to Fort Breckenridge to Fort Craig, where the boxes were opened and found to be filled with rocks and sand.

"Do you get the idea, Gallagher?"

"I do."

Artenis smiled. "Clever, was it not?"

"Aye."

The officer leaned forward. "There is one thing I want to point out to you. You are an experienced soldier. The Confederacy needs men like you who know this country. There could be a commission in it for you. The Confederacy is not as fussy as the United States. They do not require a man to be an officer *and* a gentleman."

"Like *ye,* belike?"

Artenis flushed. "I can get you a commission. We can

use you, Gallagher. We must pass through the country of Klij-Litzogue to get those weapons and munitions. You can guide us. You are the only man who can guide us. What do you say?"

"Ye have no else to do it? Ye cannot do it yourself?"

"No," admitted the officer.

Gallagher breathed out and stepped closer to the desk. " 'Tis a deal," he said firmly. He leaned forward. "Let me see that resignation."

Artenis handed it to him. Gallagher read it. It was right and proper. He took a pen, and before Artenis could stop him he had signed it as witness. He folded it, placed it inside his jacket, then smiled coldly at Millard Artenis. "Get up," he said.

"What do you mean?"

"Get up, ye traitorous bastard!"

"You're talking to an officer!"

Gallagher smiled again, tapped his jacket, and reached for the officer with great eager hands. "Ye *were* an officer, Artenis."

He dragged him clear across the desk, set him up, hit him in the belly and then on the jaw, and drove him crashing into a corner. He butted him with his head when he came up, hooked vicious blows to belly and jaw, then stood over the bleeding writhing man waiting for him to get up.

The door banged open and Mike Hallahan came in. He stared at Gallagher. "Ye've gone loco with the strain, Dan!"

Gallagher shook his head. He reached down for Artenis and raised him easily to his feet. Tenderly he braced him, smiled benignly into the battered and bleeding face, then hit him with a terrific one-two that drove the officer clear across the room and over a chair. Gallagher turned and dusted his hands.

Hallahan stared at Gallagher and then backed slowly toward the door. "Wait," said Gallagher. He took out the resignation and handed it to Hallahan, then swiftly explained what had happened.

Hallahan looked at the dust on the desert to the east. "What happens now?" he said. "We'll have to surrender."

Gallagher shook his head. "Not all of us, Mike."

"What do you mean?"

Gallagher looked at Artenis. "I'm senior noncom here. There are no officers. I'm leaving to ride to Fort Coulter on the captain's fine bay Shannon, and I'm going to find and destroy them stores."

"I knew yer mind was gone."

"Ye will stay here in command. Fire the extra stores lying in the corral. Destroy anything they can use. Keep food and medical supplies for yer men. With the honors av war, the ribils will not harm ye. I'm sorry it has to be this way, Mike."

Hallahan nodded. "Aye, Dan." He gripped Gallagher by the hand. "If any man can do it ye can." But the lie was in his eyes. He knew and Dan knew that the odds were insurmountable and that Dan Gallagher was only making a defiant gesture in the face of a grinning fate.

They worked swiftly after that. Hallahan got Shannon and saddled him. He packed rations and water and Mister Tyrel's fine Sharps carbine, as well as a brace of extra Colts. He had it all ready in twenty minutes.

Gallagher went to the captain's quarters and looked about. There was little he could take. But he must have something. Not the violin, of course. The dueling pistols were enticing but hardly worth the weight of them on such a mission. He saw a small velvet case on the mantel and took it and opened it. The lovely faces of three young girls looked up at him. He whistled softly. One of them, evidently the oldest, looked enough like the old man to be his daughter, and then the resemblance of her and the next oldest of the three girls struck him. They must be the daughters of D'Arcy Eustis. He closed the case and slipped it inside his jacket. He left the room hurriedly and returned to headquarters. Artenis was still unconscious. Gallagher grinned. He took the dispatch box and walked to the door. Suddenly he turned and looked at the guidon. That had been part of the orders, too. He took it from its stand and left the office.

Hallahan watched Gallagher attach the guidon by butt socket and leathern sling to his saddle. Gallagher mounted and looked down at Hallahan. They did not speak but gripped hands. Then Gallagher kneed the big bay away from the corporal and rode to the west. He did not see the smart salute given to his broad back by Corporal Michael Hallahan, nor did he see the growing pillar of dust rising from the east side of the mesa.

A little while later a thread of smoke arose from Fort McComber as Hallahan fired the stores. It grew and grew until it was like a huge funereal pall against the clear sky, and the Tontos who saw it wondered at it, but they did not approach the post. There were white-eyes riding toward the fort—men in gray uniforms instead of blue ones, and whose speech was different from that of the men in blue. The blues and the grays had many things in common: the set jaw, the hard look, and the easy familiarity with firearms that no Apache could ever hope to attain.

Chapter 5

THE DYING sun seemed snagged on the rimrock, and the hollows in the desert and on the mountainside had filled with lilac-hued shadows. The dull leaden shapes of the mountains seemed to brood over the desolation below them. In all that vast area there was no sign of life but for the lone man who led the big bay horse to the west. The dry wind that swept over the malpais fluttered the swallow-tailed guidon at the end of its lance.

By rights there should have been thirty-five or forty dragoons riding behind that guidon, but the big redheaded man who led the bay was utterly alone in a country where such loneliness had often driven white men mad.

Dan Gallagher raised his tired head. He had been walking for hours to let the bay rest and yet it seemed as though the western hills were no closer than they had been when he had entered the malpais country early that morning, with Fort McComber two days behind him.

He looked back at the bay. "Shannon," he said quietly, "I'm after thinking we're on a treadmill."

The dark bay tossed his proud head. Gallagher unhooked one of the three canteens from his saddle and shook it. There was hardly enough water to make a sloshing noise. It was the last of the gamey stuff he had patiently strained through his neck scarf the evening before from a rock pan where a diamondback rattler had decided to end it all.

He poured the water into his battered Fra Diabolo hat and let the bay drink while he himself touched his cracked lips with his tongue and looked west across the harsh naked country. There was really nothing to look at, nothing more than he had seen all day long. The heat from the baking rock beneath his feet came up through the soles of his shoes. That morning he had thought he knew where he was. Now he wasn't so sure. Certainly he was heading west, but he had no sure idea of how far south he was.

The bay finished drinking and looked at Gallagher almost as though to say, "I've had enough. Now it's your turn, Gallagher."

He filled his mouth with the gamey water that was left, swilled it about his mouth, then let it flow back into the canteen. "How far south?" he said aloud. "Apaches to the west and south. Ribils to the east. Unknown country to the north. A redheaded Irishman betwixt and between them, and all of them, including this cursed country, looking for his heart's blood!"

He placed the wet hat on his head, grateful for the temporary coolness of it, hooked the canteen to the saddle, then led the bay on again. The gaunt shadows of man and horse moved slowly along the harsh ground, with the fluttering shadow of the guidon above them.

The sun was almost gone when he saw the smoke. He halted and slitted his burning eyes. It was hardly visible, a faint line of darkness against the sky. Apaches in all likelihood. No white man in his right mind would betray himself in that country by lighting a fire. Gallagher took the Sharps carbine from its saddle sling and checked load and cap.

The wind shifted, bringing a new coldness with it, sweeping dust and harsh grit like a great rough broom, raking both man and horse without pity. The sun died even as they stood there. The thick darkness before the rising of the new moon would soon fill the country. Ahead of him were the first of the low, gaunt hills, like loose elephant skin lying atop the basic rock of the land. There was a pass through those hills, or at least he had seen a notch which might, or might not be a pass. It didn't make much difference. He *had* to go that way.

It was black night when he entered the first defile of the pass, and the coldness seemed to close in on him like icy clutching hands. The shoes of the bay struck against the rock and seemed to echo like cathedral bells.

The bushy-haired devils didn't fight at night. That thought at least was good. But they'd track him all night if they had caught sight of him during his march to the hills across the open malpais country, then gut him with a knife at first dawn light. Or maybe, if they had the time and the inclination, they'd haul him home to the squaws for a little clean and happy sport. He was a big powerful man who'd likely live a long time under the razor-edged knives and the burning brands. There were other things they'd do, too, and the chill thought of them sickened him.

The moon was tinting the eastern sky with silvery light when at last Gallagher reached the western end of the winding pass. He was higher now than when he had entered it. A low plain stretched to the west, where a mass of mountains etched against the sky. He reached back and got his carbine, then loosened the holster flaps on the pair of pistols that hung heavy from his lean waist. Thirteen rounds between him and the enemy—twelve for the enemy and one for himself, if it came to that.

The bay whinnied softly. Gallagher raised his head quickly. "Is it water ye smell, Shannon?"

There was a darker patch of something in the darkness ahead. "Trees, by God!" said Gallagher.

Where there were trees there would be water, but where there was water there might also be Apaches. They knew the white man's ways. He'd head for water like a thirsty sheep and stay near it while he camped, and like a sheep he could thus be slain easily.

The wind shifted, and Gallagher caught a strong smell of smoke. There was a red pinpoint of motion among the trees like a winking eye. The wind had fanned embers into life again. The fire flared up, casting an eerie flickering light on what looked to the Gallagher like a long stretch of fire-blackened wall. He rubbed his bristly jaws. This part of the country was unknown to him. He knew it well enough to the north and also further south, but this was no man's land as far as he knew. He had never heard of white people living in the area.

Thirst and hunger had allied themselves in a winning

battle against man and horse. It was almost a certainty that there wasn't any water within marching distance of the next day or so, and hardly any game to speak of. A big man and a big horse needed lots of food. Red meat for the man, grain for the horse. Most of all, they needed water.

Gallagher moved on, keeping to the low places and always watching—first to right and left, then behind, then ahead, and never stopping. To stop looking was to die . . . quickly.

He was three hundred yards from the trees when he stopped and ground-reined the bay. He padded quietly forward, surprisingly quiet for a man his size. The moon was higher now, and he could make out the structures amongst the trees. A well-built place from the looks of it, but why was it there, with no stage route through that country and no mining to speak of? The place was quiet, too quiet. There was no sound of mule or horse, no bark of dog or sound of human voice.

The wind flared up the fire, and he could see something humped lying on the ground near the wide arched gateway that led into the rectangle of buildings. A mule. A dead mule. Someone had cut deep into the flanks to rip out steaks. Gallagher felt his red hair stiffen a little, and he almost reached up to settle his hat. Appaches liked horse meat, but they liked sweet mule meat much better. If they stole horses and mules they usually killed the mules for meat.

Gallagher squatted behind a rock like a big joss idol. He was damned if he went in there and damned if he didn't. He had to have water and food. If he by-passed this place he might go on until he and the bay dropped, easy prey for the Apaches, the buzzards, or both. He peered around the rock. The moonlight touched something else. Just beyond the mule, next to some brush, lay a dead man. One clawed hand was outstretched as though he was reaching for the mutilated mule. The man's head was curiously misshapen. Some kindly warrior had let out the man's spirit by crushing his skull. Dan stood up. It was a good sign, for Dan in any case. No Apaches would stay around the newly dead at night and wait for the wandering soul to speak with the weird voice of Bú, the owl.

He padded forward, with his carbine held at chest height, while his hard blue eyes probed the shadows. But there was nothing, no sound or movement beyond the muted crackling of the fire. He saw a great blackened spot where one of the larger buildings had burned to the ground. There were embers of fire upon it like rubies on black velvet. Here and there were twisted lengths of blackened metal.

He stopped in the shelter of a big niche cut into the high wall that surrounded most of the buildings. The pair of massive and bolt-studded gates lay flat upon the hard caliche of the compound within the wall. He eyed the windows and doors of the buildings one by one. Nothing. . . .

Debris, dust, and ashes lay in the thin windrows against the walls. A pall of smoke hung over the area. Another dead man lay close to a building, both his hands tangled in the front of his bloody shirt, grasping an arrow shaft embedded in his chest.

Gallagher moved softly, keeping close to the buildings where the shadows still clung, until he reached the far end of the rectangle of buildings. An open-fronted blacksmith's shop was there. It was fully equipped. Gallagher nodded. The Apaches had touched nothing in the shop. Now he was *sure* it was Apaches who had raided the place.

The water was across the compound. It bubbled up from a rock-walled pool. His throat felt as though it had been sanded, and he couldn't resist walking toward the pool. He stopped short when he saw her, at the bottom of the pool, naked as the day she had been born. Her long dark hair floated about her ivory shoulders with the slow movement of the water. Her great staring eyes seemed to look directly at Gallagher as though to mesmerize him. The ugly wound that had caused her death showed at the left side of her shapely throat. There was a faint pinkish hue to the water about it. She had not been dead long.

Gallagher did not want to look ar her. She had been lovely, and the strange, eerie feeling that he had seen her somewhere before entered his mind.

He stepped back, one slow step after another, until his back struck a building. He turned and walked to a door, which swung easily open on its hinges at his touch. He peered into the thick darkness within. His thirst was worse now that he had seen the clear fresh water of the spring; water that he could not drink . . . for a time, at least. Later, he'd take her out of there and give her a Christian burial. But until he found the next waterhole or spring, wherever and whenever that would be, he would have a hell of a time stomaching the water he would take from this place of the dead.

He stepped softly into the room and peered about like a wary animal. He could almost feel his ears slant forward. His eyes gradually grew accustomed to the moonlit darkness. The place was a shambles. The floor was littered with ripped clothing, some of it blood stained, shattered furniture, smashed glass and crockery.

He touched his cracked lips with his tongue. There was a cabinet in a corner, and he opened it. The faint odor of spirits came to him, but the cabinet was empty. As he stepped back his left spur rang softly against glass or crockery. Likely a damned chamberpot, he thought sourly. He looked down and saw the square bottle. He picked it up and pulled out the cork with his teeth. The fruity odor struck him sweetly. "By all the saints," he said with a smile. " 'Tis brandy!"

It went down easily, then hit his empty stomach and tired brain at the same time. He sat down quickly on a chair. The second slug settled him a bit, and the third did the trick. He was just loosening his shell jacket when the cold thought came to him that his horse was still out there. Apaches might be watching the place. They wouldn't enter it that night. Still, he hadn't found any food, and if he did have to leave in a hurry he'd need it.

He sloshed the brandy about in the bottle, then raised it

toward his lips. It was then that he heard, or seemingly felt, the faint noise from the next room, beyond a closed door.

Gallagher slowly got to his feet. His breath seemed abnormally loud to him. He softly placed the bottle on a table and eyed the door. He stood there a long time before he heard a slight coughing noise. Belike a baby, he thought. His face muscles tightened. *Apaches coughed, too.*

The door latch moved a trifle, and then the door swung open with a slight sighing of hinges. Someone stood there staring at Gallagher, but not for long. One hundred and ninety pounds of tough bone and muscle struck with pile-driver power, driving back and back until both Gallagher and his quarry struck against a light table and sent it smashing against the far wall. A knife traced a burning course down Gallagher's left bicep, and he dropped his carbine to hook a shoulder into the belly of his opponent. The belly was not cord-tough like that of a warrior, but soft and full.

Gallagher fell on top of the fiercely fighting, still unseen enemy. The knife scraped across his pistol belt. He felt for the wrist, twisted it sharply, and heard the knife tinkle against the packed earth floor. A knee drove up into his groin, and he gasped in swift agony, rolling free to get to his knees. His left hand felt cloth and he gripped at it. Something ripped cleanly, and he felt the weight of a garment in his hand. A dim white figure scrambled to its feet. The mingled odor of scent and femininity came to Gallagher. His mouth gaped open. "By the powers!" he gasped. "A woman!"

She slowly moved back toward the wall.

"I'm white, ma'am," said Gallagher foolishly. "A soldier." The burning thought of that soft body stayed with him. He had not been with a woman for a long time.

The blood ran down his arm and dripped from his fingers. He placed a hand on the table, found a candle lying there, quickly drew out a block of matches and thumbed one of them into life.

"Don't light that candle!" she cried out.

It was too late. The candle flared up and he looked at her across the yellow flickering light. The dancing play of light was on her naked body, throwing the high breasts into full relief. Her dark hair flowed over her smooth shoulders. The reddened knife was again in her hand, and she held it toward Gallagher.

Gallagher looked down at the clothing he had ripped from her. It was a gingham dress. "I. . . ." His voice trailed off. He pinched out the light of the candle and tossed the dress to her as he hurriedly walked from the room.

The bottle was waiting for him. He took a stiff jolt. His arm burned like fury. He rolled up the sleeve and saw a long shallow gash in the hard flesh. He peeled off his shell jacket and undershirt.

The door swung open behind him. "I'll take care of that," she said quietly. "After all, *I* did it."

"I'd be obliged, ma'am."

She came to him in the moonlight, the dress covering the nakedness he had seen but not the sweet curves of her body. She lighted a candle and took the bottle from his hand. She poured some of the brandy into the wound.

"What a waste!" he protested.

She looked up at him with her dark violet eyes. "You're Irish," she said.

He grinned. "And what else could I be now, ma'am?"

She took a clean cloth from a rack and tore it into long strips which she used to neatly bandage his arm. "You'll live," she said quietly.

She looked up at him, deep-seated fear etched on her pale face. Then she placed her head against his chest, and the dry sobs broke from her like a torrent.

He was sure he had seen this girl, too, somewhere in the past. In Boston or New York? St. Louis or Santa Fe? He half closed his eyes. There was one thing he did know. She looked uncommonly like the girl who lay cold in death at the bottom of the pool. "Ah God," he said softly.

▶▶ *Chapter* 6

"You can relight the candles," he said over his shoulder as he finished hanging cloth over the last of the windows. He stepped down from the chair and looked at her as the light filled the room. Try as he would he could not forget her white flesh and the cups of her breasts as he had seen them.

She took her soft lower lip between even white teeth and glanced nervously at the door.

"They will not come," he said quietly.

"Why not?"

"Because of the dead. The vengeance of the spirits. They are even afraid of their own dead until they are laid to by the *diyis,* the medicine men and medicine women. That is why they will not stay near owls. They think Bú, the owl, speaks with the voice of the newly dead."

She sat down and began to mend her dress with pins and ties of cloth. "You seem to know a great deal about them, Sergeant."

"Some," he admitted. "There is one thing I do not know about them."

"And that is?"

He picked up a chair, twirled it, and then sat down in it. "What happened here. I am First Sergeant Daniel Gallagher, Provisional Company A, First United States Dragoons. Ye can call me Dan."

She looked up quickly from her mending. "Company A? But they are in New Mexico or perhaps traveling east to the war." She leaned forward. "They were at Fort McComber some months ago, were they not?"

He studied her. "How is it ye know so much about the company?"

48

"Because it is commanded by my father, Captain D'Arcy Eustis. I am Ellen Eustis."

Gallagher's lower jaw dropped. Pieces of a once-vague puzzle began to drop into place. Instinctively his right hand touched the place inside his jacket where he had placed the small velvet-covered picture case he had taken from the captain's quarters just before leaving Fort Mc-Comber.

"I came here with my two sisters Evelyn and Judith from California. We were told we could get no further east, that all United States troops had left Arizona, that there were Apaches on the warpath from the Colorado to the Rio Grande."

"They are," he said quietly. The girl in the pool was her sister all right. *But where was the third sister?*

"If you are first sergeant of my father's company you must know where he is and how he is."

Gallagher found it difficult to meet her gaze. "Yes," he said in a low voice.

"Then tell me!"

He stood up. "Of course. But we will need water for coffee."

"What coffee?"

He smiled. "The coffee I will make." He picked up a kettle for the water and reached for his carbine.

"Wait," she said as she arose.

Gallagher turned. "Well?"

"Are any of them out there?"

"Apaches?"

Her face was deathly pale. "I mean . . . white people."

The candle guttered in the draft as he opened the door a little.

"Answer me," she said.

He turned his head. "There are white people out there," he said slowly and distinctly, "but they are not for ye to see, ma'am."

A hand crept up to the smooth column of her throat. "Are any of them women?"

He opened the door a little more.

"Well, Sergeant?"

"Yes," he said at last. "There is a woman out there."

"There are three of us," she said, "as I told you. Evelyn, Judith, and myself. Evelyn is a little younger than I am and looks like my twin. Judith is smaller and blonde."

It was Evelyn in the pool then. "Ye must not follow me," he said quietly.

"One woman. Which is it, Sergeant?"

"The one that looks like ye."

"Evelyn, then." There was a long pause. "Take me to her."

"No."

"I insist!"

He turned slowly. "Ye can insist all ye like, but ye will stay here until I return."

"Is she dead?"

"Yes. But she must have died quickly. It does not look like she was abused." He walked outside and closed the door behind him. He heard a soft muted crying from inside the room.

He walked to the pool and looked at her. He hated to have to touch the body, but he could not leave her there. He could not allow Ellen to see her. He reached into the cold water and touched her. He looked away as he pulled her body from the pool and cradled it in his arms. He carried it into one of the buildings and placed it on a cot, then covered it with a rough blanket. His breath came harshly in this throat, and he felt the green bile rise. He left the room and wedged the door shut with a billet of wood.

Gallagher walked to the gateway with his carbine ready in his big hands. He looked across the moonlit plain. Nothing moved. Shadows of brush and rock were etched like black ink on the silvery earth. "There were three of us," she had said. "Evelyn, Judith, and myself."

He knew where Ellen was, and Evelyn, but where was Judith? God alone knew that.

Gallagher walked out onto the plain, damned conscious of his size and long shadow on the naked ground. Each step was like a step up the gallows ladder until he heard

Shannon softly winny. He walked to the stallion and rested his head against its neck. He led the bay toward the buildings, and each ring of hoof on that hard earth sounded like a chapel bell when the Black Mass was to be celebrated.

His heart was thudding as he led the bay into the compound and let him trot eagerly toward the pool. He could not bear to watch him drink there.

He found a butt of fresh water in one of the smaller buildings. There was a body in the room, too, that of a young boy. They had had a little sport with him before they had killed him. He had been just a little too old for them to take him for adoption. There was pure hell in Gallagher's eyes as he turned away from the body.

She was straightening up the room when he entered it. She did not speak, but as she looked at him there was a question in her eyes.

"I did not see Judith," he said at last. "I'll look about a bit while ye make the coffee."

"There is none to be found," she said. Her eyes never left his.

"A good dragoon is never without his coffee," he said. He took a small bag of the beans from his pocket.

"That is not the way the song goes," she said absentmindedly.

He squinted at her in the yellow light. "So? Ye know the song, then?"

"Yes. It says a good dragoon is never without his horse, his liquor, and his woman."

Gallagher grinned. He reached for his carbine. "Start the fire. But use only dry wood."

"They'll see the smoke, Sergeant."

"Aye, but it doesn't really matter."

"What do you mean?"

He looked quickly at her, his eyes as hard as glacier ice. "If they are close enough to see the smoke they are close enough to have seen me come here. If they are *not* that close then it doesn't matter, does it?"

"You're a fatalist, then?"

He drew out one of his pistols and began to pound

the coffee beans with the butt of it. "I have been on the frontier a long time following the guidon av the First Dragoons. There were only a handful of us out here on the frontier, perhaps one soldier against a thousand savages, if ye want to quote the odds. A man gets a little fatalistic with such odds."

"You don't have to stay in the Army, Sergeant."

He shrugged, "It is my way av life. There was nothing left in Ireland except starvation. Ireland's best export seems to be her men. They have fought all over the world under many flags. Every flag, it seems, except their own."

"Are you a mercenary?"

He finished with the beans and handed her the bag. "A fighting man, yes; a mercenary, no. I am American the same as ye, miss."

She flushed. "You were going to tell me of my father."

He stood up and shoved back his hat. "Aye."

She eyed him expectantly.

"When was the last time ye heard from him?" he asked.

"Some time last summer. At that time he expected to be transferred to California."

He nodded. "Aye. We started out, but the orders were changed."

"Then we heard he was in New Mexico, at Santa Fe."

"We were there for a time."

"He wanted us to join him. We thought we would surprise him. We took ship for San Francisco early last fall. The ship was damaged rounding Cape Horn, and we put into Callao for repairs. Then a fever epidemic started, and we did not reach San Francisco until December. I wrote to him from there before we started south. At Los Angeles we managed to join a party of traders and merchants bound for New Mexico. They did not know the Apaches held control of this territory. They decided to go to Sonora and then find their way north into New Mexico. They would not take us, saying it was too dangerous."

"They were right."

She poked up the crackling fire. "We hired guides to this place, and here we stayed. We could not go ahead, nor could we return, and we had no idea of where my father was. There was a rumor that his company had gone to Santa Fe and then to the East. We did not know."

Gallagher remembered the letter he had found in the dispatch case, addressed in feminine handwriting to the captain, in care of Fort Marcy, Santa Fe, New Mexico Territory.

"Where is he now, Sergeant?"

Gallagher felt the cold sweat break out on his forehead. Before God, she had taken enough of a beating with the death of one sister and the loss of the other. How could he tell her?

"Sergeant Gallagher?"

Gallagher touched his cracked lips with his tongue. She was alone, in the heart of hostile country, with nothing to look forward to but death, or a worse fate amongst the Apaches.

"Sergeant Gallagher!"

Wordlessly he took the velvet-covered picture case and the stained envelope from his jacket and handed them to her. She looked down at them. "This picture case. We sent it to him some years ago. How is it you have it . . . and the letter?"

"I left your father but two days ago," he said. He held up a hand at the look in her fine eyes. "There is no use in lying to ye. Ye are a soldier's daughter. Yer father passed away of typhoid fever, miss. He was on duty to the last. A fine man and soldier."

She slowly placed the letter and the case on the table and looked away from Gallagher. For a few moments she stood there, and then she spoke over her shoulder. "What will they do with her?"

She was her father's daughter, all right. She had suffered two terrible losses, but she was still alive and was now the head of the family, small as it was. Her concern now was for the living, not the dead of blessed memory.

"Judith? I do not know."

"Don't lie to me."

He leaned against the wall and felt for his pipe and tobacco. He filled the pipe and lighted it. "They are impulsive," he said at last. "There are times when they kill everything in sight like a spoiled child smashing his toys. There are other times when they take captives. Not grown men, ye understand, for they are always dangerous, and the Apache takes no chances. Small children are usually adopted or held for ransom. Some of those that are adopted, Americans or Mexicans, grow up as Apaches, and they sometimes get worse than their foster people. Men and older boys are usually killed." He puffed at his pipe and blew out the fragrant smoke. He watched the smoke ring waver and then drift toward a window. "How old is she?"

"Eighteen."

He said nothing. Most Apache women were married long before reaching that age. To them an eighteen-year-old was a fully grown woman, and if they did not take her with them to become a squaw they would have their way with her. *All* of them; half a dozen bucks or half a hundred. What would be left, if it was alive, would hardly want to live.

"There isn't much hope then, is there?" she asked.

"Quien sabe?"

"You don't like to give up, do you?"

He shrugged.

"It happened so quickly. Mister Dunlap was kind to us. This is . . . was . . . his place. He told us there was nothing to fear when we saw the smoke signals in the hills. The Apaches had never bothered him before. During times of peace he had treated some of their sick and injured. He thought that would save all of us."

"He was a good man, but either a fool or exceptionally brave," said Gallagher dryly. "It is all right to treat their sick and injured, *providing* they recover, but if they do not . . ."

She passed a hand across her forehead, brushing back her dark hair. "Mister Dunlap was trying to figure out some way to help us. Everything was so vague, so uncertain. He sent a messenger to Fort McComber several days after we got here with a message to my father."

Gallagher shook his head. "No messenger ever came from here to Fort McComber," he said.

"He said he would take us to Fort Coulter if he could not get word through to my father."

Gallagher eyed her quickly. "Fort Coulter?" He shook his head.

"What do you mean?"

"Fort Coulter has been abandoned since late last fall. Fort McComber is the only occupied post in Arizona." He corrected himself. "At least, it was. If I'm right in what I think, the Stars and Bars now flies over Fort McComber."

"But why would Mister Dunlap agree to take us to Fort Coulter if he knew that it had been abandoned?"

"Aye," said Gallagher dryly. *"Why would he?"*

She paced back and forth. "There were times when I *was* a little suspicious of him. He looked at Judith at times with more than just appreciation for her beauty."

"So?"

"He was drinking one evening and pretended that he was just being fatherly with her." The great violet eyes looked at Gallagher. "I did not think so. But there was little I could do. We were at his mercy, so to speak. There was no other place for us to go."

"Where is he now?"

She stared at him. "Isn't his body out there with the others?"

"I do not know what he looks like, miss."

"A good-sized man, not as wide as you, but perhaps a little taller. Heavily bearded. A large nose and gray eyes. His eyes, well, they seemed as though they could look right through you."

Gallagher rubbed his jaw. "There is no man out there who looks like that."

"It's possible that he might not have been here at the time of the attack."

"Aye."

The coffee had begun to brew, and she waited until it was done, then filled two big granite cups with the liquid.

"How did ye survive the attack?" asked Gallagher as he sipped his coffee.

"I was not with my sisters at the time. I heard Evelyn screaming and ran to get a gun. Then the shooting stopped, and I knew what had happened. I found a knife and ran into this building. In the room where you found me there is an opening through the wall. I suppose they threw firewood into it from the outside, then used it as they needed it from the bin built into the wall. I crawled into it and found myself just outside the walls, hidden by brush which grew alongside the building. I stayed there, listening to them as they finished everyone off. . . ."

He nodded. She had been more than lucky. The picture of her sister's body would remain etched on Gallagher's memory for the rest of his life.

She looked at him. "And you? Where do you come from and where were you going?"

He emptied his cup and refilled it. Then he told her of his mission. She was silent for a long time, and then she looked up at him. "But that is suicide, Sergeant," she said quietly.

"Captain Eustis said *the orders would be obeyed to the letter*. There was one other thing he said . . . I have not forgotten it."

"Yes?"

He looked steadily at her. "If there is *one* man left, and *one* only, *that man will return the guidon to the regiment*, Sergeant Gallagher. *But only when the mission has been completed, successfully*, Sergeant Gallagher!"

"And that is what you will do?"

He nodded. "That is what I will do."

"With the territory alive with Apaches? With the Texas mounted rifles to contend with, too? You said they intended to take California."

She was a little startled at the look on his face as he stood up and smashed his right fist into his left palm. "The guidon goes back, under the captain's conditions, if the whole Apache nation and the entire Confederate States of America, as they call themselves, stand in the way!"

"Then you had better leave at once." She walked to the door and opened it, looking back at him. "You still have time to escape. You are a veteran Indian-fighter. You can make it from here alone."

"No," he said flatly.

"I would only burden you."

"That does not matter. You have a right to ask the United States Army for protection."

She could not help but smile. *"One* dragoon?"

He seemed to be twice as big as he really was as he came close to her. *"One* dragoon. That guidon out there goes back to where it belongs. This country belongs to the United States. If there is no other flag for loyal Americans to follow in Arizona they can follow the guidon."

"The Border Guidon," she said softly.

He smiled. "Ye have a way with the words. There must be some Irish in ye! The Border Guidon! I like that!"

"But if the Apaches come back, what then?"

He picked up his carbine. "They will not attack this night. Their favorite time to strike is at the first light of dawn. If they do not come then they will not come at all."

"But would you have gone on alone tonight if you had not found me here?"

"No."

"Don't lie to me, Sergeant!"

"I'm not. The bay is tired. He needs shoeing. There is a blacksmith's shop here. Shannon needs good shoes to carry us back to the blessed Stars and Stripes, wherever that may be."

"You really believe we might make it, don't you?"

He grinned and shook his carbine. "I *know* we can!"

She watched him walk toward the big bay and take the guidon from its socket. He rested it against the wall and then unsaddled the horse. He led it to a stall near the blacksmith's shop.

She walked across to the guidon and lifted the nine-foot lance. The breeze snapped out the little swallow-tailed banner. She eyed it. "I wonder," she whispered into the night.

GALLAGHER opened his eyes. The room was still dark, but there was a subtle difference in the night air. It was getting close to dawn. He sat up and glanced toward the girl sleeping quietly on a low couch across the room. He got up and took his carbine. It was cold in the room. He crossed to her with his blanket in his right hand. Her hands rested on her breasts, and her soft lips were slightly parted. Her thick dark hair lay across the pillow. She was a beauty. He covered her with his blanket and left the room.

The compound was still dark, but there was a faint suspicion of dawn light in the eastern sky. A cold wind swept across the area, scattering dried leaves ahead of it. It would not be long before they came. They would come. He was sure of it.

He crossed to the pool, thrust aside his repugnance, and knelt to wash himself in the overflow from the big basin. The water was crystal clear and as cold as ice. Strange that such a spring could exist in so barren a country, but he had seen the same phenomenon in harsher country.

Shannon whinnied from his stall. Gallagher walked softly to the open gateway and looked out across the dark plain. It was quiet except for the swift aimless rushing of the predawn wind. He knew well enough he would never see Apaches until they wanted to be seen. They might very well be within fifty feet of him at that moment, and he'd never know it until they rushed him.

To the west was a wide plain bordered by humped hills. Once in the clear Shannon could outrun any Apache pony. The bay had hunter blood in him. Gallagher was sure he could make it to Fort Yuma on the bay, but with the horse carrying double it would be quite another matter.

Yet they couldn't stay at the station. Not that it wouldn't be pleasant enough, for a time at least. There was food in the storerooms and all the water they'd ever need. A fine looking lass for company, and there might be another bottle or two cached somewhere. A short life and a merry one if they stayed, waiting for the painted death which was sure to come.

He glanced back to the building where she slept, wondering if she'd give in to a man if she knew there was little chance of living more than a few days. "Ah!" said Gallagher, swiping hard at the empty air with his carbine and spitting angrily. "The Devil himself is whisperin' to ye, Gallagher! The lass is a *lady!*"

He walked back to the blacksmith's shop. It was well equipped, and nothing had been disturbed. He started a fire in the forge. It was still too dark for the smoke to be distinguished, and when the charcoal was glowing there would be no smoke at all. But the noise, aye, that would be quite another matter. But the horse could not go on as he was. He could hardly reach the hills before he would be crippled.

It was getting lighter as he walked to the building where she slept. He rapped on the door.

"Come in, Dan," she called out.

She was dressed and freshly washed, her skin glowing and clear. Her thick hair had been drawn together at the nape of her neck and tied with a bright yellow ribbon. Her great eyes searching his face. "Well?" she asked.

"Nothing," he said quietly. "Do not start a fire in here. There is a fire in the forge. Ye can make coffee and do yer cooking there."

"They might see the smoke! They'll certainly hear the noise of the shoeing, Dan!"

He eyed her coldly, and she drew back a little in sudden fear of this big capable man.

"What else is there to do?" he asked at last. He waved a big hand.

She caught the hard anger in his voice and did not answer. She knew his anger was not against her but against the terrible situation they were in.

She took the food to the forge and set to work, trying to forget that they might be surrounded at any moment. He walked into the shop and handed her one of his pistols. "It is loaded and capped," he said. His eyes held hers. "Don't take any chances. If I am cut down or captured do not try to reach me or to fight them off. Even if ye succeeded, which is hardly possible, there would be no way for ye to reach safety.

"Use five of the six rounds if ye must to fight them and to help me, if I need help. But listen to me, lass: *The sixth round is for yerself.* Do ye understand?"

She nodded dumbly and watched him walk toward the gateway trailing his carbine.

He was not in sight as the first light of the false dawn crept above the eastern mountains. The food was almost ready, but he was gone. For a ghastly moment she thought he might have left her and gone on by himself, but then he would not have left the big bay. *Or perhaps they had already caught him.* Her hand grew greasy with cold sweat against the butt of the pistol.

He had not said where her sister was. Evelyn would have to be buried that day. Perhaps she should be washed and laid out, for a little while at least, before she was gone forever.

Ellen walked away from the shop and into a small building. When her eyes grew accustomed to the darkness she saw the body of the boy lying on the floor. Terrified, she left the building and walked across the compound. There, she saw that a door had been wedged shut with a wood billet. She reached for it to take it away.

"Do not go in there," he said from the gateway.

She whirled and raised the pistol in sudden panic.

"Go to the forge," he said in an odd voice.

"But why?"

"Go to the forge!"

The light was clearer as she walked across the compound. She turned to look back at Gallagher, and her blood congealed in her veins. He was not alone.

Fifty yards from him, just outside the gateway, were motionless figures, like demons conjured from the gray light of the morning. She had seen such figures before. The thick manes of hair bound with dingy cloth bands; the broad flat faces with the basilisk eyes. "Dear God," she said. Her legs trembled as she walked. There was no hope for them now. He could not stop them.

They knew Gallagher was the only man there. They knew he was a soldier and would fight with a terrible bloody intensity, and they did not like to lose warriors. They would try to frighten him into surrendering, thought Gallagher. "The bloody bastards," he said between set teeth. He walked into the shop just behind the girl. The forge was a bed of glowing coals. He stripped off shell jacket and undershirt and began to pump the bellows.

She stood with her back pressed against the rear wall. "What will you do? They'll be here any minute!" There was a note of panic in her voice.

He ignored her as he worked. Sweat ran down his broad chest and back as the heat grew. He walked outside with studied deliberation and got the bay. There was no sign of the warriors now, but he knew well enough they were close by.

He began to work steadily, never looking toward the open front of the shop. There could be no escape from them by flight. He heated the horseshoes. His back was toward the shopfront, but he could see her eyes and knew they would warn him when they came.

It took all the iron guts he had to keep on with his work. It wasn't until he turned from the forge to the anvil that he saw how close they were to him, not more than ten feet away, a half dozen of them, with carbines, rifles, and shotguns pointed casually in his direction. One wrong move and he'd be riddled like Aunt Bridget's colander.

They were naked from the waist up despite the coldness of the morning air, wore the buckskin kilt and high desert moccasins tied about their knotty calves. There was no expression on any of the flat faces, and their eyes hardly moved at all.

The girl drew in her breath sharply and then steadied herself at a hard glance from him. There was no need for him to talk. *"Be silent! Don't move! Above all, show no fear,"* his eyes seemed to say.

The short hammer rang steadily against a glowing shoe, and the sparks shot toward the door. The Apaches moved a little. Gallagher seemed intent on his work, and no one could know that the cold sweat of fear ran down his muscular upper body to mingle with the hot sweat of exertion.

The hammer sang a rhythmical song against the glowing metal, the sparks showered steadily, and all the while the big redheaded Irishman seemed so intent on his work that one would have thought he was alone in the shop instead of giving a solo performance for half a dozen of the bloodiest fighters in the entire Southwest.

Another warrior suddenly appeared behind his mates. They stepped aside to let him through, and when Gallagher saw who it was it took all the steel in his belly to keep the strokes of the hammer from faltering. It was Klij-Litzogue. The half-healed wounds on his wide face gave him a look of a demon straight from the honor guard of hell. Gallagher's musketoon had smashed that already fearsome visage into something almost unreal in its terrible hideousness. The flat black eyes looked full into Gallagher's blue ones, and they seemed to clash like striking blades. Then the Tonto's eyes shifted to look at the woman, and he advanced one moccasined foot into the shop.

Gallagher snatched a glowing shoe from the forge and slapped it onto the anvil. There was no time now to do the job right. He had to hammer hell out of it. Sparks shot toward the watching bucks. Once more Yellow Snake moved a foot, and then another, until he was no more than a yard from Gallagher, and the carbine in his hands was almost touching Gallagher's broad back.

"Zastee," said Yellow Snake coldly.

"Kill and be damned to ye," said Gallagher.

Gallagher dropped the shoe into the forge, picked up

another one with the tongs, placed it onto the anvil, and began to shape it. He began to count as he struck hard at the shoe. "One! Two! Three! Four! Shut the door! Five! Six! Seven! Eight! I wish to hell I had closed the gate!"

"Zastee!" said the Apache a little louder.

The girl had placed her hands flat against the back wall of the shop, and now she swayed a little from side to side until Gallagher steadied her with a glance.

Yellow Snake came a little closer to Gallagher; the cold ring of the carbine muzzle touching the sweating flesh just above the kidneys.

Gallagher wiped the sweat from his face and resumed work.

The big hammer of the carbine was thumbed back with a click-cluck sound. *"Zastee! Zastee!"* said the warrior.

The others stood there, a faint look of fear on their broad faces. The sparks showered toward them, and they moved back a little.

Gallagher took another shoe from the forge and began to beat time as he sang:

> "Oh, the dragoon bold! He scorns all care,
> As he goes the rounds with uncropped hair;
> He spends no thought on the evil star
> That sent him away to the border war!"

The chief would have to crowd past Gallagher to reach the woman, and it would take a lot of crowding to move that muscular one hundred and ninety pounds. Yellow Snake looked up at Gallagher. The Irishman brought the hammer down hard so that the hot sparks danced against the warrior's naked chest, but Klij-Litzogue did not wince or speak. Once again the eyes clashed like crossing blades. Then the Apache looked at the woman. He crooked a finger at her in silent command to come to him. She did not move. Her hands were behind her, holding the pistol. Was it now? Should she shoot herself quickly, before he reached her and before the rest of them swarmed over the mad Irishman who shaped horseshoes in front of a bloodthirsty audience as though they did not exist? *Now?* Her hand tightened on the gun butt slippery with sweat.

Gallagher snatched another glowing shoe from the forge, slapped it down on the anvil, and began a frenzied beating on it so that the station rang with the sound and sparks showered the interior of the little shop. The warriors drew back, covering their mouths with their hands in awe. Yellow Snake tried once more to get past Gallagher, but this time a glowing shoe was held up in the tongs a foot from his naked chest, and even an Apache couldn't ignore that! His eyes widened. He glanced at the woman he wanted, then back at the huge Irishman. Then he spat full in Gallagher's face.

Gallagher dropped the hammer from his right hand, badly as he wanted to crack the Apache's skull with it. He doubled a huge freckled fist, and the blow traveled short and true, catching Yellow Snake flush on the jaw, lifting him from his feet and driving him back against his mates.

Gallagher wasted no time. He snatched a shoe from the fire and advanced toward the wide-eyed bucks. *"Ugashe! Ugashe!* Go! Go!" he yelled at the top of his voice, brandishing the glowing shoe in their very faces.

"Pesh-chidin!" one of them cried. He turned and fled, followed by the others. *"Pesh-chidin! Pesh-chidin!"*

Gallagher dropped the shoe into the forge, wiped the sweat and spittle from his face, gripped Yellow Snake by the heels, and dragged him outside. He looked at the backs of the warriors as they ran toward the gateway. Then he looked down at the unconscious chief. The devil in Gallagher wanted him to strip the bastard naked and throw him out on the ground beyond the gate, but there would be hell to pay and no pitch hot if he did. He gripped the warrior by the heels and hauled him to the gateway, then he propped him against the outer wall, wiped his hands on his trousers, and walked back to the shop.

The girl was gone. Where? . . . Then he saw her. She had fallen in a dead faint behind a work bench. He bathed her face, but she did not move. Her breasts rose and fell, and her body was warm and soft in his thick arms. He clumsily brushed her dark hair back from her pale face. She opened her eyes. "I don't understand it," she murmured.

He picked her up easily and placed her on the bench. Then he grinned. "It was a colossal bluff," he said. "They look on blacksmiths as being allied to spirits. The witch, or ghost of iron, I expect. . . . *Pesh-chidin*."

Her face was as pale as a lily. "That face of his. Like a devil peering through the smoke of hell itself."

"Aye! Ye have a way with the words. Ye are sure ye are not Irish?"

She smiled wanly. "My grandfather was North Irish."

His face fell a little. "An Orangeman? Ah well, it cannot be helped, and even an Orangeman is an Irishman in a *sense*." He grinned. "But it was close when he spat in me face."

She nodded. "That was when I fainted. I think I hit the floor just as he did."

Gallagher ruefully eyed his big freckled fist. "Ah," he said quietly, "if I had him alone. . . . But then it would be no fun. Say two of them, or perhaps three, with no knives and no holds barred. 'Twould be a real Donnybrook!"

"What happens now?"

He shrugged. "I do not know."

"Will they be back?"

"Not likely. For a time at least. In that time we must get ready to leave."

"To go out there?"

"There is no other place to go, and we cannot stay, lass. Tonight, when it is dark, before the rising of the moon, we'll pull out of here. Do ye go now and find food and canteens. Round up any weapons ye can. Meanwhile, now that I have no audience, so to speak, I'll shoe me bay."

She placed a hand on his naked shoulder and stepped down to the floor. For a moment she looked up into his face, then she took his head between her hands, bent it forward gently, and placed her soft lips against his cracked ones. Then she was gone, leaving a faint trace of her scent behind her while he slowly touched his lips with

thick fingers. "What a lass," he said. He looked at the bay.
"Shannon! Ye're to be shoed! We've got to get the lass to
California."

The bay looked at him quizzically.

Gallagher threw up his hands. "How do *I* know what
will happen then, ye great booby?"

THE SUN was dying in the west, leaving a great wash of rose and gold against the sky. Dan Gallagher smoothed the last of the graves he had dug and filled. He had not let Ellen see the body of her sister despite her pleading. He wiped the sweat from his naked torso with a huck towel. The day was almost gone. A cool wind swept through the bosque, rustling the leaves. It would be cold that night.

They had not come back, or at least he had seen no signs of them. But Klij-Litzogue would never forget Dan Gallagher as long as he lived. He would thirst for his vengeance, and it would be a terrible and bloody thing if he achieved it.

He picked up the spade and walked toward the buildings. The bay was saddled and loaded with cantle and pommel packs, an extra carbine, and half a dozen canteens. The guidon had been thrust into its socket and the arm strap tied to the saddle. It fluttered in the breeze, seemingly anxious to get back to the regiment where it belonged. Gallagher swung up the spade in a saber salute as he passed it.

She was waiting for him dressed in male clothing that had probably belonged to the boy who had been killed. The gunbelt about her slim waist was weighted down by the Colt he had given her. She had cut her hair shorter and had tied it at the nape of her neck with a bright-yellow ribbon. She wore a low-crowned, flat-brimmed hat. "How do I look?" she asked.

"Fine. But the ribbon is the wrong color."

"So?"

He placed a finger on the orange stripe alongside his blue trousers. "The dragoon color, although it pains an

Irishman such as meself, is orange. The cavalry wear yellow, and the mounted rifles wear the blessed green."

She flushed a little. "I wasn't thinking of the dragoons, Sergeant, when I tied my hair."

It was his turn to flush. "They are buried," he said to cover up his confusion. "Is it in yer mind to say a few words over them?"

"No. I can't do it, Sergeant."

"Then I will. Come."

She glanced at him curiously as he led the way to the graves. There were many unusual facets to the character of this big rough man, and they constantly surprised her.

Gallagher picked up his undershirt and jacket and put them on, then removed his disreputable hat and bowed his head. For a moment he stood there, as though groping for words, and then he spoke in a soft fine voice that was almost in direct contrast to his usual sharpness of speech: *"The Lord is my shepherd; I shall not want. He maketh me to lie down in green pastures: he leadeth me beside the still waters. . ."*

When he had finished it was dark and the wind was stronger.

"Do you soldiers always do such things?" she asked quietly.

He placed his hat upon his head and looked off into the unseen distance, almost as though he were eying other times and other places unknown to her. "Over the graves of many comrades. The lonely resting-places scattered in Utah and in Texas; in New Mexico and Arizona. Perhaps *they* do not hear it, but it gives the rest of us who are still living a little comfort." He turned quickly and walked away from the graves.

When she was alone she realized he had left her to be with her sister. She knelt beside the mound, said a quiet prayer, passed a soft hand across the grave, then got quickly to her feet and walked toward the big man who seemed to be all she had left.

He led the way from the quiet place. The water bubbled up steadily in the pool. A shutter banged in the rising wind. The black patches where the blood had soaked into the thirsty caliche showed up dimly in the darkness.

They did not look back as they passed from the bosque into the open plain. The wind snapped out the guidon. Gallagher looked ahead as he walked. Fort Coulter was to the southwest to the best of his recollection. He could have found it easily enough following the stage route, then the wagon road, then cutting off through a little-known pass in the Diablos. But now he wasn't so sure. Fortunately, God had fashioned a built-in compass in his brain, and many a time on forced marches in the old days, when everyone was a little panicky with the fear of being lost in unknown country, Gallagher had led the way with the true instinct of a homing pigeon.

It was the girl who worried him. There was no going back for Gallagher. He would cast the dice the hard way and live or die depending upon which way the ivory cubes fell. He would not cry out if he lost. That was not the way of a dragoon. But for her he felt a twinge of his deep-seated pity. She was strong, but not strong enough for what lay ahead of them. Few women, and not too many men, could live in that country even in times of peace. During war, especially against the Apaches, it was only the toughest fighters who survived.

Yet he felt better for having her with him. He knew he was a fool. She'd never live to see the Stars and Stripes snapping in a fresh breeze over a post of the United States Army. One way or another she would have to die, and the way of dying would be hard indeed. By thirst or by weakness; by hand of Apache or perhaps her own hand. Perhaps, and this was the worst thought of all, it would have to be by *his* hand.

"Supposing she comes back to the place?" she asked out of the darkness.

He glanced at her dim face.

"I mean Judith, Dan."

They strode on for fifty yards.

"Dan?"

He looked away from her. "She will not be coming back, lass," he said in a low voice.

The moon washed the country in silver light, etching
sharp shadows upon the harsh earth. Now and then Gallagher looked back. There had been no sign of them since
the two had left the buildings. It was odd and a little bit
eerie, plodding across the moon-washed ground, like sil-
houettes in a shadow theater, easily seen from a mile or
two away, and yet nothing else moved in the cold bright
moonlight.

"Will they follow us?" she asked.

"Yes."

She looked back over a slim shoulder. "I don't see any
of them," she said.

"That is the time to expect them, Ellen."

"What is ahead of us?"

"The Diablos. They are half hills and half mountains."

"What is beyond them?"

"To the south is Mexico; to the west, a long way off, is
the Colorado."

"And to the east?"

He hesitated. "Apache country."

"But isn't this all Apache country?"

"In a way. But they have strongholds just as we have
forts."

"Whose stronghold is closest?"

"Klij-Litzogue . . . Yellow Snake . . . the one who tried
to get to ye in the blacksmith shop."

She made a disagreeable sound. "He must hate you for
what you did."

He shrugged. "He hated me long before that." He eyed
her. "This man Dunlap. Ye are sure he planned to take ye
to Fort Coulter?"

"That is what he said."

"Tell me: Did he have any features a man would remember well after having seen him once?"

She was silent for a little while, then said, "It was his
eyes, I think. One could never forget them. He was like
one of the prophets of old at times. He knew the Bible
from cover to cover, it seemed."

Gallagher glanced quickly at her. "What was his first
name?"

"I can't remember. Everyone called him *Mister* Dunlap.
It was a name of biblical times, I think."

"Like Elijah?"

She smiled. "Yes! That was it! Elijah Dunlap!"

A strange cold feeling crept over Gallagher.

"Did you know him, Sergeant?"

"I think so."

How could he tell her of Elijah Darris, for that was the
man he was sure. Elijah Darris. Jackleg preacher. Member of some little-known and almighty strange religious
sect. A man who had been driven from more civilized
areas because of the unholy practices in which he delighted. A man who gave allegiance to no recognized
creed and no country, only allegiance to himself and his
strange perverted tastes. One of those tastes had been for
women, particularly young girls.

"What do you know about him?" she asked.

"Very little." He had to lie to her. If Judith had been
killed or captured by the Apaches her fate would be easier
in a sense than it would be in the rough hands of Elijah
Darris. There were other stories about the man, of his
dealings with the Apaches; one of his friends had been
none other than Klij-Litzogue.

Gallagher eyed the clear sky against which the moon
hung like a silver salver. He glanced back along the way
they had come. He thought he saw a faint quick movement, but then all was devoid of life again. They were
back there, all right, and on each flank, and in all probability some of them had forged easily ahead to complete
the ring about them. They would close in when the time
was right, like howling wolves in the wild steppe country of Russia closing in on a sleigh drawn by tiring
horses.

"I think she is still alive," Ellen said suddenly.

"Judith?"

"Yes."

"Why do you think so?"

She tilted her head to one side. "Because Judy has a
way of doing things just like that."

"This is not a game they play out here."

"I know."

"If she is in their hands it would be better if she had died as Evelyn did."

She wrapped her arms about her shapely knees. "Judy likes men," she said thoughtfully.

"They are not such men as she might have known."

"She has known rough men. On the ship coming to California. On the stagecoaches to Los Angeles. Other places."

Gallagher looked back over his shoulder. There was something puzzling about this trip. The Apaches could have kept them penned up at the station, yet they had let them leave. Klij-Litzogue must have his revenge. If he did not he would lose face amongst his people, and they had no place in their stern way of life for such a leader or such a man.

Somewhere to the south a coyote howled softly. A moment later the call was answered by another coyote far to the north. Gallagher raised his head. The call came again, this time from the east. Ellen shivered. "They sound so lonely," she said.

"Yes."

The fourth and last call came as he had expected it to, from the west, and it sent the cold sweat trickling down his sides. There was no advantage in telling the girl that those were not coyotes out there, but Apaches, and that they had completely surrounded Gallagher and her with an unseen and deadly escort.

IT WAS just before the false dawn when Gallagher stopped walking and looked at Ellen. "There is something I must do," he said quietly, "and ye must help me."

Her face was dim in the faint light. His heart went out to her, for he knew she was badly frightened. "What is it, Dan?" At least her voice was steady. She had good control.

"I am going back to bleed them a little."

"I don't understand."

He drew her close. "It is better to outflank an advancing enemy than a retreating one. I am going back. Ye will go on, for they will hear the horse. It will not be easy for ye to be alone in the darkness, knowing they are close, but it is close to the dawn, and they might jump us then. They will not expect me, Ellen." He smiled wryly. "At least I hope not."

"And I'm to be the bait."

"Aye."

He was as ready as he'd ever be, with Sharps carbine, twin issue Colts, and a long-bladed bowie, which was not issue, but few veteran Indian-fighters were without one of the heavy-bladed gutters. "Ellen," he said quietly.

"You don't have to tell me, Dan. I have the pistol ready." She smiled wanly. "If anything happens to you I'll take the guidon back to where it rightfully belongs. With the First Dragoons."

"That's the dragoon spirit!" He lowered his voice. "Do not be afraid if ye hear shooting. I hope it will be *my* shooting. Now go on, traveling at the same pace we have kept up all night."

She placed a cool hand against his rough cheek and

touched her lips against his. "Good luck, dragoon," she said, and suddenly she was gone into the dimness.

Gallagher removed his spurs and placed them in a pocket. He padded back with carbine at hip level. His eyes darted back and forth, eying and evaluating each shadow, each faint movement. Then he saw the place—a low swale rimmed with thorny brush. To the left of it, fifty yards away, was a low mound of rock that thrust itself up above the flat ground like an angry boil ready for eruption. To the right was a low ledge that extended for about two hundred yards. To the northeast the ground sloped down, and it was almost barren of brush.

He entered the swale and removed his hat, letting it drop onto his back, hanging by the strap. He took out one of his Navy Colts, cocked it, and placed it on a flat rock near at hand. Now there was nothing to do but wait . . . and think.

They might expect an ambush. They were tophole fighters themselves, masters of the unseen ambush, the spit of a rifle from concealment. Just as they were masters of the ambush, they also feared it more than any other form of attack. It was logical for them to be on the lookout for an ambush near the low mound to Gallagher's left. At least he hoped so. The mound unconsciously drew the eye on that flat plain.

They were in sight before he realized how quickly they were moving—seven of them, mounted on their ponies, following the unseen trail to pass between mound and swale. Gallagher wet his dry lips. Seven of them. He had thirteen rounds between carbine and two pistols. Twelve of those rounds were in the Colts, hardly a weapon for long-range or even middle-range shooting. Then, too, there would be more warriors within earshot.

She would be moving on, trending to the southwest. What if he was killed or captured? She would go on then until they showed up silently waiting for her. She might put up a fight, but it would not be for long, and then they would have her, and she would die by her own hand.

"Ah, God," he said softly and drove the thoughts from

his teeming mind. There was work to be done. His chosen trade, fighting the enemies of his country.

Gallagher eased back the big hammer of the Sharps to full cock. He lowered his head and rested his cheek against the stock, sighting on the last rider. Closer and closer they came until the lead horseman was not more than fifty yards from Gallagher. Gallagher took in the slack of the trigger, steadied the carbine, picked up the broad chest of the brave on the knife-blade front sight, settled the front sight in the notch of the rear sight. Then he touched off the carbine.

The Sharps bucked back against his shoulder, driving a puff of smoke toward the Apaches. The slamming report of the shot seemed to roll across the flat plain. The warrior was driven back off the rump of his horse by the impact of the big .52 caliber slug.

Gallagher reloaded, lowering the breech, slipping in a linen-covered cartridge, raising the block to shear off the rear of the cartridge, capping the nipple, all in swift well-timed movements, so that when he sighted again the Apaches were still milling in confusion.

The second shot struck a yelling Apache in the left shoulder. The third knocked a buck from his horse, and the fourth round killed a horse. Then Gallagher was gone, running swiftly along the ledge, bent low so that he could not be seen, reloading as he ran, leaving a cloud of drifting smoke to mark the place where the Apaches had begun to plant lead.

Gallagher hit the ground fifty yards up the ledge, thrust the carbine forward, sighted, and squeezed off. The slug creased one of the bucks, who fell as if dead. The lead Apache screamed as he jerked his lance from its sling, couched it, and raced toward Gallagher, who was reloading.

"Trying to make a bloody hero out of yerself, is it?" grunted Gallagher.

He raised the carbine and sighted. The chest of the buck got bigger and bigger, and then Gallagher pulled the trigger. The Sharps misfired. There was no time to reload. Gallagher jumped to his feet and jerked out his

Colt. The lance was ten feet from his chest when he fired twice, then dived over the ledge and rolled away. The lance blade drove into the ground inches away from Gallagher. The warrior was pitchforked from his horse, landing with a dull thud a few feet from his quarry. He raised his head, and then dropped it as Gallagher's knife sank in deep, probed for the heart, and drove in another inch or two.

Gallagher reloaded his Sharps and gripped the dead buck's pony by the hackamore. He swung up into the rough saddle. The pony reared and fought viciously, but a hard blow atop the head from the steel-shod butt of the carbine brought him around. Gallagher slammed the carbine barrel against the flanks of the pony and rode like a fury, to the west, but as he turned to look back he saw the face of the buck he had dismounted by killing his horse. It was the face of Yellow Snake.

"*Zastee! Zastee!* Kill! Kill!" yelled Gallagher.

The pony's hoofs drummed on the hard earth. There was a trace of the false dawn in the eastern sky. The wind picked up. Behind Gallagher, near the low swale, lay two dead warriors, two wounded warriors, and a dead horse. The big White-eye had not only ambushed skilled ambushers but had added insult to injury by stealing an Apache horse right under the noses of Yellow Snake and his best men.

She was waiting near an upthrust shoulder of rock, the pistol in her hand. She raised it as she saw the lone horseman bearing down on her, then lowered it again. No Apache was *that* big."

He slid from the horse. "Mount!" he snapped, jerking his thumb toward the bay. "We can get a good lead on them now. They will not be anxious to close in." He slung the carbine over his shoulder and fought to get the excited Apache horse under control until at last he brought a huge fist down atop the head of the horse. It seemed to the girl that the legs of the horse wobbled a little from the effect of the blow.

They rode to the southwest as the light grew, and there was no sign of the enemy. She looked at him as she guided the bay past broken ground. "Have you nothing to say?" she demanded at last.

He looked at her in surprise. "What do ye mean?"

"What happened back there?"

He grinned reminiscently. "It was a fine fight. A bit onesided, ye might say, what with one Irishman against the seven of them."

She paled. "Seven of them?"

"The odds were a little on my side, lass."

"But you are not marked!"

He waved a hand. "They never had a chance to mark me, Ellen."

Then he thought back on that hot little fight . . . the misfiring of the Sharps and the lance attack of the warrior. It had been a close thing. The reaction from it made his stomach roll over within him. It had been too damned close for comfort.

"To the right," he said.

She guided the bay closer to his mount.

"See the dark line against the earth? That is a draw, or an arroyo, and we can shelter there. God help us if they have gotten there first!"

They reached the lip of the draw as the sky lightened fully with the dawn. Gallagher whistled softly. The draw seemed to drop into the very bowels of the earth. It was deep and not very wide, fifty yards at the most. Gallagher looked back over his shoulder. "Into it, lass!" he ordered. She hesitated. He drove the horse at it, leaning forward as it slid down the steep decline in a shower of gravel and stones. He could not see the bottom. Perhaps it was a sheer drop after a time, but if it was it was too damned late, for Gallagher was on his way down.

The girl followed him, riding the big bay easily, but her heart was in her mouth as she saw Gallagher's broad back vanish into the darkness below her. She could hear the rocks rumbling past her, loosened by her descent. Dust billowed up, choking her.

Then she saw him standing beside his horse, holding its head and looking up at her with drawn face. He caught

the bay by the mane as it reached the place beside him.
"Do not look down!" he said to her.

But she couldn't help it. They stood on a narrow ledge,
hardly more than eight feet wide, beyond which there
was nothing, a sheer drop into blackness. She closed her
eyes and swayed in the saddle, feeling his arms about
her as he helped her down. "We must move on," he said.

"Let's rest. I'm frightened, Gallagher."

"Get on with ye! There is no time to waste! We have
been lucky so far! Get on with ye!"

She stumbled along the ledge ahead of him. He looked
down into the chasm they had almost fallen into. "Jesus,"
he said softly as he led the two horses on after Ellen.

The light of day filled the canyon. The ledge was wider
now, and it sloped downward, but still the bottom of the
chasm on the right was a long way down.

Gallagher could see that the girl was almost exhausted.
Once again he looked over his shoulder for signs of pur-
suit. It would have been easy for them to roll rocks over
the brink high above the two white people, like playing a
deadly game of skittles. But there was no sign of them. A
hawk hovered high overhead, almost at ground level with
the lip of the canyon. He did not seem afraid, almost sure
sign that there was no human life up there.

It was strange, but then there had been a number of
strange things about the journey he and the girl had made
from the station. It would have been easy for the Indians
to pen the two whites in the station, or to cut them off on
the open plain; finally, they could have followed the lip of
the canyon, knowing well enough they had their quarry in
a great natural prison.

Gallagher looked ahead. There seemed to be no way
out of the place, yet there might be unseen openings that led
up to the ground level to the east. There had better be . . .

They reached the bottom of the canyon. Ellen Eustis
turned. "Look," she said quietly.

Ahead of them, beneath a great rock overhang, were
tinajas, rock pans of water filled by seepage from some
hidden source. The water rippled in the cool morning

wind of the canyon. Shannon whinnied. Gallagher held onto the horses and looked about. The place was as dead as an Egyptian tomb. Not a sign of life. The brush and scrub trees moved uneasily in the wind. Gallagher looked above them. Nothing but the jagged rimrock and the blue sky, dotted with a few hurrying clouds.

He shook his head as he led the horses to the water and let them drink their fill. It was almost as though they had wandered off the earth to some unknown and deserted planet.

They made their camp up a talus slope, in a deep cave protected by great fallen rocks. There was a seepage of water at the rear of the cave—enough to keep them alive for days if they were besieged in the cave.

She dropped onto the blanket he had spread for her and fell asleep almost immediately.

Gallagher had led the horses into the cave. He rubbed them down and let them feed on dried grasses he had pulled. He walked to the mouth of the cave and looked out across the peaceful sunlit canyon. It was a nice place. Quiet and peaceful looking. Far to his right, almost due south, it seemed as though the canyon widened and formed a vast Y, and he could have sworn he saw sunlight sparkling on running water.

On the far wall of the canyon he saw a rather even line, a fault perhaps, with a curiously irregular pattern of light and dark rock. He stared at it and then struck his right fist into his left palm. "By God," he said. "I wouldn't have believed it! This must be Canyon Encantado! There is no other place like it in this country. And if it is Canyon Encantado, then we are safe from the Apaches, for the place is taboo to them!"

He rubbed his bristly jaws. It was sheer good fortune. They would be safe enough in there . . . for a time at least. Some time soon they would have to leave it if Gallagher carried on with his mission. His face tightened. The mission! There would be a reception committee awaiting them when they left the canyon. Men with thick black manes of hair and greasy tearing hands holding hard-edged knives ready for soft white-eye flesh.

Chapter 10

THE GREAT canyon was filled with the sun and warmth of midday. A fitful breeze felt its way along the canyon and rustled the foliage. Dan Gallagher awoke with a start. He glanced at Ellen, who was still asleep. He cursed himself softly as he gathered his weapons. If it was not Canyon Encantado the Tontos might have crept up on the two of them.

He walked to the front of the cave and stood just inside the entrance, just short of the light of the sun, eying the floor of the canyon and the far wall. It was castellated, a curious conglomeration of spires, domes, towers, and battlements. With half-closed eyes and a little imagination the formations appeared man-made, lacking only banners and men-at-arms, with their armor shining in the sunlight.

There was no sign of life. Gallagher worked his way out of the cave by crawling through a jumble of rock and brush. He lay for a long time studying the great trough of the canyon. The trail by which they had entered was but a hairline against the sheer salmon- and yellow-colored rock wall.

He eased his way down the talus lope, taking advantage of every scrap of cover and shade, until he found himself in a tangled labyrinth of rocks and brush where the going was slow but the cover was excellent. It took him an hour to reach a place where he could see the stream. It was wider than he had expected and ran between grassy banks overhung by tree branches. A rabbit moved from one patch of cover to another. A small bear prowled about a meadow.

Gallagher walked around a huge naked shoulder of rock and then stopped short. A hundred yards from him was a high-walled corral build of fieldstone. A rough track led from it toward the stream, then continued on the other side of the ford.

Dan scratched his growing beard. Indians would never have built such a corral. Peeled poles were good enough for them. It was obviously the work of white men . . . but no white men lived there! At least he had never heard of white men living there.

He squatted in the shade of a boulder and scanned the rough trail that followed the far side of the stream until it vanished into a wall of greenery that lay like a thick dam across the width of the right-hand branch of the Y.

Gallagher shrugged. He walked slowly back to the cave. Fort Coulter was about twenty miles from this place, as best as he could estimate. He'd have to go there. Taking the girl along was out of the question. This place was as good as any in which to leave her. If it was Canyon Encantado the Apaches would certainly leave her alone. But the corral was a puzzler. He looked back toward the great Y. Maybe Mormons had built it. They built well, and this was their kind of country, for they were more farmers than cattlemen or miners, but it was a long way south from their home base.

She was waiting for him inside the entrance to the cave, with gunbelt about her slim waist and the heavy carbine across her lap. "Are you sure there are no settlements around here?" she asked.

"None that I know of."

"What is this place?"

"Canyon Encantado."

She looked up at him. "Charmed Canyon?"

He squatted beside her and took up a handful of dirt in his great hands. "More likely 'Enchanted Canyon,' Ellen." He looked up at her as he let the earth fall from one hand to the other. "They tell strange stories about this place. It was the Spanish conquistadores who named it, as ye can guess. But even before their time, according to what yer father once told me"—here he looked down at his busy hands—"the Apaches shunned this place."

"But why?"

He gestured with the empty hand. "See yon rock

formation across the canyon? See the alternate lights and darks av it?"

"Yes."

"Look closely then. If ye cannot see sharply enough yer father's fine Vollmer glasses are in one av me saddle-bags."

She stared at the wall, then looked strangely at him. "But it is man-made," she said wonderingly.

He nodded. "Yon great crevice is filled with fieldstone work. Room after room av them. Far back into the crevice. With windows and doors. The T-shaped openings are the doors."

"But who built them?"

He shrugged. He dropped the earth and dusted his hands. "The 'Hohokam,' I think they are called. The old ones. The people who were here long before the Apaches, it is said. They left. No one knows why. Perhaps famine, disease, lack of water, any number av reasons. But leave they did."

"Why did they live in a place like this?"

"Water. Tillable soil. Natural protection."

"Against the elements?"

He looked up at her. "Partly."

"What else would there be to be frightened off?"

He stood up and looked out upon the peaceful canyon. "The same thing we came in here to get away from . . . the Apaches."

She paled a little. "Will they come after us?"

He shook his head. "But we cannot leave without running into them again. It will be like a great prison for ye until I get back."

She stood up slowly. A slim hand traveled to the white column of her throat. "What do you mean?" she faltered.

Gallagher's face grew hard. "I am not going to deceive ye, lass. I am on a mission, ordered to it by yer own father, and I must go."

"They can't expect one man to carry out such a mission! Forget about it, Dan."

"Ye will be safe here. God knows I don't want to leave ye, but I must go."

She looked up into his face. "You're a brave man, Dan Gallagher, but as big a fool as any I have ever met!" She walked away from him toward the rear of the cave.

Gallagher shrugged. It was always the way. Explaining such a thing to a female was like butting your skull against Blarney Castle. It would not give.

Gallagher went outside and eyed the canyon walls. That corral still bothered him. But they had seen no sign of life. No fresh horse or mule droppings. No Apaches, either. It was Canyon Encantado all right; it had to be!

He cocked an eye at the sun, still high in the sky. He would have to leave this evening, before the moon arose, or bide his time until it was gone and he could scale his way out of the canyon. He looked up at the great sheer walls. Here and there they had crumbled and left wide notches in the rimrock. It would not be easy for a man to scale the walls, and with a horse to get up there, too, he'd have the devil of a time of it. But he had to have a horse, and he could not leave by any of the canyon entrances. The Tontos might not have the guts to come into the place, but they had the patience and the time to wait outside for Gallagher.

All the strange stories of this fabled place came back to haunt him as he stood there. He shivered a little as the breeze slowly reversed itself to flow down canyon as it always did at nightfall. But it was more than the cool wind that made him shiver. There was *something* in that canyon besides animal life and the decaying bones of cliff-dweller structures. *Something. . .*

They ate in the darkness. Gallagher had lighted a candle in a niche around a curve in the cave wall long enough for her to prepare their supper, and then he had insisted on extinguishing it. She wondered why. He had said that the Tontos would not come in there no matter how badly they wanted the two of them. But she knew something was bothering him.

He busied himself after they had eaten, getting his gear ready for his trip to Fort Coulter. There was feeling of dread within her, not so much for her own safety, even though the prospect of being left there alone was frightening, but for his. They did not speak to each other, but each of them knew what the other was thinking. At least they thought they knew. Each of them individually had begun to sense an inner stirring, a feeling that had not been present until they had returned to the cave, but neither of them knew the same feeling was in the mind and soul of the other one.

"When will you leave?" she asked at last.

He sheathed one his Colt. "As soon as I saddle the bay."

She leaned against the wall of the cave, slowly letting down her damp hair to dry it. "That soon?"

"Yes. There will be darkness before the coming of the moon. By the time it is gone I will be in the open."

"But can you escape them then?"

He grinned in the darkness and patted his Sharps and one of the Colts. "I am not worried."

"But the horse. Can their ponies outrun him?"

"Shannon?" He laughed. "He is a Denmark breed, lass. Yes, ma'am, a direct descendant of old Gaines Denmark himself, he is!"

"Oh," she said vaguely.

He gathered his gear together and looked down at it in the darkness. She slowly dried her hair. "How long will you be gone?"

"Not long," he said. He walked to the rear of the cave and lighted the candle, making sure he concealed the glow of the light from the rest of the cave by hanging a blanket in front of it. He took out the dispatch that concerned his mission and read it slowly so that he could memorize the contents. Then he concealed the dispatch in a niche of the cave wall. He turned and snuffed out the candle, then dropped the blanket. As he did so he felt her close to him. "I'm afraid, Dan," she said in a little voice.

He placed his hands on her shoulders and felt the soft dampness of her hair. "Ye will be all right," he said.

"It's not for myself," she said, "but for you, Dan."

They stood there in the darkness, and then she placed her hands against the sides of his face and drew it down so that his mouth met her lips. She had kissed him before but never like this. His arms went about her and he lifted her off her feet, feeling the softness of her body against him, and he remembered her as he had first seen her in the guttering yellow light of the candle, naked and with a knife ready in her hand.

He carried her to the mouth of the cave and kissed her again. They did not speak for a long time as they sat there close together, the wind whispering softly down the canyon.

"I will be back, lass," he said at last.

She clung to him and rested her head against his shoulder.

"Ye are a soldier's daughter. Ye must know that I have to go, Ellen. It is my duty."

"Yes."

He kissed her and drew her tightly to him, and his hands felt the softness of her. Then he stood up and reached for his weapons.

"Look, Dan," she said.

He turned. There was a faint suspicion of soft silver light against the eastern sky, above the notched rimrock of the canyon. He could not leave her now; not for some hours; not until the moonlight was gone. He walked to her and drew her close.

They lay down upon the blankets and watched the silvery glory of the new moon as it rose. They talked in low voices, and Dan Gallagher knew he was deeply in love with her.

The moon traveled swiftly, it seemed to Dan, and when the cave mouth was in thick shadowy darkness he knew it would not be long before he would have to leave her. By the time he found his way out of the canyon the moon would be gone and he could travel in the darkness.

But her arms would not release him, and he felt a powerful surging within him. He had not been with a woman for a long time, far too long to be tempted like this, and she did not resist when his hands became more intimate. At last there came a time when both of them knew there could hardly be a turning back.

There was no need to talk. She was there for the taking, and he knew she would not resist. He hovered on the verge, covering her face with kisses while he fumbled with her clothing. Then he noticed that her face was wet with her tears as well as with his kisses.

"What is it, Ellen?" he asked.

She drew herself closer to him and clung to him tightly. "Ellen?"

"Go on, Dan," she said almost fiercely.

He started again, and then he stopped. He rolled back a little and looked down at the dim loveliness of her oval face. She was ready for him, she would not resist, but something held him back. He suddenly knew why she would let him take her. He mentally tore himself away from her, kissed her gently, then stood up.

"Dan?"

"Yes?"

She hesitated. "Don't you *want* me?"

"Aye! With all my heart."

"Then?"

He gathered his gear and walked to the mouth of the cave. He stood there for a few minutes looking out in the moving shadows. He could hear her irregular breathing. She would have given herself to him because she thought she'd never see him again. But why? Because he was a man going to his death and she was sorry for him? Because she loved him and wanted a last eternal memory of him?

"Dan," she said tenderly.

He turned and walked to her. She was sitting up. He took her face in one great hand and raised it, kissing her gently, without the hot passion of before, and she knew by this token that his love for her was far deeper than even she had realized.

He walked quickly to the mouth of the cave and looked back. "Thanks," he said quietly.

"For what, Dan?"

"For ye. For yer love. For my being a man and ye being a woman. I will be back, Ellen. Nothing can stop me.

It is then that we'll know a love greater than this we know now. Goodbye, love."

Then he was gone, with hardly a sound of his passing, and she was alone, yet not alone in the darkness. For wherever she would be, and whatever might happen, she loved Dan Gallagher and knew she was loved by him. Nothing else quite seemed to matter anymore.

►► *Chapter* 11

FORT Coulter, or what was left of it, was now garrisoned by the bat, the owl, the mouse, and the rattlesnake.
The thought was Dan Gallagher's as he lay on his lean
belly and studied the ruins through the captain's field
glasses. The fine German lens seemed to draw the buildings in close, sharp and clear, under the bright morning
sun. There wasn't a sign of life about the place.

Tumbleweeds were stacked in windrows against walls
and in the corrals. The flagpole had been shattered and
riven and now lay across the parade ground. Even the
post cemetery had not been spared. The mounds had
been lowered by the keening winds and the headboards
driven aslant and weathered by wind and pelting rain.

Gallagher lowered the glasses. Somewhere about that
post, certainly not *in* it, would be the weapons and
supplies, if they had not been moved elsewhere. He rested
his chin on his folded arms and studied the terrain. The
rutted wagon road ran northeast, trending to Gallagher's
left and by-passing the great canyon he had left the night
before. To south, west, and east were rugged hills, masses
of decomposing rock, stippled with scrub trees and thorny
vegetation. In the whole area there was hardly enough
water to wet a cricket's throstle.

Gallagher rubbed his whiskered jaws. Now that he was
here he really didn't know where to start looking, but he
had to start, that was sure. He walked back to the tired
bay and led him down into an arroyo, where, after a
watering, he picketed him. Gallagher took carbine, field
glasses, and a canteen, then left the bay. Shannon *might*
be there when he got back.

He worked his way through the draws and arroyos,
looking for telltale signs, but found nothing of value.

He circled the entire post. Nothing. He did not want to enter the fort proper, but it had to be done. Artenis would hardly have been able to conceal the small arms, the six howitzers, and the mass of equipment within the post, but Gallagher had to see for sure.

He poked about in the buildings. They had done a good job when they had left the post. A great mass of ashes, humped with blackened iron and charred wood, lay in the middle of the parade ground. The dispensary was a stinking depository of broken medicine bottles and pots of lotion mingled with dirty bandages and other hospital items.

There was nothing of value on the post. Wanderers had conceded that fact in past months, leaving as proof of their disappointment piles of human fecal matter within the buildings.

Gallagher walked to the eastern edge of the post proper and looked toward the hills. There wasn't any place in the open where the materials could have been hidden. They must be in the hills, but that would have been dangerous, because the Tontos would have seen such activities.

Gallagher squatted and balanced on his heels. A lone hawk hung in the sky. Dotted against the sharp clear blue of the sky were small clouds, and their shadows raced across the open country ahead of them in a race that was never won and never lost.

Gallagher leaned back against the building with his carbine across his thighs. He drove the thought of Ellen from his mind. He was worried about her, but his mission came first. The sooner he accomplished it the sooner he would be able to return for her. What would happen then was in the hands of the fates.

Where in God's name could that slinking bastard Artenis have hidden those weapons and supplies? A man could spend a lifetime looking through those hills if the Apaches let him live that long.

What had Artenis said? "We can use you, Gallagher. We must pass through the country of Klij-Litzogue to get those weapons and munitions. You can guide us. You are the only man who can guide us. What do you say?"

The country of Klij-Litzogue. What had he meant by that? The whole Diablo country was the country of Klij-Litzogue. Only Fort Coulter had held him in check. The country of Klij-Litzogue. Miles and miles of rugged hills and tangled canyons, fanged mountains and barren deserts. Then Gallagher slapped his hands against the sides of his head. "Jesus God!" he said hoarsely. There was only one place those weapons would have been safe other than on a military post. *Canyon Encantado!*

Klij-Litzogue would not dare enter the canyon, but the Texas mounted rifles would, if they had managed to pass through Apache country safely. That was why Artenis had wanted Gallagher to throw in his lot with the Confederacy.

Gallagher left the fort and hurried to Shannon. He cursed himself as he pulled out the picket pin. Ellen was safe enough from the Apaches as long as she stayed in the canyon; even if the rebels found her in there Gallagher did not fear for her. But if they tried to get out of that canyon under the very noses of Klij-Litzogue and his warriors they wouldn't have a chance. If Gallagher got there in time he could guide them out of the Apache country, but he'd be damned if he'd help the rebels get out of there safely with enough weapons and munitions to sway the balance between victory and defeat for the Union on the deserts of the Southwest.

He led the bay along the arroyo, hoping to God the Apaches would not spot him before dusk. He wanted to wait until darkness; every fiber in him warned him that that was the safest course, but the black dog was upon his back and would stay there until he reached Canyon Encantado.

The moon was not up yet. Gallagher stood poised at the brink of the great darkness-filled trough of the canyon. He tested the night with his senses. There had been no sign of the Apaches as he had crossed the country to get to the canyon. Maybe they were watching the Texas mounted rifles. He grinned at the thought. What a game they were all playing in that country! It reminded him of the fights they used to have in the barracks to while away the boredom and loneliness of outpost forts. They would snuff out the lights, and each man would strike out at anyone he could hit, noncom or private, big or little, friend or enemy. There was one big difference between those fights and the one that was coming up in Canyon Encantado. This one would be to the death. Three parties feeling for each other in the darkness and the loneliness.

The rebels wanted the weapons before Gallagher could get to them. Gallagher wanted to destroy them before the rebels got them. The Apaches wanted the weapons and the horses of the Texans, and they wanted the heart's blood of Daniel Timothy Gallagher. It might yet end up in a bloodletting merry-go-round.

The moonlight touched the eastern sky with a faint promise of light to come. Gallagher looked back over his shoulder. The wind whispered through the brush. Shannon nickered softly. Gallagher closed a hand on the bay's windpipe. There was something back there in the black velvet of the night.

He led the bay slowly forward. He had cased the bay's hoofs in leather and cloth. Gallagher felt for the faint trail he had found the night before. It was pitch black beneath him. Thank God he could not see over the brink, for he knew he could not march that thread of trail if he could see what was below him.

He eased his way down on to the trail like a cautious bather wading into icy water. He was fifty feet down the dangerous way when he felt that something, or someone, was standing at the head of the trail. He looked back past the horse and for a long moment or two thought it was a boulder or perhaps some form of vegetation about the height of a man. Then he remembered there had been nothing like that when he had been up there.

He continued downward, feeling his way, his thudding heart seemingly trying to leap out of his chest. Now and then he heard the harsh pattering of gravel and small stones dropping from the brink of the trail. He looked back again—the dim something up there seemed to have grown. In the faint promise of the moonlight to come he could see the thick manes of hair and the broad deep chest and shoulders of the mountain people. But they would not follow him down. Was it because of the danger? Or because they feared ambush? Or because the dark trough below him was actually the taboo Canyon En-cantado?

Gallagher went on. He heard a distant scuffling sound, and something struck the trail twenty feet behind the horse. The bay reared, and Gallagher fought him, drag-ging his head down with the bridle reins. "Aisy, boyo!" he pleaded.

Something struck far below him, then again and again. He knew what it was: they were rolling rocks over the brink. The rocks could go where the Tontos did not dare to go. The cold sweat poured down Gallagher's sides, and for a moment blind panic seized him, urging him to plunge down that trail which would lead him straight to hell the hard way.

The rocks seemed to pour down upon the trail, striking hard, bounding off into space, then striking again and again to shatter the decomposing rock of the canyon slopes below.

A shard struck the bay, and he whinnied sharply.

"For God's sake, Shannon!" cried Gallagher.

A rock struck just ahead of Gallagher, and fragments of it struck him like a dose of canister. He staggered with the impact. Another rock struck beside the bay. Shannon surged forward, driving Gallagher to one side, pinning him against the canyon wall. Then the bay was gone, thudding down the trail while Gallagher stood there pressed against the wall listening to the devil's cannonade of rocks crash-ing and splintering, bounding and rolling, awakening the canyon echoes, slamming them back and forth be-tween the walls. Gallagher closed his eyes and for the first time since he had been a boy in Ireland he prayed with all his heart and soul.

There was no sound from the bay. Dead, perhaps, or

lying with splintered ivory bones protruding through his bleeding hide.

Gallagher at last inched his way down, with the dust of the trail coating his face and drying up his throat and nostrils. Then he was at the bottom, and the rocks were dropping farther and farther away as the Tontos moved in the opposite direction.

Shannon nickered from the darkness. Gallagher walked to him, gripped him about the neck, and buried his face in the mane. He stood there for several minutes while the sweat ran down his body and soaked his dirty trail clothing.

He led the bay toward the cave area. The moon was lighting the western wall of the canyon, but the very bottom of it was thick in whispering darkness. An uneasy feeling crept over him. There was no sound from the Tontos.

He tethered the bay to a shrubby growth, then took his carbine and lowered the breech to remove the cartridge in the chamber. He thrust in a fresh cartridge, closed the breach to shear off the end of the round, then half cocked the hammer and placed a cap on the nipple.

He walked softly up the rough talus slope toward the cave. The moonlight was already bathing the rock wall above it, although the mouth of the cave was hardly more than a darker patch against the shadowed wall. He looked back. The canyon was quiet except for the ceaseless rushing of the wind.

He reached the wall and stood there listening. Nothing. Gallagher walked softly toward the cave mouth and waited again. There was no sound or sight of the girl. He walked to the entrance and whistled softly the dragoon song. She must be sleeping soundly.

He walked into the cave and leaned his head forward, trying to probe through the darkness. Ellen," he said softly.

"Ellen?"

A mouse or some other small creature scurried for cover over his feet.

"Ellen?"

Nothing.

Gallagher walked to the rear of the cave, past the turn in the wall. The place was as empty as last night's whiskey bottle.

Maybe she was playing with him.

"Ellen!"

There was nothing but the soft rushing of the wind past the cave entrance.

It was the same in the area outside of the cave. The Apache horse was gone, too. Everything was gone except the sweet memory of her and of how she had lain in his arms the night he had left, willing to let him have her body as well as her soul.

He cursed himself blackly with all the inborn skill of an imaginative race for having left her there at all.

THE GREAT canyon was silver bright with cold moon-light which etched trees, brush, and boulders against the ground and the walls of the canyon. The cold waters of the stream rushed swiftly along, murmuring between the grassy banks. The wind swayed the tall trees of the thick bosque that blocked off the right-hand branch of the canyon.

Gallagher picketed the bay, then waded across the stream, hardly feeling the numbing effect of the cold water, with his eyes on that dark bosque. He walked slowly toward it, Sharps at hip level, full-cocked, finger drawing up trigger slack.

He stopped in the thick shadows of the first trees to look and listen. The place was quiet and peaceful, but to him there was a brooding quality about it.

He passed quickly through the wood and reached the far side, stopping while still within the shelter of the trees to look out upon the more open reaches of the branch canyon. Then he caught the faint bittersweet odor of woodsmoke. He looked to his left, up a long gradual sloping of the canyon floor, and his eyes widened as his jaw dropped.

There were several buildings on a broad rock shelf that overlooked the lower portions of the canyon. Smoke drifted lazily up from a chimney at one end of the biggest structure. Water flowed from a large square opening at the floor level of the west building and poured into a rock-walled pool, then overflowed to follow a narrow rock channel down toward the stream at the bottom of the canyon.

The main building was made of great hewn stones, neatly mortared together. There were a few small, secretive windows on the ground-floor level of the two-story house, and between the windows were loopholes. When Gallagher focused the captain's glasses on the scene he saw that the main building was actually two similar structures about fifty or sixty feet apart, connected by a two-story wall which formed a courtyard between the buildings. A great bolt-studded gate was set in the wall closest to Dan.

The place was like a small fort, much like some of the old fortifications in Dan's native Ireland. There were outbuildings, too, placed against a high rock ledge. Corrals were evident beyond this ledge.

High above the main building was a great crescent opening in the live rock of the canyon wall, and he could see a fine example of cliff dwellings placed within the shelter of the huge opening, with dark smoke stains showing clearly against the salmon-colored rock. A thread-like trail which seemed to hang against the side of the canyon wall made its way up to a wide terrace in front of the pile of cliff dwellings.

Gallagher looked away; no one had lived in them for hundreds of years. The other place was different. It looked deserted, but there was that smoke rising from the chimney. Was it possible that the place had been recently abandoned? All of Arizona was in the grip of a cold fear now that the troops had left. The people had either fled to California or to New Mexico. But someone had built a fire in that building.

A cold feeling crept over Gallagher. Stories of haunted canyons and ruins eased insidiously into his teeming mind, and the Celtic superstition of the man began to take hold. It was a curse, and one who is not of that talented yet infinitely superstitious race can ever know what the fertile imagination of such a people can bring to life.

He waited a long time, knowing that the moon soon would be on the wane, leaving him alone in the darkness with that cold-looking mysterious block of buildings. But she might be in there, or whoever lived there might know where she was. One thing was certain: Apaches would not be in the buildings.

Gallagher stood up and cased the field glasses. He took the carbine and worked his way up the slope within the cover of the woods until he stood about a hundred yards opposite the big gateway. He was now impressed not only with the layout of the place and the excellent manner of its construction but with its great potentialities. A man could live like a feudal baron there. There was everything in plenty—water, fish, grazing, shelter from the heat of summer and the cold winds of winter, timber, and plenty of game.

He eyed the tiny windows and the slitted loopholes. Nothing. Even the mysterious smoke had vanished. The moon now slanted its cold rays down upon the western face of the building next to the wide pond. Gallagher wet his lips. He suddenly looked quickly behind him. The long forgotten lines of "The Ancient Mariner" came drifting silently and quickly into his mind to plague him.

> ". . . walks on,
> And turns no more his head:
> Because he knows a frightful fiend
> Doth close behind him tread."

Gallagher cast the gruesome thought from his mind. "Get on with it, boyo!" he said sharply to himself.

He walked out into the clear moonlight toward the gate. The big man had a set look on his hard Irish face and the glinting of ice in his blue eyes. The crunching of his feet on the hard earth and the sound of his breathing seemed abnormally loud to him, as though he could easily be heard within those walls. *But by whom?*

There was a small doorway cut into the right-hand side of the huge gate. Gallagher stopped and stretched out a hand to try it. It swung open easily at his touch. He hesitated, then quickly stepped inside, swinging head and carbine muzzle from side to side, ready to fire in a split second. There was nothing to fire at. He stood at one end of a deep-walled courtyard between the two massive buildings. Roofed porches ran the entire length of the second floor of each building. Small paned windows looked out upon the porches.

The ground of the courtyard seemed as hard as stone. A huge soap-rendering kettle stood on a stone fireplace. A wagon had been drawn into the yard. The bed had been removed and a number of heavy logs slung to the frame of the running gear. Here and there tools were stored in racks; harness hung from pegs driven into crevices in the stone walls. At the far end, in a corner, a small smithy had been fitted out complete with tools.

Gallagher looked uneasily about him. It was the second time since he had left Fort McComber that he had stumbled onto a place such as this. But there had been dead bodies at Dunlap's place, along with the very live body of the woman Gallagher had grown to love. Here there was nothing but soft furtive echoes.

He looked up over his head. A sentry walk ran from one building to the other just over the gateway, with the top of the wall acting as a solid breastwork. Another such walk ran across the far end of the courtyard. Gallagher nodded in appreciation. Whoever had built this place in remote Canyon Encantado had built a small citadel, ready for a long stay.

He padded forward and stopped in the middle of the courtyard. The place was as quiet as a tomb. He shook his head and walked back toward the little gate. Gallagher poked his head outside and looked about. He wanted no one walking up behind him. He stepped outside and walked a short distance from the wall. It was as deserted out there as it had been when he had reached the buildings.

Gallagher shrugged. He had to go through those buildings, much as he hated the very thought of it. *She* might be in there.

He stepped inside the courtyard and advanced a few feet. The door closed quickly behind him. He whirled. There was no one there. Then he looked up. He saw four bearded men, two on each opposite porch, with rifles in their hands and cold menace in their eyes. They did not speak. For one awful moment Gallagher thought they might be ghosts. Then one of them laughed; laughed right in Gallagher's staring face. Somehing landed hard against his skull, just behind his left ear, and as he felt his carbine fall from his hands and as the ground rushed up at him with incredible swiftness he heard all of them laugh.

Water splashed against Gallagher's face. He opened his eyes to look up into the hard face of a young man. "You weren't hit that hard, bucko," he said with a grin.

Gallagher felt the egg behind his ear and withdrew his hand to look at the blood upon his fingers. "It was me that was hit, not you, boyo," he said sourly.

"Get up. The boss wants to see you."

"Who's the boss?"

"You'll see. Now get up!"

Gallagher got dizzily to his feet. A man stood on the sentry walk over the gateway through which Gallagher had entered. The wind ruffled his beard, and the moonlight glinted from the polished barrel of his rifle.

They had stripped Gallagher of his weapons. He shook his head. He had walked neatly into this mess. Rebels probably, he thought as he walked toward a door indicated by his guard.

The guard opened the door and spoke close to Gallagher's ear. "Don't get any ideas, soldier. We've got enough men to take you apart piece by piece."

"So?"

"*So!*"

"Go . . ." breathed Gallagher.

"Like all the Irish you talk a good fight," said the man as he closed the door behind them.

Gallagher turned slowly, and there was pure cold hell in his eyes. "Maybe ye'd like to try me, boyo?" he asked thinly, and his accent was as thick as porridge.

"Get on with you!" said his guard. "Walk or be driven!"

Gallagher felt a pistol muzzle against one of his kidneys. He walked.

He opened another door at a command from the guard and stepped down into a big room ceiled by huge handhewn beams. A fire had been blazing in the massive fireplace, but now had died to a thick bed of ashes from which a ruby ember eye peered now and then. The room was comfortably warm. A man sat in a chair near the fire with his big veined hands resting on his thighs. His eyes held Gallagher's. There was a cold look about the man despite the warmth of the room. His eyes were cold, his beard was gray, and his thick hair was heavily shot with gray. There was a cold grayness about the man, thought Gallagher, the cold grayness of death. The eyes seemed to clash against Gallagher's as though the man were trying to force his will upon him.

"It was easy, Elijah," said the young man behind Gallagher. "He walked into the trap like a schoolboy." He laughed.

Then Gallagher knew who the man was. It was Elijah Darris, the man who had used the name Dunlap with Ellen. Elijah Darris . . . jackleg preacher, member of some obscure and unsanctified religious sect of strange and outlawed practices, a middle-aged lecher with perverted tastes.

"You know me?" asked Darris.

Gallagher was startled. It was almost as though the man had read his mind. "No," he said quietly.

"You're lying."

"Who . . . me? Ye mistake me."

"I'm Elijah Darris."

"So?"

"You've heard of me?"

"Can't say that I have."

"You're lying again."

Gallagher shrugged. The man seemed a little mad, perhaps insane. From what Gallagher had heard of him it was quite possible that he was mad.

"Who are you?"

"First Sergeant Daniel Gallagher, Provisional Company A, First United States Dragoons, although they call us cavalry now, but I . . ."

"Shut up."

Gallagher reddened and closed his big hands, but the

pistol nuzzled his back like a bloodthirsty kitten snuggled close.

"What are you doing in my country?"

"Yer country?" The pistol muzzle jambed Gallagher's kidneys. He winced. "I'm on me way to California."

"On what business?"

"Why, on me own business! I'm to report to the nearest military post there. Fort Yuma, it would be." Gallagher smiled. "That was the last orders of me commanding officer."

"Where is he?"

"He died."

"And the rest of his command?"

"They will be along soon."

"He's lying again, Elijah," said the man behind Gallagher. "He came into the canyon with the woman, and the Tontos were breathing down their necks. There are no United States troops within hundreds of miles of here. They've all pulled out of Arizona."

Gallagher nodded. They knew as much as he did . . . perhaps more than he did. If they had been watching him all that time they were as good as Apaches, maybe better, for he had never seen them.

"Why did you leave the woman behind?"

Then Gallagher knew they had found her. "I could not take her with me."

"You deserted her?"

"I . . ."

Elijah cut him short with a wave of his left hand.

Gallagher stepped forward. "If ye have the woman ye must turn her over to me for safe conduct to Fort Yuma."

Elijah yawned. "How was Fort Coulter?" he asked.

Gallagher half closed his eyes. He felt like a child in front of this man.

"You might have known there would be no weapons and munitions left there, Sergeant."

"So? Then ye know where they are?"

Darris nodded. "They are safe in my keeping."

"They are the property of the United States. Those supplies must be turned over to me."

"So? Your uniform and stripes do not give you authority over Elijah Darris, Sergeant."

"I can place this area under martial law," bluffed Gallagher.

A cold smile fled across the bearded face. "No . . . you can't. You and your country have no authority here."

"This is part of the United States."

Again the frigid smile. "The United States? They have no authority over a domain they cannot hold. Where are your soldiers, Sergeant Gallagher? Where is your flag?" A thickly veined hand passed back and forth as though brushing away everything he had mentioned. "Gone like an evil stench!"

Gallagher tilted his head to one side. "Ye think so? What are ye then? Mormons?"

"No."

"Rebels?"

"No."

"*Then who are ye?*"

"I am Elijah Darris!" The fanatic looked at Gallagher as though his short statement would explain everything.

Gallagher wet his lips. The pistol was not against his back, but he could almost feel it. "Ye have the woman here?"

"Yes."

"And her sister Judith?"

There was a queer look in the piercing eyes. "She is here, too."

"Ye took her from the station before Klij-Litzogue struck it?"

"Yes."

"And the other sister?"

There was a strange look on the bearded face. "She would not come peacefully with me."

"Did she die by her own hand or the hand of the Apaches?"

"No, Sergeant."

The answer struck Gallagher like a gun-butt blow. He stared at Elijah Darris, the man who had brutally killed a beautiful young woman because she would not accompany him.

"You understand, Sergeant?"

"Ye filthy woman-chasing lecher!"

Darris stood up. "Get out of here! Your time will come, and the way of your death will not be pleasant. Klij-Litzogue will give much to get his hands on you."

Gallagher froze. He remembered now that Elijah Darris had been known to deal with Klij-Litzogue.

Darris smiled thinly. "It frightens you, doesn't it, Sergeant Gallagher?"

Gallagher did not answer. The man was right. Gallagher felt panic rise in his gorge. He left the room with the guard behind him, who locked him into a small room with a tiny window that looked out upon the pond.

He lay down upon a cot. He was bone-weary. He'd never leave the canyon alive unless it was to be delivered to Klij-Litzogue like a steer for bloody slaughter. But there was a greater sickness underlying even that thought. The idea of Ellen Eustis being a captive in this outpost of hell, a helpless victim of Elijah Darris and his strange lusts, filled him with terror and anguish.

▶▶ *Chapter* 13

THE GREAT house was quiet. It was deepest night, perhaps getting on toward dawn. Gallagher got up off his cot and walked to the door. The wind scrabbled along the eaves and rattled a shutter somewhere. Gallagher reached down for his left shoe and took it off. He bent the sole into an arc and worked the shoe back and forth until the built-in steel brace worked out of the leather. It was good spring steel. He got down on his knees and listened. Not a sound came from the corridor. They would not have left a guard. The walls of the room were thick and strong, and the window was too small.

Gallagher worked silently and patiently, probing into the guts of the door lock with the steel. An hour went past before the end of the piece of steel caught hard on something. He eased the end of it down. There was a dull click. The door opened silently in his grasp.

He stepped into the corridor and took off his other shoe. He tied the shoes together by their laces and hung them about his neck. Gallagher padded to the door which led into the great room where he had first talked to the madman. He padded about looking for a weapon, but there was none to be found.

He crossed the long dining room and tried the next door. It opened into a low-ceilinged kitchen equipped with a great fireplace and several stoves. He armed himself with a heavy-bladed knife, then went back through the rooms to his cell. He rolled the blankets to make it look as though he was asleep, then left the room to work his way down to the end of the corridor.

He eased the door open and looked out into the moonlit courtyard. It was empty of human life, but a fire still glowed in the forge. He was sheltered beneath the second-floor porch. Then he heard the steady thudding of feet on the sentry walk over the north gate, and he knew he'd be spotted as soon as he stepped out into the bright moonlight.

There was another door behind him. He opened it and stepped down into a low-ceilinged room which was damp and smelled like a dairy. He heard the noise of moving water. Moonlight streamed through the loopholes, and he saw that the spring that fed the pond and channel in front of the west building actually started from underneath the house.

He shook his head. They had thought of everything. No Apaches or troops, unless equipped with artillery, could ever take the place by attack or siege. He'd be willing to bet on the deadly marksmanship of those cold-eyed bearded men.

He could see a hint of moonlight on the water at the west end of the stone trough through which the spring flowed to the outside of the house. The water was like the overflow from a glacier, so icy it was. But it was the only way he could get out of his prison.

He took a deep breath, rolled his big body into the trough, and felt his breath leave him as the water closed about his body. He worked his way along the trough until his head stuck out into the moonlight and he saw the flat surface of the pond shining in the light. He pulled himself forward and went head and shoulders down into the pool. It was like bathing in a tub of ice cakes.

He forced himself to swim silently underwater to the far side of the pool, then crawled out on the bank beneath low overhanging trees. He shivered until he could have sworn the sentry could hear his teeth chattering.

The canyon was quiet and still. The wind had died away. Gallagher worked his way through the trees to the south end of the buildings, passed the end of the pond, and flattened himself against the building. The steady tread of a sentry sounded on one of the walks within the courtyard. He bellied along a ledge, then through thick brush until he reached a low line of buildings, where he stopped to look and listen. He had no idea how many

men were in the buildings. He was pretty sure how many'
women were in them, though. Two: Ellen and Judith
Eustis.

Gallagher studied the lay of the land. The easternmost house had been built on the hill slope, so the rear
of the first floor was below ground and the second floor
was at ground level. He could see a doorway at the south
end of the second floor. He crawled through the brush.
The windows were all heavily shuttered. He could go
neither north or south without the likelihood of being seen
by guards at either end of the courtyard.

He reached the side the house and looked up at the
low eaves. He stood up, gripped the edge, then swung
himself up easily to lie flat on the roof. He moved slowly
up to the ridge of the roof and peered down into the
courtyard from the shelter of one of the large chimneys.
He waited until he could see both sentries to make sure
they were still at their posts, then slid down the roof,
dropped lightly to the ground, and flattened himself
against the wall. He edged toward the door, tried it, found
it locked.

Gallagher worked his way through the brush to the far
end of the low buildings. He walked into the shelter of
some trees growing in a low place that led to the stream.
He stopped on the bank and suddenly remembered Shannon. He looked up toward the buildings. They could see
him if he crossed from his shelter to the big bosque that
closed the way to the other branch of the canyon. There
was nothing else to do but to swim that frigid stream.
He went right in, waded for a moment, then swam with
a slow easy breath stroke to the far bank. His teeth were
chattering loudly enough to alert everyone in those moonlit buildings on the slope. Gallagher walked quickly into
the trees and struck out for the ford where he had left
Shannon.

The great bay was gone, as Gallagher had expected. He
squatted in the shelter of a boulder. They would know he
had escaped when morning came. They'd beat the bloody
canyon for him. He knew too much now for them to let
him get away. But it was a long time until daylight.

Gallagher set off with long swinging strides. He passed through the bosque and the trees that thickly lined the side of the stream opposite the buildings. Then he reached an area where the stream wound in great loops across flat lands, thickly stippled with brush and scrub trees. He could see the wide mouth of the canyon when he caught the pungent odor of burning mesquite wood. It was certainly an easier way to enter the canyon than the ones he had used.

Gallagher worked his way through the trees like a wraith while the odor of the smoke grew ever stronger. When he saw the huddled figures lying on the ground on the far bank of the stream his blood seemed to congeal. Apaches! A lot of them. Gallagher softly hit the ground and lay on his belly eying the camp. He needed weapons, and they had weapons. There were at least a score of them, however, and few white men could creep up on a camp of these warriors without being discovered.

He was damned if he did and damned if didn't. There wasn't any doubt in his mind that Darris was in close accord with Klij-Litzogue. For Gallagher it was either be caught by Darris to be turned over to Klij-Litzogue, or be caught by the Tonto himself. There was a third alternative. Gallagher could run, strike out for Fort Yuma on his lonesome and to hell with everything.

He rested his tired head on his arms. The mission had not been accomplished. Ellen Eustis had been lost to him and was now in the hands of Darris. To go back was to face such odds that his chances of succeeding were hardly worth thinking about.

The low voice seemed to come from the ground, then from the air, and Gallagher raised his head to listen while the cold sweat burst out upon his body. *"The company has been assigned a dangerous mission . . . most likely a hopeless one . . . but we will obey those orders to the letter . . . if there is one man left, and one only, that man will return the guidon to the regiment . . . but only when the mission has been completed successfully, Sergeant Gallagher!"*

"Yes, sir," he said softly.

There was another voice, that of a woman, the woman he loved. *"Don't you want me?"*

Gallagher's mind reeled. He looked into the sky and caught the first rays of the false dawn. Now there was only one course for him to take. He staggered off into the brush to find a hiding place before the sun came up. He wasn't worried about the Tontos, as long as he kept within the bounds of the forbidden canyon. But Darris and his men would surely be combing the area for him once his escape was discovered.

There was another voice, that of a woman, the woman beloved. "Don't you hear me?"
Gallagher stirred and raised. He looked into the sky and beyond ... into ... into ... drum ... drum ... drum ...

▶▶ *Chapter* 14

IT WAS morning. Gallagher opened his eyes and looked down into the canyon. The stream rushed along far below his position. The ledge he lay upon was hardly wide enough for a man of his build, but he felt safer up there.

He could see the Apache camp. Gallagher shivered at the thought of what Yellow Snake would do to him if he caught him.

But the big, bone-weary, dirty-faced redheaded dragoon was too stupid to quit trying to represent the entire United States Army west of the Rio Grande and east of the Colorado.

A gecko lizard eyed Gallagher brightly as the sun arose. "Are ye fat enough for a meal?" asked Gallagher. The lizard knew when it was in trouble. It vanished into a cleft.

It was then that he saw the horsemen riding down the canyon. There were four of them. White men. The last man of the quartet led a heavily laden pack mule. The eyes of the men constantly scanned the canyon walls and the area beyond the stream. Gallagher knew well enough who they were looking for. He crouched down. His red head would be like a flame in the bright morning sunlight.

They reached the place where the invisible boundary line stretched across the canyon; the taboo line. There they stopped and waited. Some of them lighted pipes and smoked as they waited. The bluish tobacco smoke rose in the windless air.

Klij-Litzogue came through the brush with some of his warriors, and they stopped fifty feet from the waiting white men. During the next half hour one of the white men and the Tonto chief carried on a conversation, principally in sign language. At last the pack mule was brought forward and unloaded, the contents of the packs being laid out on a flat slab of rock. Gallagher whistled softly. Carbines and ammunition boxes, and he was willing to bet he knew well enough the place they had originally come from.

The white men rode back up the canyon as the sunlight began to fill it. The Tontos were examining the fine weapons. Suddenly Yellow Snake raised one and fired it. The report echoed flatly down the canyon, and the slug slapped against a rock not two feet from Gallagher's head. Gallagher winced as tiny shards of lead and rock struck his face. It was a good five minutes before he realized that the Tonto had just fired the carbine at random to try it out, not to plant a slug between Gallagher's bloodshot eyes.

The Tontos carried the weapons and ammunition back to their camp, where the smoke of the cooking fires was now rising straight in the air. They had the canyon corked as far as Gallagher was concerned.

He had other ideas.

When the long day had crept past and the walls of the canyon were thick with shadows he crawled stiffly from his eyrie and headed toward the stream. He lay beside the stream for a long time, alternately sousing his head and drinking deeply of the pure cold water.

The wind was cold when he started up the canyon. He had no fear of the Tontos as long as he stayed within the invisible taboo boundaries, but the men at the buildings were quite another matter. They were potentially as dangerous and a great deal more shrewd. They knew he had little chance of getting past the Tontos. They also knew what he needed no matter what he decided to do. He needed food and weapons first. He needed a horse. He might steal a horse and even some weapons, but in order to accomplish his mission he had to find those weapons. The weapons and the women would be bait enough for Gallagher.

He could see the buildings plainly. There were horses and mules in the corrals. Smoke rose from a chimney.

The dying sun glinted dully on the barrel of a sentry's rifle. Shannon was in the corral, too. There was no mistaking the big bay. There was something else in the corral, lying in the mud and filth in one corner, the once bright colors stained and dull. It was the guidon. "Ye dirty bastards," said Gallagher. He shook a fist at the buildings. "I'll wipe the dung from it on yer faces," he promised.

He crawled through the woods until he could see the foot of the trail which climbed the canyon wall behind the buildings to the cliff dwellings. The place looked peaceful enough, like a country holding in his native Ireland, but to Gallagher there was an aura of obscene evil about it. These men owed no allegiance to their country; they traded weapons to Apaches; they would hold a woman against her will.

It was dark in the canyon when he reached the top of the trail. Yellow light shown from the loopholes and small windows of the buildings far below him. The noise of the stream came to him, and now and then he thought he heard voices, but he was not sure.

The cliff dwellings had been neatly tucked into the great arched opening in the live rock of the canyon wall. It was a far greater ruin than Gallagher had realized. There were several towers, some of them three stories high. Row after row of one-room houses extended the full length of the area, with their tiny windows and distinctive T-shaped doorways. Here and there along the terraced front of the building area he could see the openings that led down into the rounded chambers beneath the ground, with crude ladders protruding from the holes.

The moon had begun to flood the canyon with light. Some of the buildings had collapsed into mounds of adobe and rock from which shattered wooden beams and poles protruded. Most of the other rooms were empty except for smashed pottery, dried bones, and animal droppings.

He entered the ground floor of the tower at the end of the row of dwellings and ascended a thick log that had been notched like a chicken ladder. From the top story he had a fine view of the buildings below, the canyon, and the moonlit stream. There was a second row of buildings behind the first. He descended the ladder and began to look through the rest of the rooms. The moon shown down on the terrace almost as brightly as though it was daylight.

He was at the end of the row, and there was only one big dwelling left to explore. His heart was sick within him. He had been so damned sure the weapons would be stored in the dwellings. He looked into the room. The back wall seemed to be of better construction than any of the other rooms he had been in. The stones were larger, better shaped, and more evenly laid. It wasn't until he was closer to them that he realized his search was over.

They were not stones at all but rather large wooden boxes of a type he knew well. He undid the thumbscrews of the first box and whistled softly when he raised the lid. The bellies of four carbines were there, neatly nested in wooden supports, with the metal covered with grease. They were slant-breeched Sharps carbines, with patch boxes and Maynard tape primers, Caliber .52. "Model 1855," said Gallagher. They looked as though they had never been used.

He looked along the rows of boxes. They were all the same. Beyond the row of carbine boxes were piles of ammunition boxes, several cases of single-shot and revolving pistols, sabers and scabbards, bayonets, boxes of caps, as well as other impedimenta and accessories.

Beyond was another room, the back wall of which was formed by the slanted roof of the cave. Here were racks of Springfield .58 caliber rifles. Gallagher peered through a door on the right. He whistled again, this time louder. Six brass mountain howitzers stood wheel to wheel, with their caissons behind them. Piled against the walls were rammers, buckets, cases of powder charges, rounds of shot, canister and grape, boxes of friction primer tubes, and all the odds and ends necessary to service and fire the stout little pieces.

There was enough armament in the dwellings to arm a flying column, and arm them as well as any United States troops at Fort Yuma—or anywhere else in California short of the forts along the seacoast. With this stolen equipment the rebels had a good chance to accomplish their mission to take the Pacific coast.

Gallagher walked to the terrace and looked down upon the other buildings. What game was Darris up to? He recognized no authority, neither of the United States nor of the Confederacy, and he dealt openly with the Tontos. But the equipment he held belonged to the United States of America, and the United States Army was the only organization that was entitled to use those weapons, *or to destroy them if need be.* The destruction would be undertaken by First Sergeant Daniel Timothy Gallagher, Provisional Company A, First United States Dragoons.

He needed to arm himself before he started his work. So he would draw his weapons from the U. S. property in the dwellings. He walked into the first of the rooms and opened a box of Colt revolving pistols. He was wiping the grease from one of them when he heard the quiet voice behind him.

"Darris is waiting to see you, soldier. Just drop the pistol like a good boy and turn around with your hands in the air." The words were followed by the greasy sounding click-cluck of a gun hammer being cocked close behind Gallagher's back.

Elijah Darris was seated in his big chair, his veined hands resting on his muscular thighs. His cold gray eyes fixed themselves upon Gallagher and sent an eerie crawling sensation along his spine.

"Did you really think you could escape, Sergeant?" asked Darris at last.

"It was worth a try."

"Very clever. But the Apaches drove you back, eh?"

Gallagher could not but help grin at the memory. "I did a little drivin' meself, old whiskers."

A carbine barrel struck him alongside the neck. Gallagher winced with the blow. "Ye scut," he said in a low voice.

Darris leaned back in his chair. "You are getting to be a problem to us," he said quietly.

"You can always let me go."

"We cannot free you, nor can we keep you here."

"Not very popular, am I?"

"The only alternative is death."

"That's what I thought."

"You know too much."

"Aye."

Darris glanced at the fire and studied the leaping flames. "So ye deal with the Apaches," said Gallagher slowly.

"You saw that?"

"Aye."

"Your tongue is your undoing, but then that has always been the way of your people."

" 'Tis true enough," agreed Gallagher wryly. He set his jaw. "Ye've done great harm, Darris. Ye've murdered a young woman who would not yield to ye. Ye've set yerself up here against the United States of America. Ye are keeping two young women here against their wills. Ye keep me a prisoner—a noncommissioned officer of the United States Army on official business. Worst of all, ye not only plan to supply arms and munitions to the ribils, but ye are also giving them to the Tontos. For what purpose, Darris?"

There was a long silence, and the cold gray eyes touched Gallagher's sensitive nerves like the slimy tentacles of some evil creature. "Is there any more to come from that loose mouth of yours, Sergeant?" asked Darris.

"Much more."

Darris looked at Gallagher's guard. "Take this man out into the courtyard. Tell the men to gather there. Yes, and get the women, too! This will be a lesson for all of them."

He was taken out into the moonlit courtyard. The men were there. Two of them stood on the sentry walks. The others leaned against the walls or the posts that held up the second-floor porches. On the porch of the easternmost of the two buildings were two women. One of them he had never seen, but the other he knew well enough. It was Ellen Eustis. The other must be her sister.

"Bart!" called out Darris from the porch of the western building.

A man swaggered forward from the shadows. He was a real broth of a boy, thought Gallagher. "Yes, boss?" asked Bart.

"The lash," said Darris shortly.

It was done quickly. Stripped to the waist, Gallagher was tied to one of the stout posts that supported the porch of the western building. The wind was cold on his flesh as he stood there, the tips of his toes barely touching the ground.

"How many?" asked Bart.

"A dozen, for a start."

Bart took a lash from a hook and ran his thick fingers through the tails of the thing to free them from each other. Then there was a long pause. There was no movement amongst the men or women. It was quiet except for the distant murmuring sound of the stream and the sighing of the night wind about the buildings.

The first stroke hit him when he least expected it. It drove the breath from his body. His back and belly quivered involuntarily as he waited for the next stinging blow. But Bart was a master of his trade. The second, third, and fourth blows came at varying intervals, and each of them struck hard enough to drive what little wind he had left from his body so that his mouth hung open gasping for the thin air.

One of the watching men laughed, then stopped as Gallagher's pain-shot eyes sought his—the pure Irish hell in them was enough to quiet any man.

The blood coursed slowly down his back. "Enough!" cried Ellen Eustis.

Gallagher looked back at her. Her dark hair hung over her shoulders, and her eyes seemed to sparkle in the moonlight.

The next stroke seemed to cut to the very bones. The blood seeped down past the waist band of his trousers and ran slowly down the backs of his legs.

It was timed neatly. The last stroke hit him like a searing tongue of lightning, and at that instant one of the men cut the rope that held him up. He sagged to his knees. Bart walked around in front of Gallagher, passing his fingers through the tails of the lash, freeing them of blood and bits of skin. He started back a little when he saw the look on Gallagher's face. *"Some day, boyo,"* said Gallagher slowly and distinctly, *"I will have the hide and bones av ye for what ye have done to me."*

Bart spat in Gallagher's face, raised a big foot and drove it at Gallagher, catching him on the side of the head and driving him to the blood-spattered ground. He spat again, and there was a low growling sound deep in Gallagher's throat. He came up from the ground like an uncoiling spring. His left fist caught Bart in the belly, and the right came across like a triphammer to meet the downcoming jaw.

Bart swung at Gallagher's face with the lash, but Gallagher twisted it free and began to lay it about the head and shoulders of the man like he was chopping wood. Bart screamed hoarsely.

Three of the men were on Gallagher, but he drove them back with the lash. He brought up a knee into the groin of one of them, smashed the thick handle of the whip down on the head of another, kicked the third man in the belly. Bart rushed in to meet a left to the jaw and a vicious crack alongside the head with the whip handle.

They drove him back at last, fighting savagely in an insensate fury that made him impervious to pain and fatigue. Finally he struck a wall and was driven into a corner. They rushed him, and the overpowering weight of their hard bodies carried him down until he could not move.

"Let me have him!" yelled Bart insanely.

"No!" said Darris. "The water cure will take the heat from him, if it doesn't kill him."

He almost screamed in agony as they dragged him by the legs across the harsh ground to the pond. They hurled him in and stood there grinning as the breath went out of him in a great spluttering gasp.

He sank quickly to the bottom of the icy pool and

then came up to meet hands that thrust him down again and again until he knew he was going to die. And all the time, when he could hear them, they were laughing as though it was some kind of monstrous joke, and the loudest of the laughing ones was the man named Bart.

He was almost gone. He came up for one last fighting try and saw the hard face of Bart close to his. "Had enough, *hombre?*" sneered he.

Gallagher spat full into his face. A fist hit him and drove him under. The water cascaded over the edges of the pond and swept down the slopes as he fought his last fight. He came up for his last sight of the world.

"That's enough!" said a sharp cold voice.

A man stood at the south end of the pond with a long-barreled rifle held at waist level. His wide-brimmed hat shielded his face.

"Who the hell are you?" demanded Bart.

"Luke Ainsley."

"We been expecting some of you boys."

"What are you doing to him?"

"Punishing him," said Bart with a grin.

"Pull him out."

Gallagher lay quietly getting back his breath. "Hello, Luke," he said at last.

"Good God! It's Gallagher himself!"

"The same," said Gallagher wearily.

"They said you were dead."

"Who did?"

"Them back at Fort McComber."

Gallagher looked quickly at the man. "They tried hard enough to kill me. Lucky you came. Matthew, Mark, *Luke,* and John, they guard the bed I lie upon."

"Very funny," said Bart. He looked at Ainsley. "Darris ain't going to like you butting in like this, Ainsley."

The man spat. "I'm worried," he said quietly.

They eyed the lean man and his steady rifle. They shuffled their feet.

"Take him to one of them buildings over there," said Ainsley, jerking his head toward the row of low structures.

"Darris won't like this."

The rifle hammer clicked back. "Move!" snapped Ainsley.

They carried him to the end building and dumped him on a dusty cot. As they left he was sure he could hear the thin screaming of a woman from somewhere in the bigger buildings. He tried to get up, but Ainsley came in and shook his head. "Stay put, Gallagher," he said. "Even *you* can't fool around with these bearded bastards."

Gallagher cursed and lay flat. The raw meat of his back was seared by the rough blanket on the cot. He was sick and exhausted, but that scream struck through his mind worse than the pain of his big body.

▶▶ *Chapter* 15

AINSLEY squatted beside the door and lighted a candle. "They've been looking for you, Gallagher."

"Who?"

"Them at Fort McComber."

"They couldn't look for me, Luke. No horses. Hardly enough men to penetrate Tonto country anyways."

Luke shielded the guttering flame. "You mean *your* company?"

"Aye."

"That's not who I meant."

Gallagher winced as his body warmed up a little.

"Roll over," said Ainsley. He felt in a pouch at his waist and brought out a small pot. He came to the cot and began gently to rub ointment on the raw back. "Jesus God," he said. When he was done he bandaged the back and covered Gallagher with a blanket.

Gallagher wiped the cold sweat from his face. "Listen, Luke," he said quickly. "These men have the missing stores from Fort Coulter. They are trading guns to the Tontos, and I think they will sell or trade the rest of the weapons and stores they have to the ribils. Now look ye! Ye are like a ghost in the deserts and the mountains. Go ye to Fort Yuma and get troops to come back here and destroy these weapons!"

"You're talking loco, Gallagher."

Gallagher stared at the man, and his mind began to clear. How would Ainsley know about the missing weapons from Fort Coulter? He had been a civilian scout for the Army before the war, but he had not been around for some time.

Ainsley squatted on his heels again. "Just what is this you want me to do?"

119

"There are weapons stored here, Luke. Weapons that can turn the Tontos into a scourge that will sweep all of Arizona, or weapons that will help the rebels conquer Arizona and the Pacific Coast! Get to Fort Yuma and get troops!"

"Why should I go?"

Gallagher stared at him. "Ye can see I can't go! Besides, they mean to kill me."

"So?"

"Ye are an Army scout, Luke. It's up to ye!"

"I'm a scout all right, Gallagher, but not for the United States Army. I am scouting for Captain Hunter Sherrod, commander of G Company, Sixth Texas Mounted Rifles, Army of the Southwest."

"What 'J' Company outfit is that?" Then a cold light dawned in Gallagher's mind.

Ainsley smiled. "You have quite a distinction, Gallagher, as Lieutenant Artenis said, a little sarcastically of course. There are no United States troops left in Arizona except *you*, Gallagher, and the prisoners at Fort McComber, and most of them are dying of typhoid."

"Artenis?"

Ainsley nodded. "What the hell did you do to him, Gallagher?"

The big hands closed and opened, closed and opened. "Nothing to what I'd like to do," said Gallagher softly. He looked at Ainsley. "And they sent you ahead to this place to find the weapons."

"They were never lost, mick."

"Aye."

"All's fair in love and war, Gallagher."

"Aye. But the Tontos? They hold the mouth of the canyon. They will not come in here. But they will not let the ribils pass into here either, will they?"

"Darris has arranged that."

"I might have known," breathed Gallagher. He closed his eyes.

"We can use good men, Gallagher. You know this country better than I do. I would have thought Lieutenant Artenis might have persuaded you to join us. I was surprised when he sent for me. You're on a losing side, mick. Reconsider."

"What do ye offer me?"

"They said they had a commission for you. What do you say, Gallagher? Captain Sherrod authorized me to tell you that, if I found you."

The blue eyes opened and held Ainsley with a terrible gaze. "I came here from Ireland, a starving kid, without a seat to me breeches or a shilling in me pockets. They tuk me into the Army and made a man out of me. I earned me three stripes and diamond the hard way. I've worn the blue and served under the blessed Stars and Stripes too long to change now."

"You're a fool! If I leave you here with Darris and his men they'll kill you or turn you over to Klij-Litzogue. You know how badly *he* wants you."

"Aye." Gallagher sat up and gripped the edge of the cot. "Let them kill me, or torture me, but they will do it when I am wearing *blue*, Ainsley! Now get out of here before I break yer goddam traitorous neck between me hands like a matchstick!"

Ainsley shrugged. He closed the door behind him and shot the outer bolt.

Gallagher bent his head and held his battered face in his hands. There was more connivery going on than he had realized. Now he had rebels, Tontos, and Darris and his men to contend with. One man, *one* United States dragoon, was still left with enough life within him to fight on.

The thought of Ellen Eustis came swiftly to him. Maybe it had been her who had screamed so desperately. Maybe Darris was already pawing her soft white body. Gallagher's big hands opened and closed spasmodically, and the power in them was terrible to see.

His back had stiffened, and it was an agony to get up and peer from a window. He could see a sentry pacing the length of the southern walkway. The moon was waning swiftly. He looked up the trail that led to the cliff dwellings and the invaluable cache of arms that might mean the difference between victory and defeat for the Union in

California if the rebels got them. There was no hate in Gallagher for Luke Ainsley and Sherrod Hunter, for they were sworn rebels doing their duty as they saw it. It was the others like Millard Artenis and Elijah Darris whom he hated with all the venom in his soul.

He gripped the bars of the window. They were solid. They were solid all right, *but they were made of wood.*

He knew well enough he could not cut through that dense, close-grained wood with the spring steel from his other shoe, but Gallagher set to work anyway.

It was pitch dark when he heard the soft footfall. He stopped cutting and flattened himself against the wall.

"*Tsst! Tsst! Tsst!*" came the sibilant Apache scout warning.

Gallagher wet his dry lips.

"*Tsst! Tsst! Tsst!*"

Something brushed against the outside of the wall. "*Mick?*" came the soft question.

"Ainsley?"

"Yes. Come close to the window."

He could just make out Ainsley's head and shoulders against the darkness.

"They are changing the guard," said the scout.

"So?"

"They mean to do away with you."

"That's not surprising."

There was a pause. "I can't stand by and let them do it, mick."

"*Gracias,* Luke."

"Take this."

Gallagher touched the cold steel of a heavy bowie knife.

"I'm heading back to Captain Sherrod's camp out beyond the canyon. We'll be coming back tomorrow for the weapons. I overheard Darris tell Bart to do away with you."

"So?"

Another pause. "Bart means to turn you over to Klij-Litzogue."

"Jesus God!"

"Now listen to me: Cut your way out of there. Go north up the canyon. Somewhere up there is a hidden trail that will take you out of this accursed canyon. Get out of here and head west to Fort Yuma."

"What about the women?"

Ainsley shifted a little. "Forget about them."

"I can't do that, Luke!"

Ainsley looked back over his shoulder. "Look," he said harshly. "I've given you a chance to live. Get out of here. Go back to the Army. Forget the women. You hear me, mick?"

"Aye."

"I sure wish you'd join up with us, Gallagher."

"Not a chance."

"*Adios*, then."

"*Adios*."

The scout was gone like a ghost.

Blood was running down Gallagher's fingers when he cut through the last of the hard wooden bars. It was black as the pit outside. The wind had died away.

He eased his big shoulders through the window and felt with his raw hands for the ground. He worked his slim hips through the opening and lay flat upon the ground. The main buildings showed as a dark mass against the cliff. He bellied slowly away, gripping the knife. A nocturnal animal scuttled for cover. An owl flitted silently overhead. Somewhere far up on the canyon a coyote howled.

He wormed his way up the slopes until he lay in a hollow not far from the easternmost of the two buildings. It took all of his guts to force himself to work toward the house. If Bart caught him and turned him over to Klij-Litzogue . . . he remembered too well some of the bloody human wreckage he had seen after Apache torture sessions—Old Man Willis, who had been cooked alive over his own stove at Vaca Creek; Corporal Harris of Company A, who had been captured in the lonely Grindstones and staked naked on a hill of big vicious Sonoran ants, with a trail of honey leading to his mouth that had been propped open by a stick sharpened at both ends. As an added touch they had sliced off his eyelids so that the intense sunlight would burn away his sight while he still lived.

He slid down the slope, driving all such thoughts from his mind. If he kept on thinking about them he'd run like a craven for the shelter of the northern canyon and the hidden trail.

He reached the small door. It was still locked. He swung himself up onto the shingled roof and lay flat. He didn't know what to do now. Then a questing hand struck a raised portion of the roof. He investigated it by feel. "By the powers," he said softly, "a trapdoor, and the bloody thing is not fastened!"

He lifted it gently, and the warm air flowed up about him. He slid it back and peered into the darkness. He was almost sure he could smell the soft aura of feminine flesh. He listened and heard nothing.

Gallagher chewed at his lower lip. He hated the thought of going down into that pit of darkness, but he had to go if he wanted to find those women. Gallagher lay flat, listening and peering down into the rectangle of darkness. It was as quiet as a graveyard, and the simile sent a cold shiver across Gallagher's lacerated back. It was too damned quiet to suit him. Maybe they had set a trap for him down there. But then they didn't know he had escaped again . . . or did they?

The big Irishman gripped the edges of the trapdoor and let himself down easily. His legs swung back and forth feeling for obstacles and a landing place. He breathed a short prayer and let himself drop to the unseen floor. As he rose to get his balance he felt arms wrap themselves about his body from the rear and felt a soft body press tightly against him. Gallagher reacted like an uncoiling spring, turning and gripping for the throat, and his hands brushed naked breasts and long hair.

"Please get me out of here," she said.

Gallagher's heart slammed back and forth within his rib cage like a frightened bird. "Ellen!" he gasped.

"No. It's Judy. Judy Eustis, Ellen's sister."

He gently loosened her arms from about his waist. She was naked he well knew. "Have ye no clothing, lass?" he asked hoarsely.

"No. They stripped me and kept me locked up. I managed to get free and find my way up here. I couldn't find any clothing."

He stared at the vague dimness of her face. "What have they done to ye?"

She looked away. "It was *him*," she said quietly.

"Darris?"

"Yes."

He nodded. Darris had a reputation for such things. Maybe Ellen was next. "Where are we?" he whispered. "Tell me the layout av this house."

"This is an attic. We are almost in the middle of it. There is a door in the wall behind you that leads to a large storeroom. At the far end of the storeroom there is a ladder leading down to the second floor."

"Where is Ellen?"

"I'm not sure."

"Think!"

She seemed to stiffen in the darkness. "Why should I? If it hadn't been for her this would never have happened."

"I don't understand. She was much concerned about ye."

"Oh certainly! Ellen always has been concerned about me! That's why she hauled Evelyn and me out to this hell on earth! Evelyn is just as bad. She doesn't care what happens to me."

"Evelyn is dead, lass."

"She's well out of this mess then! I've heard these men talk about you, Sergeant. They're afraid of you. They say if you escape you'll have the Army down on their heads."

"Aye."

"Will you take me away from here?"

"I'll try."

She came closer to him. "Then let's go! Right now!"

"I must find your sister."

"If you look for her they'll catch you."

He placed his hands on her smooth bare shoulders. "It is a risk I must take, Judith."

She sobbed softly, and he drew her close to comfort her. Her arms crept about his neck, and he felt her breasts and belly press against him as though she was a bordello girl from Tucson. "Forget about Ellen," she said softly. "Just get *me* out of here. You won't be sorry, Sergeant. Help me get up through that trapdoor. They say you know this country as well as any Apaches do. I can hide out in the canyon until you get horses. The Apaches won't come in here. Surely you can find some way to get me back to civilization if anyone can."

A slow flame crept up his belly and back. He pushed her back a little. "Ye're daft, lass."

"Am I? Are you a big enough fool to try and find her in this hellhole?"

"Aye, that I am," he said simply. "I brought Ellen into this mess, and by the powers, I intend to get her out of it! As for ye, shameless little baggage that ye are, I'll take ye along, too, gentleman that I am." He walked about the little room. "Are there no clothes here at all?"

She laughed. "Nervous? There's a blanket over there."

He tossed it at her.

She laughed again. "You want me to wrap myself in this filthy thing?"

" 'Tis better than being mother naked in front av a man, is it not?"

"Oh Sergeant! I really don't know!"

He slapped her across the face. "Ye little slut! Wrap yerself in that blanket!"

She moved quickly. Her fingernails raked his face, and he felt the blood run. He gripped her by an arm, twisted it, turned up her bare bottom, and with one calloused hand struck true and flat on the soft rounded flesh and with the other hand gripped across her mouth. He winced as her teeth dug into the hand.

Gallagher released her and walked to the door. He eased it open and walked across the next room, bowie knife in hand. The ladder was there, as she had said it

was. A trapdoor had been neatly fitted about the opening
in the floor. He lay down and pressed his ear to one of the
cracks. There was nothing to hear.

She was close behind him as he stood up. "What is
below?" he asked.

"A large room. Some of the men sleep there."

"Are any of them down there now?"

"I'm not sure, but I don't think so."

He pulled up the trapdoor and eased himself down the
ladder. Embers glowed in a fireplace, but there was no
sign of man in the place. Several bunks had been built
against a wall. He crossed to a door leading to the next
room and held his ear against it. Nothing. He eased it
open and walked into another big room, empty except for
a few boxes and some bundles of rags.

It was the same in the next room. A stairway led downstairs from one corner. He went softly down the stairs
and found himself in a small room wherein a candle
lantern flickered on a table.

The building seemed deserted. He gently opened a door
to the courtyard.

He heard the shuffling of the sentry's feet. Judith
pointed upward and opened her mouth to scream. He
looked away, then crossed the yard like a great lean cat,
close to the wall, with the girl just behind him. They
stopped beneath the porch of the western building. They
had not been seen.

He wanted to get away from this place and away
from Judy Eustis, but Ellen was still a prisoner and in
the hands of Darris, and if what Gallagher suspected
was true there was no time for him to waste.

▶▶ *Chapter* **16**

GALLAGHER entered the room where the spring water flowed through the stone trough. The girl shivered in the dampness. "Are ye glad now ye put on that blanket?" he asked with a malicious grin.

"Are you?" she boldly asked.

He walked to the next door. She was hardly more than a girl, yet her actions could be those of a much older woman, one with a helluva lot more experience. Then he remembered the words of Ellen Eustis when she had spoken about her youngest sister. *"I think she is still alive. Judy has a way of doing things just like that. Judy likes men."*

Judy Eustis was a bit of a wanton, he knew now. She thought only of herself. She had a way of working a man. He remembered how she had pressed her young body against his and the shameless words she had used. She could make a man forget quite a bit—his duty, his honor, and his soul. God help the man who took her for his wife.

The entire first floor of the western building was empty of life. There was a big kitchen in the southern end with a stairway leading up to the second floor. Gallagher softly ascended it. Judy was not behind him. There was no time to look for her. He reached the top of the stairs and found a sort of sitting room. There was a door on the far wall, and as he walked toward it he heard the distinct sound of flesh striking flesh. Something clattered on the floor. He heard the sound of heavy breathing.

"Get back, you devil!" said a woman. It was Ellen Eustis.

Gallagher hit the door with a shoulder and hurtled into the room. Ellen Eustis stood against a far wall, her dress hanging in rags about her waist and her arms covering

128

her bare breasts. Her face was scratched and bruised.
Sweat dewed her flesh. She held a heavy wrought-iron
candlestick in one hand.

Elijah Darris stood facing Ellen, reaching out for her
with big veinous hands. He whirled in time to meet a
smashing right to the whiskers that drove him back
against the wall. Gallagher grunted deep in his throat and
hit the older man again. Elijah Darris went down on
one knee, snatched up a heavy stool, and threw it with all
his strength at Gallagher. It bounced off Gallagher's
head, almost stunning him, and then the older man
closed in, kicking, striking, and cursing.

The old bastard was strong, with muscles like steel
wires. He drove Gallagher back toward a great bed and
pushed him heavily on top of it. The musty sour smell of
the bedding sickened him. He rolled away and planted a
foot in the older man's lean belly just as the stool smashed
down on the place where Dan's head had been an instant
before.

The air went out of Darris with a rush. He hit the
wall and bounced back right into a rocky fist that smashed
lips and nose together in a bloody froth. He opened his
mouth to yell and shut it again as a left sank into his
lean belly. Then Gallagher remembered how Darris had
stood on the porch like a god and watched his back being
lashed into tatters. A right seemed to whistle as it hit the
older man. Darris' legs flew up from under him, and he
hit hard on the floor with his mouth gaping and blood
smeared on his yellow teeth.

She was in Gallagher's arms, forgetting her half nakedness. "Oh, Gallagher," she sobbed. "That man. The awful
things he said. He's mad!"

"I've found Judy. We've got to get out of here!"

He led her down the stairs and through the kitchen
and the other rooms. Judy was gone. He looked back at
Ellen. "Judy is quite a lass," he said.

She nodded. "I can tell you know her, Gallagher."

"She is not like ye, Ellen."

"She is not my real sister. My father brought her home
when she was just a little girl," she said quietly. She

looked away. "We never really knew whether she was his natural child or. . . . My mother accepted her. She was like that. She never spoke about it, but it broke her heart. Judy has always been trouble for us."

He drew her close. "Ye must know the chances of us getting out of here are almost nil. I can get ye and yer sister out of these buildings, but it will not be long before they scour the canyon for us. They will not harm ye and Judy, but as for me. . ."

Her eyes were fierce in the dimness. "Harm us? If they do catch us, Gallagher, I hope they kill us! That old man is evil itself!"

He grinned. "Spoken like a thoroughbred!"

They stopped in the damp spring room, and Gallagher padded to the door and looked out. The courtyard was deserted, but he could have sworn he saw something move just inside a door across it. Judy. He turned to Ellen. "Ye must follow me close, directly beneath the sentry walk. If I stop ye must stop. If they jump me ye must make a break for it, lass. There are ribil troops coming into the canyon tomorrow. Try to get to them, *but do not go too far*. The Tontos are at the canyon mouth. They will not come in, but do not stray into their camp."

"I won't leave you, Gallagher!" she whispered fiercely.

He kissed her. He stepped outside, flattened himself against the wall, and looked toward the southern sentry walk. It was empty. They crossed the courtyard and entered the small armory room. Still no sign of Judith.

They walked quietly up the stairs. Judith stood in the room, waiting for them. Her face was set. "What do you expect to do now?" she coldly asked Gallagher.

"Get the both of ye out of here."

"Two of us? It will be almost impossible to get *one* of us out of here, and you know it!"

"I know who I'd like to leave behint," he said under his breath. "What do ye expect me to do? Sprout wings and fly out av here?"

"Take *one* of us," she said in an odd voice.

He thrust his face close to hers. "Listen to me! I'm

taking the two av ye from here. I will do the best I can. But both of ye will go!"

She smiled coldly. "Choose between us, Sergeant."

"Ye're mad!"

"You must choose!"

He looked back at Ellen. "What is wrong with her?"

"I don't know. She acts strangely at times."

"I do?" spat out Judy.

Gallagher placed a hand across her pretty mouth. "Come," he said to Ellen. He released his grip on Judy. "Will ye be quiet now?"

"You won't choose then?"

"If I did," he said slowly and with emphasis, "it would not be *ye*."

Her face became a terrible, almost degrading thing to see, and then she emitted a piercing scream that could have aroused the dead.

"Mother av God!" said Gallagher hoarsely. He gripped Ellen by the arm and drove a door aside with his shoulder. Judith was still screaming like a soul demented.

"Wait for her!" said Ellen.

"Are ye mad, too?"

He reached the door that led out onto the side of the slopes and fumbled with the bar across it. He jerked the door open and jumped through the opening, hauling Ellen behind him.

The rifle muzzle struck his chest right at the sternum and held him poised on one foot like a ballet dancer in a tableau. "Stay right where you are," said the man who held the rifle.

"I wasn't thinking of going anywhere," said Gallagher as the cold sweat broke out on his body.

"Back into the building!"

Gallagher and Ellen were marched through the building and into the courtyard. Elijah Darris stood there fully dressed with pure icy hell on his bearded face. "I should have let them kill you," he said.

"Kill me then, ye lecherous old bastard!"

There were four more of the men in the courtyard now.

There was death in their eyes. Gallagher's string had run out for sure this time.

Darris raised a hand. "You've broken too many of our laws to live, Sergeant," he said quietly.

"Get on with it, ye old blackguard! Don't prate to me of yer laws. Yer day will come, and though I be dead, me ghost will come back to watch that day."

"I make the decisions and laws here."

Mad as a hatter, thought Gallagher. He was a man trying to build a world of his own because he could not live in the world of other people.

"I sentence you to life imprisonment."

Bart stepped forward. "Kill him and be done with it," he said. "Or still better, turn him over to Yellow Snake."

"When I said 'life imprisonment' I did not say how *long* that life was to be."

They were all watching Darris now. There was something evil about the older man. He smiled, but there was no mirth in his eyes. "There are many small rooms up on the cliffs," he said at last. "Some of them are fitted only with doors. Some of them are placed far back into the rock."

An aura of stinking evil seemed to hover about Darris, somewhat like the foul stench of his big bed. "Throw him into a cell," he said. "In the morning we will wall up this great hulk of a man in a room so small he will hardly be able to move. We will leave a breathing hole and perhaps a hole big enough to admit enough water and hard bread to keep him alive long enough to repent his sins. But he will go mad long before he dies."

They drove Gallagher into a cell and slammed the door behind him. He dropped onto the bare cot and lay for a long time with his hands locked behind his head, staring at the ceiling, waiting to hear the first scream from a woman.

They came for him in the morning and hustled him out of the building and up the trail. The canyon was beautiful under the bright light of morning. The trees waved gracefully in the wind. The stream rippled and flashed under the sunlight. Everything was sharp and cameo clear. It was a hell of a day for a man to know his future as Gallagher did.

The place they had picked for his prison was seemingly wedged into a great crevice. A small T-shaped door led into a room hardly large enough for a man of Gallagher's size to fit into, much less move around in. They dragged him into it and cut his bonds.

"Wall him in!" snapped Darris.

They worked quickly and well, fitting in the lower stones and mortaring them thickly. Higher and higher went the courses until there was but one stone left to be slipped into place. It didn't seem real, this mad business, and yet it was happening.

The wind shifted, and Gallagher could have sworn he heard faint voices in the distance.

"It's Hunter Sherrod and his boys," said one of the men.

Gallagher's heart leaped.

"They're early," said Bart.

"Tell them we are busy," said Darris.

"Too late. Sherrod and Ainsley are coming up the trail."

"Finish the job!" snapped Darris. There was a pause. "Leave no opening."

"Ah, God!" said Gallagher hoarsely.

"What are you doing there, Darris?" asked a soft Texas voice.

"It doesn't concern you, sir," said Darris.

"Likely they're hiding some of the weapons," said Ainsley. "They've been trading some of them off to the Tontos."

"Don't place that last stone," said the officer.

"This is my land," said Darris, "and my business. Let be!"

There was a moment's silence. "What exactly do you mean by that, Mister Darris, suh?" asked the officer.

"This is my country. My domain. I make the laws. I rule. You have no right to tell me what to do, Captain."

The officer's voice was level. "Ainsley told me something about this situation. This territory is now part of the

Confederate States Territory of New Mexico, by conquest. As such, the laws of the Confederate States of America apply here, and as the chief representative of those states here in Arizona I warn you that any claims you make that this is your land and your country are entirely contrary to the laws of the Confederacy."

Gallagher managed a croaking sound from his dry throat.

"What was that?" asked Captain Sherrod.

"Place the stone!" said Darris.

Something clicked—a gun hammer being cocked. "Let me just take a look in there," said Sherrod. "I have twenty-five men down in the canyon, Darris."

Gallagher croaked again. He saw the opening get blocked and for one awful instant thought it was the last stone. "Christ!" he screamed.

"Jesus God!" said Sherrod. "There's a man in there!"

"I have a damned good idea who it is, too," said Ainsley.

"Rip out those stones," said the Confederate officer.

"No!" screamed Darris. "This is my country! I make the laws. I punish transgressors! I am the ruler here! Seize these two men!"

Ainsley spoke in a low voice. "The first man who moves will trigger a bullet into this loco old bastard's back. *Now move those stones out of there!*"

The stones were torn out one by one, and Captain Sherrod reached in, gripped Gallagher beneath the armpits, and dragged him outside into the bright blessed sunshine. The officer unhooked a canteen from his belt and held it to Gallagher's cracked lips.

"For God's sake, Gallagher," said Luke, "I've seen you in some bad situations, but nothing like this!"

Gallagher grinned crookedly. "I have a way of doing these things it seems."

The officer and the scout helped Gallagher down the twisted trail. Sherrod's Company G lounged about on the ground beside the big houses. They wore slouch hats and badly fitting dusty gray uniforms, but they were all fine looking men, young and vital.

"G Company, Sixth Texas Mounted Rifles, Army of the Southwest," said the officer with a note of pride in his voice.

Gallagher, as a professional, noted their weapons, and he knew now why they needed the hidden arms so desperately. Some of them were armed with double-barreled shotguns, some with muzzle-loading Enfield or Springfield musketoons. A few of them had revolving pistols, but most of them carried one or two muzzle-loading single-shot pistols converted from flintlock to percussion lock. Klij-Litzogue and his Tontos were better armed by far than this outfit.

There was another officer standing near the pond, holding the bridle reins of a fine gray horse, and his hard eyes studied Gallagher. It was Millard Artenis wearing Confederate gray. The warmth of the sun and of his miraculous release from the tomb suddenly left Gallagher under the cold thrust of those eyes. Faint bruises still showed on the handsome face of the officer, bruises placed there by the smashing fists of Dan Gallagher. He knew Artenis's warped sense of honor would have to be satisfied, wiped out in the blood of the man who had beaten him and humiliated him.

"Sergeant Gallagher," said Artenis mildly. "We meet again."

"Aye."

"I did not think you could survive, but somehow you did."

"The luck av the Irish, sir." The "sir" had slipped out.

"Maybe your luck has run out at last. The last man of Company A."

"So?"

"The rest are dead, dying, or are prisoners."

"Aye."

Artenis placed a hand on the holster flap of his sidearm. "So stand to your glasses steady," he said softly. "Here's a health to the living. Hurrah for the next man to die."

Elijah Darris and his men had come down the hill and entered the courtyard of the twin houses. The thick gates had closed behind them, and the bars falling heavily across their supports. Now Darris appeared on the sentry walk and looked down at the Texans.

Captain Sherrod looked up. "I'll get those weapons and be on my way, Darris. I'll sign a form authorizing you payment for the storage of the weapons and accessories. My government will reimburse you. I want to get out of this canyon as quickly as possible. I don't want to make camp for the night until I've put a lot of miles between me and those Tontos."

Darris did not speak.

The officer slapped his gauntlets against his thigh. "I'll need water and rations. We'll pay for the rations."

There wasn't a sound or a movement from Darris.

"Do you hear me, suh?"

Darris said nothing but pointed up toward the cliff dwellings. The sun glinted on gun barrels thrust over the terrace wall, and the wind moved the beards of the men who were behind those rifles watching the Texans.

Sherrod looked up at Darris. "What does this mean, suh?"

Gun barrels protruded from the loopholes of the buildings. The troopers slowly got to their feet and backed away from the menacing muzzles.

Darris rested his forearms on the wall. "I have told you that this is my country . . . that I make the laws. Those guns in storage are mine, to do with as I see fit."

Sherrod had been neatly foxed. A hundred men could not have taken those massive twin buildings by assault.

"I can go back south," said the officer easily, "and bring up more men and artillery."

There was a cold, knowing smile upon the bearded face. "Do," said Darris politely, "but it is only fair to warn you that Klij-Litzogue and his Tontos block the canyon mouth, and he will continue to do so until I send word that you may pass."

Ainsley whistled softly. He looked at Gallagher. "He has us by the short hairs, mick."

"Aye," said Gallagher dryly.

"What is it you want from us, Darris?" asked Sherrod.

"You and your men may camp beside the stream, but

no closer than two hundred yards from this western house. I will sell you food."

"Agreed."

Darris clasped his veinous hands together. "In return, I want an assurance from you that my men and I will not be bothered by you or your men, nor forced to obey the laws of the Confederacy."

"You will not be bothered by our forces if you turn over the weapons that rightfully belong to us. I cannot assure you, suh, that you will not have to obey our laws."

Darris straightened and pointed toward the stream. "Go and make your camp. I'll give you until moonrise to agree to my terms."

"What do you intend to do with those weapons?"

Darris smiled crookedly. "Everybody seems to want them. The United States, the Confederacy, the Tontos, and Mister Artenis."

"Mister Artenis is an officer in my command. It was he who made the deal with you to bring those weapons here in good faith, Darris."

"Oh *did* he?"

Hunter Sherrod turned slowly and looked at Millard Artenis, and there was a cold set look on his face. "Well, suh?"

Artenis waved a hand. "I expect something for my services, Captain."

"What, for example?"

"A higher rank in the Confederate Army, for one thing. Payment for these weapons . . . in gold."

The Texan's face whitened beneath his tan. "I understood that you, suh, were a patriot."

Artenis smiled. "Oh, I am! I am indeed! But I'm also a poor man, Captain. Gambling and drinking, you know. The Confederacy needs those weapons. I can make a deal with Darris so that you can have them."

In the silence that followed Hunter Sherrod dropped his hand to the butt of his pistol. "Sergeant Gerry," he said quietly.

"Yes, suh!"

"Arrest that man!"

Gerry turned, but Elijah Darris leaned over the wall. "If anything happens to Mister Artenis there will be no deals of any kind. There will be no food for your men. Klij-Litzogue will be told to hold your command back, Captain Sherrod."

Sherrod's hand dropped. He nodded shortly.

Artenis walked slowly toward the small gate set in one of the big gates.

"Damned traitor!" said a red-faced corporal.

"Twice," said Gallagher softly. "Twice."

"One other thing, Captain," said Darris clearly. "By moonrise you must turn over to me the person of Sergeant Gallagher to do with as I see fit."

"Move out!" snapped the officer. He looked up at Darris, slapped gauntlets against thigh, and then followed his command. Gallagher followed the officer, noting that a trooper fell in close behind, his carbine held casually pointing at Gallagher's back.

There were black looks on the dusty faces of the young Texans as they made their camp. Now and then they looked at those strong buildings bright in the sunlight. It had been a long journey from Mesilla to Arizona, and a more dangerous one to Canyon Encantado, and now they had failed in their mission, as Gallagher had failed in his.

►► *Chapter* 17

DARKNESS was settling into the great trough of the canyon. The Texans lay about their fires, frying their bacon in iron spiders, brewing strong issue coffee, the while eying the cold stone walls.

Gallagher ate with Captain Sherrod and Luke Ainsley. "The moon will be up before long," said Sherrod softly. "Maybe we can rush them with volunteers."

"Not a chance," said Gallagher. "The place is like a citadel."

Sherrod eyed Gallagher. "You think he'd really turn those Apaches against us?"

"Without a doubt, Captain."

"They were watching us all the time we rode into the canyon," said Ainsley.

"I didn't see any of them," said Sherrod.

"They were there, Captain."

"Who is this Darris anyway, suh?" asked Sergeant Gerry as he stopped beside the fire.

Sherrod looked at Ainsley.

Ainsley was filling his pipe. He placed it between his teeth and lighted it. "He's wanted in half a dozen states for white slavery, larceny, forgery, and murder, too, as far as I know."

"He's a murderer, all right," said Gallagher. He had his memory of Evelyn Eustis.

"Darris found out that the Mormons who had built this place wanted to move on. He bought it from them, lock, stock, and barrel."

"And Artenis made a deal with Darris to store the weapons here," said Sherrod. "Neat as mutton."

The sergeant nodded. He looked up at the buildings. "And where does it place us, suh?" he quietly asked.

It seemed to all of them that the wind had suddenly become quite chilly.

"I must have those weapons!" said Sherrod. He smashed fist into palm.

Gallagher emptied his coffee cup. "Seems as though ye will need all the luck ye can get to escape from this canyon alive, sir, much less try to get those weapons."

They were miles and miles from safety. There were few enough Confederate troops in Arizona. In fact, from what Gallagher had heard Sherrod's Company G was about the only rebel force in the territory.

"I can lie to him," said the officer thoughtfully . . . "give him a written assurance that he will not be bothered by our government."

"Aye," said Gallagher. " 'Twould be fair enough in war."

"He wants you, too, as part of his deal, Gallagher."

"Aye."

"You know what that means."

"I do."

"Take the oath of allegiance to the Confederacy and it will place you squarely under the protection of my government."

"And if I don't?"

They all looked at him.

Gallagher shook his head. "Ye would not turn me over to him. Ye may be ribils, but ye are men."

The officer nodded. "I won't do it," he said. He eyed the big redheaded noncom. "But reconsider, Gallagher. I need officers. If I get those weapons I'll get all the recruits I need. I will be advanced in rank and probably be given a semi-independent command here in Arizona. I can't think of a better man, from what I have heard, to be an officer in my command, Gallagher. Give me your hand on it!"

Gallagher stood up. "That I cannot do, sir. I am a soldier of the United States Army and I will not break my oath of allegiance to my country."

Sherrod dropped his hand. "I didn't think you would break it."

"However," said Gallagher thoughtfully, "there are two

women in that hellhole up there that I must save. I cannot do it alone. I will form an alliance with ye, sir. Federal with Confederate—until such time as we no longer need each other."

"What can you offer us, Sergeant?" asked Sherrod.

"I want those women, and ye want those weapons. Neither of us gives a fiddler's damn what happens to Darris and his bloody crew, including Millard Artenis. Agreed?"

"Yes."

"Then I have a plan."

Ainsley grinned. "I knew it!"

Gallagher lowered his voice. "The moon will rise before long. Darris will be expecting you. Take me up there under guard and turn me over to him. Agree to everything he says."

"You're loco!" said Ainsley.

"Listen, dammit! I am not talking through me hat! There is a way into that western house that I don't think they know about. When I am inside those walls I will try to make my presence interesting enough so that the sentries will not be on the alert. Sergeant Gerry and Luke can take a party av picked men, the real boyos of yer command, and move up through yon trees and brush to a place near the pond.

"The spring water pours into the north end av the pond. The spring starts under the eastern house, runs through a tunnel under the courtyard, enters a stone trough in the end room av the western house, then out av the room into yon pond. Ye can enter the pool when the sentries are not looking, crawl into the house where the trough comes out, and be inside the westerly house."

Gallagher took a stick and sketched out the layout of the great house on the earth. "When ye move in ye must move fast! Once ye get yer hands on Darris and Artenis we might be able to dicker with the boys who are on guard up on the cliffs."

Gerry rubbed his lean jaw. "Sounds loco, but it might work."

"Ye have any better idea?" asked Gallagher sarcastically. "I tell ye it will work! It has to work!"

Sherrod nodded. "We'll go through with it."

Gallagher looked at Gerry and Ainsley. "Ye must leave enough men to move about these fires to make it look as though none of ye are missing."

The officer looked up at the canyon wall. "The moon is rising," he said quietly. He looked at Gallagher. "Whatever it is you plan to do inside those walls, I hope to God it works, or none of us will get out of this place alive."

Gallagher nodded. "One thing ye must all remember: Those men are good fighters and they will fight. Kill or be killed. *Deguelo*."

"What do you mean by that?" asked Gerry.

"No quarter," said Gallagher. There was a hard look on his face.

The moon was touching the rim of the canyon when the rebel officer came to Gallagher. "Ready?" he quietly asked.

"As much as I'll ever be, sir."

"Come on then. Everything is ready."

They walked up the slope until a sentry on the wall called them to halt.

"I am here to see Darris," said the officer.

The two men stood in the moonlight waiting. In a little while the small door set in the gate was opened, and as they passed through they were examined for weapons. Sherrod was relieved of his pistol and knife.

Elijah Darris stood in the courtyard with his men about him, their faces as hard as glacial ice. Millard Artenis stood on the balcony porch of the eastern house looking down on the scene with a faint smile on his handsome face.

"Have you agreed to my terms?" asked Darris.

Sherrod nodded. "I have no other choice. I have written out an agreement to the effect that you and your people will not be bothered by my government. I have also written that payment, in gold, will be made for those weapons."

Darris half closed his eyes and glanced at Gallagher,

and the hairs on Gallagher's neck seemed to rise stiffly. Darris was too shrewd a fox to be taken in lightly.

"And where is the gold, may I ask?" said Darris.

Sherrod flushed. "I don't carry that much money with me," he said. "I have several thousand dollars in Confederate money, however, and I will turn that over to you, upon receipt of the weapons."

"Trash," said Darris contemptuously.

"What is that, suh?"

"I say your Confederate money is trash."

Sherrod started forward, then stayed himself as their weapons were raised. "What is it you want me to do then?" he asked in a strained voice.

Darris shrugged. "Klij-Litzogue promises me raw gold. It means nothing to them. They have no use for it. He promises me burro loads of the ore in exchange for the weapons."

The Confederate officer paled. "But you know what that means, suh! The Tontos will cut a bloody swath throughout Arizona with those weapons."

Darris smiled faintly. "And what did *you* expect to do with them, Captain?"

"He has ye there, Captain," said Gallagher out of the side of his mouth.

"Whether you obey the laws of the United States or the laws of the Confederate States of America does not matter, Darris," said Sherrod, "but there are greater laws. The unwritten laws of humanity. You cannot sell those weapons to the Tontos."

Darris walked slowly forward. "I will sell them to whom I please, soldier."

Sherrod looked up at Millard Artenis. "Can't you do anything about his attitude, Artenis?"

The man shook his head. He was watching Gallagher. "I don't give a tinker's damn for the Confederacy *or* the United States, Sherrod. I'm only interested in Sergeant Gallagher."

"Do tell," said Gallagher.

"It seems as though everyone wants a crack at you, Gallagher," said Artenis.

"I didn't know I was that popular," said Gallagher with a grin.

"I told you once that it was a pity that we two could not meet on the field of honor because of our social levels."

"Do tell."

Artenis casually flicked dust from the sleeves of his neat shell jacket. "But I have arranged something that will repay me for the beating you gave me at Fort McComber."

Gallagher raised his two fists. "Ye'll fight me, Artenis?" he said eagerly.

"No. But I have paid someone to fight for me. Someone to whom you also owe a debt."

The big barrel-chested man named Bart stepped forward, spat into both palms, and slapped his hands hard on his muscular thighs. "Me, you Irish son of a bitch," he said with a grin.

Hunter Sherrod looked at Darris. "This is foolishness," he said. "We have business to take care of."

Darris raised a hand. "It will be a pleasure to see this arrogant bragging swine beaten to a pulp before we throw his bloody body to the Tontos."

Sherrod stepped forward. Again the guns came up, but the Texan was not afraid. "This man is not in good condition," he said. "Look at him! You've done everything you can to break him."

Gallagher spat. "And failed," he said. He caught Sherrod's eye. The silent message sped between them. This was the chance; the opportunity for Gerry and Ainsley to get into the building.

"Get the women," said Darris thinly. "Let them see blood."

The moon was at such a height that it flooded the courtyard with light. Bart slowly stripped to the waist. His chest hair and beard looked even blacker in the moonlight against the white skin.

Gallagher peeled off his shirt and undershirt. The rude bandages that swathed his upper body were dirty and encrusted with dried blood. Gallagher stripped them off, wincing as the rough cloth tore loose from the scabs. Blood began to trickle from some of the deep welts.

"Good God!" said Sherrod. "Who did that, Gallagher?"

Gallagher turned slowly, and his face was a terrible thing to see in the pale moonlight. He jerked a thumb toward Bart. "Him," he said softly, almost gently, and the hidden menace in his voice struck home to Sherrod.

A door opened on the second-floor porch of the easterly building. Ellen and Judith Eustis came out and stood by the railing near Millard Artenis.

"Time," said Darris.

They advanced toward each other. Bart was heavy and meaty, and his muscles were thick and wide. There was a terrible power in him. Gallagher hoped to God he could stay on his feet until the Texans attacked.

Bart spat and reached out a toe to mark a line on the hard earth. Just as he did so a rock-hard fist caught him under the left ear and drove him back. "Damn you! It ain't time!" spluttered Bart.

Gallagher grinned. "Old whiskers said 'time' clearly enough, or would ye rather draw pictures on the ground?"

Bart rushed in, throwing hard short punches, and Gallagher was driven back as the blows battered at rib cage, face, and belly alternately. He bumped into Sherrod, and the officer shoved him back toward Bart. He sank a left into Bart's thick belly and measured him for a smashing right cross. The backs of Bart's legs struck the edge of a water trough and he sat down heavily.

Gallagher was upon him before he could get to his feet. He struck him viciously on the head two or three times, then gripped the man's thick hair and soused him under while the overflowing water soaked his own legs. He pulled up the dripping head. "Have ye had enough, *hombre!*" he roared into a wet ear.

Gallagher jumped backward as Bart kicked out. The big man struggled to his feet, but Gallagher hit him with a perfectly timed one-two that dumped him back over the trough.

Gallagher stepped back. He was tiring. He had drained too much stamina from his body in the past few days.

Bart got up slowly, water dripping from his clothing and forming little puddles beside his big feet. He rounded the trough, pure hell on his face. He plunged toward Gallagher with short little steps, swinging both arms in vicious hooks.

"*Now*, Bart!" yelled Artenis.

It was as though he was chopping wood with short smashing blows of the ax, and when he was done Gallagher lay sprawled on the ground with blood running brightly in the moonlight from nose and mouth. His brain reeled sickeningly. He was licked. God how he was licked!

Bart straddled Gallagher. He moved slowly, reaching with big bloody hands for Gallagher's face, while the stubby powerful thumbs felt for the eyeballs. Darris laughed. "Let him go blind to his maker," he said.

"Gallagher!" screamed Ellen. "The guidon! The Border Guidon! It must go back to the regiment!"

Her words called forth Gallagher's last reserves. He twisted his head free from the terrible hands and bent it forward, then drove it up with all his strength into Bart's groin. The man grunted in sudden agony. Gallagher got to his feet. Bart charged right into a fist that Gallagher held out in front of him. Bart reeled, and he was helped in his downfall by a right-handed crusher that drove his beak of a nose up half an inch. His head cracked dully against a porch post on the way down. Gallagher booted him. It was a mistake, for Bart gripped the leg and up-ended Gallagher. The two of them thrashed over and over across the hard earth of the courtyard until they were almost at the feet of Darris.

Then they were up on their feet with science thrown to the night wind. It was hit, knee, gouge, and bite—and never let up, for if you did you would no longer resemble a man.

They broke free at last and staggered away from each other, blood running from their faces to form little black pools on the moon-silvered earth.

Their eyes were wide in their heads, but they did not hesitate to close in again. Bart drove Gallagher back. Gallagher covered up and kept retreating, but his legs were fast weakening, and they shook with the strain of him staying on his feet. He was almost beaten by this bearded rock of a man. Then, beyond the sweating hairy shoulders of Bart, he saw the end door of the western building open a little. Ainsley and Gerry! It had to be!

Gallagher drew upon an unknown source of power and threw it into the scales. Blood flew from the battered face of the big man as he slowly retreated. Sergeant Gerry was out in the open now, running lightly toward Darris with a pistol in his hand. Then Ainsley was out in the courtyard followed by dripping Texans. Someone cursed to break the spell. A carbine cracked, and a Texan died. Gun shots crackled out through a weaving shifting veil of smoke. A man raised a rifle to shoot at Gallagher, but Captain Sherrod snatched up an iron bucket and threw it hard and straight to drop the rifleman.

Bart reached down and snatched up a length of heavy wagon chain. He whirled it over his head like a terrible flail and advanced on Gallagher as the shooting crackled fiercely from both sides and echoed back and forth between the walls of the two buildings. Sherrod ran to the south gate and threw the bar to the ground, then pulled open the gate. The rest of Company G poured in.

As the chain clipped Gallagher on the forearm he screamed like a woman. He darted behind a post, and the chain wound viciously around it. Gallagher kicked Bart in the groin, then followed up with the last punch he had in the locker, snapping it up under the thick beard. Bart's head struck the stone wall. There was the sound of a dropped melon, and Bart dropped sideways. His eyes were wide in his head, but he did not see. He would never see again.

Darris yelled in a mad frenzy as he darted in through a lower door in the east building. Gallagher looked up toward the women. They stood there together, frozen. Millard Artenis was running toward the north wall of the courtyard. Gallagher raced for the stairs and caught the heel of a boot on his chin. Then Artenis placed a hand on the wall and vaulted cleanly to land on the hard earth below. By the time Gallagher got to the top of the stairs the man was gone.

Gallagher thought of Darris. He burst a door open with a shoulder and looked through one room after another until he found the man. The man was on his knees. Tears streamed down his face and trickled into his beard. "Don't punish me!" he screamed.

Gallagher spat. He twisted a hand in the heavy beard and dragged Darris after him, bumping him cruelly down the stairs to the smoke-filled courtyard. The fight was over. The Texans stood around grinning. "Two dead, three wounded, suh," reported Sergeant Gerry. The grins vanished.

"And the others?" asked Sherrod.

Gerry turned with an odd look on his face. *"Deguelo,"* he said. "No Quarter." He jerked a thumb at Darris. "Just him, suh." The sergeant cocked his pistol.

Hunter Sherrod wiped the sweat from his face. "Thanks, Gallagher. Without you we could never have managed it. But for a time there I thought he surely had you . . . until the woman called out."

Gallagher wiped the blood from his face with his free hand. "Aye," he said quietly, "it was a near thing, that."

"The rest of them are coming down the trail, suh!" yelled a corporal. "Do we open fire?"

There was a strange look on Sherrod's face. "We take only the women from this hellhole," he said clearly.

So it was. Texans have a habit of shooting straight. They waste no ammunition. When the last echo of the battle died away down the canyon the only man left alive outside of Millard Artenis was Elijah Darris, the old devil himself, and the madness that had always hovered behind his icy eyes had full control now.

Chapter 18

THE Texans were piling food and stores together beside the buildings. Horses and mules had been rounded up to carry the supplies and weapons from the cliff dwellings. Luke Ainsley had slipped down the canyon to scout the Apaches. Sergeant Gerry had sent a detail to bring down enough Sharps carbines and Colt revolving pistols to arm the company adequately. The troopers grinned as they handled the fine weapons. "Sure kin go through them Yankees west of heah like crap through a tin horn," said a big corporal.

"Where's Gallagher?" asked Captain Sherrod.

"Went to get his hoss and his damned old Yankee guidon, suh."

"Won't do him any good hauling that guidon to a prison," said Sergeant Gerry.

Ellen Eustis stood close to the wall watching the troopers. Judith sat on a chair some distance from her sister. They did not speak to each other. There was a coldness between them that would never be replaced with the warmth of sisterly love.

Hunter Sherrod looked toward the corrals. "Gallagher has been gone a long time," he said suddenly.

"He wanted to bathe," said Ellen.

The officer nodded. He eyed her appreciatively. No wonder Gallagher had fought so hard. She was a beauty. A thoroughbred. The other one? Well, she was a beauty, too, in a different sort of a way. A man knew where she was headed. "I don't know how we can get you two ladies through the Apache lines," he said quietly.

"I can shoot," said Ellen.

The moon was on the wane now. Gallagher came up the slope from the stream. "What now, Captain?" he asked.

"We'll have to break through. The Confederacy needs these weapons. We'll lose men, but we came here for weapons, and we must pay a price for them."

"Not a chance," said Gallagher. "Ye do not know Yellow Snake. He'll not fight ye in the open, but will use the swift ambush when ye least expect it. He'll cut down yer men one by one."

"I have no recourse but to try and break through."

Ainsley came up the slope. "They're still there," he said quietly. "They've picked out two positions, one on each side of the canyon, and they can cover every inch of the bare ground between them with rifle fire. We can't get out that way, sir."

"There is no other way," said Gallagher, "not for ye and yer heavily laden horses and mules. Even if ye did get part of yer command past them they'd cut ye down in the desert country."

Hunter Sherrod slapped his gauntlets against his thigh. Indecision was written across his tired face.

"I'll make a deal with ye, sir," said Gallagher.

"Go on, Sergeant."

"I do not want to go to a ribil prison, sir. If I get ye past the Tontos will ye free me and the lasses with horses, weapons, and supplies?"

"How can you get us through?"

Gallagher smiled slyly. "First, the word of an officer and a gentleman, which I know ye to be, sir."

"On my honor, Gallagher."

Gallagher grinned. "There are some brass mountain howitzers up there, sir. I can show ye a place to set one av them up not far from the mouth av the canyon. When the time comes for ye to make yer break the howitzer can be fired into the Tonto ambush. I have yet to see Indians who would stand up to well-served artillery."

The officer eyed him. "But the men who stay behind to serve the gun will surely be lost."

Gallagher grinned again and cocked an eye. "I did some time in the artillery when I was a recruitie. The gun can be placed within the taboo limits av the canyon. They will not try to rush it."

"You'll need help."

Ellen came forward. "Gallagher can teach me," she said.

There was stark admiration in Sherrod's eyes. "Damme, what a woman! Begging your pardon, ma'am!"

Judith swaggered up to them. "Don't count me in," she sneered. "I'm not going with *them*."

"What do you mean?" demanded Sherrod.

She looked archly at Sergeant Gerry, who turned away with reddening face. "I think I'd prefer living under the Stars and Bars rather than the Stars and Stripes. Is there any objection?"

"None," he said quietly.

Gallagher saluted the officer. "And now, if the captain is ready let us get the gun and move it into position."

"But the other howitzers?" said Sherrod wearily.

Gallagher shrugged. "Ye cannot get them out of the canyon, sir."

"No." Sherrod smiled. "But neither can the Federals."

The horses and mules were laden with the supplies. Box after box after box of Sharps carbines, Colt revolving pistols, ammunition and caps, followed by one of the stubby brass howitzers. Gallagher checked its accessories—powder charges, shells, friction tubes and lanyard, rammer, and wads. "Artillery section all correct sir," he said to Sherrod.

"No chance of you joining the 'ribils' is there, Gallagher?"

"None, sir."

Sherrod indicated the laden mules and horses. "That equipment will sway the balance in our favor in this territory, Sergeant. I'm sorry that you will end up on the losing side."

Gallagher shook his head in mock sadness. "I have me loyalty to think of first, sir, win or lose."

Sherrod flushed. "Move out!" he commanded.

Gallagher followed the troopers and the mule train with his gun being hauled by two mules. Behind the gun rode Ellen on big Shannon, leading another horse and a laden pack mule. She had bound her hair with a yellow ribbon. "Cavalry colors," Gallagher had said sadly as he led out his section.

The false dawn lightened the eastern sky. Sweating Texans had silently hauled the gun up the western wall of the canyon to a wide rock shelf that overlooked the canyon mouth. Gallagher fiddled with the elevating screw for a time, then blew a breath upon the fat breech of the gun and solicitously polished it with a very dirty sleeve.

Ellen sat on a rock beside the gun with the rammer across her lap and the wads, shells, and powder charges piled neatly beside her.

It grew lighter. Sherrod had said he would charge after the first shot from the howitzer. The sky was tinted with rich gold. Gallagher placed a friction tube in the vent of the loaded gun and attached the lanyard to it. "Ye will remember what to do?" he asked her.

"Yes."

"Yes, what!"

"Yes, Sergeant!" She smiled thinly. "Now, Sergeant?"

"Now," he said as he stepped to one side and gave the lanyard a hard clean pull. The little gun roared valiantly and rammed back in recoil. The smoke blew out in a perfect ring, and the shell burst in a red-orange blossom shrouded in thick white smoke right in the center of one of the Tonto positions.

Gallagher heaved the gun back into position and thumbed the vent. "Sponge!" he snapped.

She moved like a veteran redleg, plunging the sponge end of the rammer into the water bucket, driving it into the smoking muzzle of the gun, then withdrawing it, steaming blackly.

"Load!"

Powder charge and wad went in and were rammed home with a thud by the brass end of the rammer staff. The shell followed, with another wad behind it. Gallagher placed the friction tube and attached the lanyard. "Stand clear!" he roared and jerked the lanyard. The gun spat flame and smoke. Far below them they could hear the thrilling piercing yell of the Texans as they charged.

The thunder of pounding hoofs filled the canyon with sound. Hand guns sparkled death in the growing light as Captain Hunter Sherrod led G Company, Sixth Texas Mounted Rifles, through the gap, while a redheaded Irish dragoon and a raven-haired girl worked as a gun team that sowed red fire blossoms in the Tonto positions, spewing hot metal and sudden death through the chapparral. The dry brush flared up, and in a few minutes the fresh wind was fanning the flames higher and higher. The yelling Texans burst through the thick wall of smoke and were in the clear, with the pack mules thudding along behind them, braying in terror.

The last shot from the howitzer struck just behind a running warrior, lifting him upward with arms and legs splayed out like a human sacrifice, and before he struck the ground Gallagher knew Klij-Litzogue was on the way to the House of Spirits.

Gallagher neatly spiked the little gun and heaved it over the side of the cliff. It bounced and crashed its way to the rocky bottom.

"Come on, lass," said Gallagher as he wiped the sweat from his battered face.

They walked down the trail to where they had left the horses and the mule. Ellen looked through the rifted smoke to the thread of dust rising from the hoofs of the Texans' animals. "Those weapons might win the war for them, Gallagher," she said.

"Aye, they *might*. . ."

"You don't seem concerned, Gallagher! This isn't like you!"

"There is no time to waste talking! Mount!"

"I'm not a dragoon!"

He drew his fingers across his tattered faded stripes and diamond. "Ye see these? I'm the first soldier here and don't ye forget it!"

"How can I?" she retorted. But she mounted quickly enough to follow him through the thick brush. The faded guidon snapped in the fresh breeze.

The sun was well up when they reached the deserted buildings. "Look!" said Ellen suddenly.

A naked figure danced about one of the roofs, his beard waving in the wind. Thin, maniacal laughter echoed from the canyon walls.

"Darris," said Gallagher. He shivered.

They could still hear his laughter as they spurred through the quiet woods.

They did not see Millard Artenis until they had cleared the woods. He stood in the trail with a cocked pistol in his right hand. They drew rein. "Well, Gallagher?" said the ex-officer.

Gallagher eyed the man. "Get out of the way. Yer Texan friends are gone. The United States will not have ye. Where will ye go, Artenis?"

The man's face worked. "I'll get out of here," he said. "Past the Tontos?"

The color drained from his face. "Damn you, Gallagher! At least I can finish *you* off!" He raised the pistol. Something cracked deafeningly alongside Gallagher's head, and stinking powder smoke swirled past his face. Through the smoke Gallagher could see Artenis gripping his right wrist with his left hand while the gun dropped from nerveless fingers. Blood leaked between the fingers of his left hand. He stared at the girl.

Ellen lowered her smoking pistol. "Let's go home, Gallagher," she said quietly.

They rode past the white-faced man. He opened his mouth. "But what about me?" he shrieked.

Gallagher grinned. "Yes," he said. "What about ye? Go back to the buildings, *Mister* Artenis, ye'll have good company there."

They rode on, never looking back.

It was middle afternoon when Gallagher found the dim trail that would lead them from the canyon to the trail to Fort Yuma. They stopped to rest the animals. The big pack mule was very tired.

Ellen lay back and looked at the bright sky, shading her lovely eyes with her hands. "Those guns," she said quietly. "In a few months I expect to hear that the rebels have conquered the territory—and perhaps the Pacific Coast—with them, Gallagher."

"Aye," he said.

"You puzzle me! Wasn't there something we could have done?"

"Aye."

"What?"

He walked to the mule and stripped two heavy bags from it. They clinked as he lowered them to the ground. He opened one of the bags and took out a metal object which he showed to her.

"What is it? What do you have in those bags?"

He whistled softly. "Breechblocks from Sharps carbines and cylinders from Colt revolving pistols, lass. It seems as though Gallagher was a very busy boyo up in those dwellings whilst the trusting Texans were down below thinking only of supplies for their bellies. Sure, they have the fine weapons, but without these breechblocks and cylinders they will be of no use, and ye cannot frighten the mean Yankee soldiers with such weapons, can ye now?"

She roared with laughter. "Now I know why you were gone bathing so long and still did not smell like a rose when you came back with grease on your fingers!"

He nodded. "Poor Captain Sherrod. A hero he will be until the giniral finds he has brought back useless weapons for the all-important campaign. And, to me knowledge, the only spare breechblocks and cylinders in the whole Southwest are in the hands of the Yankees, and they won't part with 'em, lass."

He carried the bags to the stream and dumped them in a deep hole. He stared down into the water, then walked upstream a little way to a riffle. Then suddenly he waded in and scooped up some of the sand. It glittered in his big hand. He walked back to her and placed the sand in her hands. "Gold," he said quietly. "The stream is full of it."

She looked up at him. "What good is it to us, Gallagher?"

He looked up the bright canyon at the soft waving

trees and the flashing stream laden with yellow riches. "The war will not last forever," he said at last. "A man could come here and make a fine home."

"But it is haunted," she said. "Darris and Artenis."

"They will hunt each other down and they will die, one way or another. Or, if they are still here when I come back I will hunt them down meself."

She shivered a little. "If a person lived here they would still be haunted of nights by those two men, Gallagher."

He smiled. "There is one thing that can drive them away, if their spirits haunt this place."

"So? What is it?"

He bent and kissed her gently. "The laughter of little children, lass," he answered. "Nature will cleanse this place. It always does."

She got to her feet and walked to her horse. She fumbled with her hair. "Gallagher!" she called out.

He walked to her.

"Tie up my hair," she said. She handed him an orange ribbon.

The guidon snapped in the breeze as they rode toward the trail. She looked up at it. "The Border Guidon," she said. "It knows it is going home to the regiment."

They rode up the trail side by side. The last United States soldier in Arizona Territory was leaving. But he'd be back before too long, and he would not come alone. He and his comrades would follow the Border Guidon back to where it belonged—on the fighting border between the United States and its enemies, whoever they might be.

SIGNET Westerns by Ray Hogan

(0451)

- [ ] THE COPPER-DUN STUD   (125711—$2.25)*
- [ ] THE RENEGADE GUN   (125215—$2.25)*
- [ ] THE LAW AND LYNCHBURG   (121457—$2.25)*
- [ ] THE RENEGADES   (119282—$2.25)*
- [ ] DECISION AT DOUBTFUL CANYON   (111192—$1.95)*
- [ ] THE DOOMSDAY BULLET   (116305—$1.95)*
- [ ] LAWMAN'S CHOICE   (112164—$1.95)*
- [ ] PILGRIM   (095766—$1.75)*
- [ ] RAGAN'S LAW   (110307—$1.95)*
- [ ] SIGNET DOUBLE WESTERN: OUTLAW MARSHAL and WOLF LAWMAN   (117441—$2.50)*
- [ ] SIGNET DOUBLE WESTERN: MAN WITHOUT A GUN and CONGER'S WOMAN   (120205—$2.95)*
- [ ] SIGNET DOUBLE WESTERN: BRANDON'S POSSE and THE HELL MERCHANT   (115910—$2.50)
- [ ] SIGNET DOUBLE WESTERN: THREE CROSS and DEPUTY OF VIOLENCE   (116046—$2.50)
- [ ] SIGNET DOUBLE WESTERN: DAY OF RECKONING and DEAD MAN ON A BLACK HORSE   (115236—$2.50)*
- [ ] SIGNET DOUBLE WESTERN: THE VIGILANTE and THE REGULATOR   (124561—$2.95)*
- [ ] SIGNET DOUBLE WESTERN: THE DOOMSDAY MARSHAL and THE DOOMSDAY POSSE   (126238—$2.95)*

*Prices slightly higher in Canada

Buy them at your local

bookstore or use coupon

on next page for ordering.

Exciting SIGNET Westerns by Ernest Haycox

(0451)

- [ ] **STARLIGHT RIDER** (123468—$2.25)*
- [ ] **BUGLES IN THE AFTERNOON** (114671—$2.25)*
- [ ] **CHAFEE OF ROARING HORSE** (114248—$1.95)*
- [ ] **RETURN OF A FIGHTER** (094190—$1.75)
- [ ] **RIDERS WEST** (099796—$1.95)*
- [ ] **SUNDOWN JIM** (096762—$1.75)*
- [ ] **TRAIL SMOKE** (112822—$1.95)*
- [ ] **TRAIL TOWN** (097793—$1.95)*
- [ ] **CANYON PASSAGE** (117824—$2.25)*
- [ ] **DEEP WEST** (118839—$2.25)*
- [ ] **FREE GRASS** (118383—$2.25)*
- [ ] **HEAD OF THE MOUNTAIN** (120817—$2.50)*
- [ ] **SIGNET DOUBLE WESTERN: ACTION BY NIGHT and TROUBLE SHOOTER** (123891—$3.50)*
- [ ] **SIGNET DOUBLE WESTERN: SADDLE & RIDE and THE FEUDISTS** (094670—$1.95)
- [ ] **SIGNET DOUBLE WESTERN: ALDER GULCH and A RIDER OF THE HIGH MESA** (122844—$3.50)*

Prices slightly higher in Canada

SIGNET Westerns by Lewis B. Patten

		(0451)
☐	VENGEANCE RIDER	(126211—$2.25)*
☐	THE ANGRY HORSEMEN	(093097—$1.75)
☐	A DEATH IN INDIAN WELLS	(112172—$1.95)*
☐	POSSE FROM POISON CREEK	(095774—$1.75)*
☐	RED RUNS THE RIVER	(097378—$1.95)*
☐	RIDE A TALL HORSE	(098161—$1.95)*
☐	TRACK OF THE HUNTER	(110315—$1.95)*
☐	THE TRAIL OF THE APACHE KID	(094662—$1.75)
☐	SIGNET DOUBLE WESTERN: KILLING IN KIOWA and FUED AT CHIMNEY ROCK	(114256—$2.75)*
☐	SIGNET DOUBLE WESTERN: SHOWDOWN AT MESILLA and THE TRIAL OF JUDAS WILLEY	(116313—$2.50)*
☐	SIGNET DOUBLE WESTERN: REDSKIN and TWO FOR VENGEANCE	(119290—$2.75)*
☐	SIGNET DOUBLE WESTERN: THE HIDE HUNTERS and OUTLAW CANYON	(122526—$2.95)*
☐	SIGNET DOUBLE WESTERN: THE CHEYENNE POOL and THE TIRED GUN	(124928—$2.95)*
☐	SIGNET DOUBLE WESTERN: DEATH STALKS YELLOWHORSE and THE ORPHANS OF COYOTE CREEK	(125223—$2.95)*
☐	SIGNET DOUBLE WESTERN: AMBUSH AT SODA CREEK and MAN OUT-GUNNED	(125738—$2.95)*

*Prices slightly higher in Canada

Buy them at your local
bookstore or use coupon
on next page for ordering.

Wild Westerns by Warren T. Longtree

(0451)

- [ ] RUFF JUSTICE #1: SUDDEN THUNDER (110285—$2.50)*
- [ ] RUFF JUSTICE #2: NIGHT OF THE APACHE (110293—$2.50)*
- [ ] RUFF JUSTICE #3: BLOOD ON THE MOON (112256—$2.50)*
- [ ] RUFF JUSTICE #4: WIDOW CREEK (114221—$2.50)*
- [ ] RUFF JUSTICE #5: VALLEY OF GOLDEN TOMBS (115635—$2.50)*
- [ ] RUFF JUSTICE #6: THE SPIRIT WOMAN WAR (117832—$2.50)*
- [ ] RUFF JUSTICE #7: DARK ANGEL RIDING (118820—$2.50)*
- [ ] RUFF JUSTICE #8: THE DEATH OF IRON HORSE (121449—$2.50)*
- [ ] RUFF JUSTICE #9: WINDWOLF (122828—$2.50)*
- [ ] RUFF JUSTICE #10: SHOSHONE RUN (123883—$2.50)*
- [ ] RUFF JUSTICE #11: COMANCHE PEAK (124901—$2.50)*
- [ ] RUFF JUSTICE #12: PETTICOAT EXPRESS (127765—$2.50)*

*Price is $2.95 in Canada

SIGNET Westerns You'll Enjoy

Buy them at your local

bookstore or use coupon

on next page for ordering.

SIGNET Americana Novels of Interest